D1011609

THE
RETURN

THE
RETURN

JOSEPH
HELMREICH

ST. MARTIN'S PRESS
A THOMAS DUNNE BOOK
NEW YORK

THOMAS DUNNE BOOKS.
An imprint of St. Martin's Press.

THE RETURN. Copyright © 2017 by Joseph Helmreich. All rights reserved. Printed in the United States of America. For information, address St. Martin's Press, 175 Fifth Avenue, New York, N.Y. 10010.

www.thomasdunnebooks.com
www.stmartins.com

Designed by Omar Chapa

The Library of Congress Cataloging-in-Publication Data is available upon request.

ISBN 978-1-250-05219-3 (hardcover)
ISBN 978-1-4668-5350-8 (e-book)

Our books may be purchased in bulk for promotional, educational, or business use. Please contact your local bookseller or the Macmillan Corporate and Premium Sales Department at 1-800-221-7945, extension 5442, or by e-mail at MacmillanSpecialMarkets@macmillan.com.

First Edition: March 2017

10 9 8 7 6 5 4 3 2 1

*For Alan Helmreich, a wonderful brother and
a brilliant dreamer. Your memory continues to inspire.*

THE
RETURN

CHAPTER 1

If the conspiracy theorists are right and it never happened, then the day it didn't happen began innocently enough. The night before had yielded little morning news, and, in fact, it had been a slow news week in general. A conservative mayor somewhere in Indiana had accidentally outed himself through a risqué text message sent to the wrong aide. Several dozen people had been buried in an earthquake in La Viña, Chile, a city few people in the United States could name, let alone empathize with. An up-and-coming pitcher for the Dodgers had been caught cheating on his wife, whom he turned out to be estranged from, anyway. In short, watercoolers across the country were, if anything, quieter than usual that afternoon. The calm before the storm.

Still, almost any story would have been preferable to the one Bill Allenby found himself saddled with that Tuesday, a lunar eclipse that would be taking place from around 8:35 to 9:35 P.M., PST. Roy Hanson, his ineffectual producer, had explained that it had been several hundred years since an eclipse had occurred on the occasion of a winter solstice, making this what experts liked to term a "rare

celestial event." To Allenby's mind, that hardly made it worth dragging a whole crew up to Bernasconi Hills, which was expected to
offer the best views of the sky in the Southern California area. And
what exactly was he supposed to talk to Andrew Leland about, and
where the hell was Leland, anyway?

"Celestial events" were not what Allenby had gotten into jour-
nalism for, and Hanson knew that. But several months earlier, a
segment in which he had badly mispronounced the name of German philosopher Immanuel Kant had gone viral, and he was still
paying the price. Though no one ever said so explicitly, until that
embarrassing flub was fully lived down, high-profile trips to dangerous war zones and coveted interviews with world leaders would
have to wait. For now, someone like Dr. Andrew Leland was probably a good catch. And not even the Leland of the late '90s, either,
who'd been hailed as the heir apparent to Stephen Hawking, but
the watered-down Hollywoodized Leland of today, a notorious self-
promoter whose name was more likely to be found in the pages of
Entertainment Weekly than *Scientific American*.

"Easy near the eyes," Andrew Leland requested as an attractive
young woman applied foundation to his cheeks and forehead inside
the hair and makeup tent.

"Well, if you kept them closed like I asked, this would be a
whole lot easier," she said.

"If I close them, I can't see your pretty face."

She rolled her eyes.

"What's your name?"

"Maureen."

"Maureen, I'm Andrew."

"I know who you are. My husband used to watch your show on
the Discovery Channel."

"So he was the one!"

She smiled and removed a lint brush from a table.

"Your husband's a man of science?"

"He's a man of TV," she answered, applying the brush to Leland's sports jacket. "Course he thinks he's a poet. The next Pablo Neruda, he says. I don't even know who that is."

"Me, neither, but I'm actually something of a poet myself. Except I don't deal with words; I deal with numbers and laws. Equations. You might call me a poet of the universe."

She smiled. "I might call you full of shit."

"That right? Here, I'll write something special for you right now you can keep."

He removed a pen and small ticket stub from his pocket and jotted something down on the back, then handed it to her.

"What is it?" she asked, staring at the ten digits he'd scrawled there.

"A rare series of numbers unique in all of math and science. I call it the 'Leland Sequence.' If you're ever in the Silver Lake area, feel free to bring it along and use it."

She arched an eyebrow, shook her head with mock reproach, and quickly shoved the phone number into her purse.

As production assistants and interns pitched tents into the hard, uncooperative earth, Bill Allenby paced back and forth, going over in his head the questions he'd be asking Leland. He still wasn't sure why they'd gone with a physicist instead of an astronomer, but then who ever heard of a famous astronomer in the twenty-first century, and Roy Hanson was a sucker for talking heads anyone might recognize. Meanwhile, about forty feet from the edge of the cliff where the interview would be taking place, Hanson and several uniformed young men were guiding the camera crew on usage of the Astral HDR-8K, a sophisticated new camera that had been loaned from the U.S. Naval Observatory and would be able to capture both Allenby and Leland, on the one hand, and the celestial imagery taking place in the sky behind them, on the other, with equal clarity. Allenby watched for a few moments, noting how hard Hanson was pretending to be in control, while obviously letting the naval officers do all the work.

Allenby then stepped toward the edge of the precipice and gazed out on the vista. From where he stood, he could see the imposing black silhouettes of the San Gabriels and Bernardinos in the far distance, the twinkling lights of Fontana, the winding roads that snake their way from Moreno Valley back to Los Angeles, all of this somewhat less visible tonight, but illuminated nonetheless by the stars and the portion of the moon no longer in shadow.

Jesus, he thought to himself. He was forty-five years old, hardworking, extremely ambitious, intelligent. If he was no Anderson Cooper, he could carry himself well enough in an expensive suit. And here he was covering the fucking moon!

"Up yours, Kant," he muttered to himself, mispronouncing the name again, this time on purpose.

At 9:25, as the segment producer called out "Stand by," Allenby and Leland got themselves into position, moving to where the moon, now a burning orange-red, would be visible directly behind and above them.

"And now we go live to Bill Allenby, on location in Bernasconi Hills, watching the sky as the moon is just about to exit the eclipse," his colleague Tammy Simon informed viewers from their studio in downtown LA.

The segment producer gave him the signal.

"Thank you, Tammy," Allenby began, staring into the surprisingly clunky-looking Astral HDR-8K. "That's right, the moon is about four minutes from exiting the eclipse, and standing with me now is celebrated physicist and recent author of *A Little More Space*, Dr. Andrew Leland. We thank him for being here, and we also want to thank the U.S. Naval Observatory for lending us the extraordinary camera we're shooting with tonight."

He turned to Leland. "Now, Dr. Leland, what can you tell us about the significance of tonight's eclipse?"

Leland smiled warmly. "Well, first of all, Bill, I would just like to say that it is a great pleasure to be on your program, and thank you very much for having me."

"Pleasure's ours," Allenby responded.

"Tonight's eclipse, Bill, is taking place on the occasion of the winter solstice. That means Earth's tilt is at its maximum distance from the sun, about twenty-three degrees toward the plane of its rotation."

"And it's the shortest day of the year, is that right?"

"The shortest day and the longest night, yes. But a lunar eclipse on a winter solstice is really a very special thing. In fact, the last time these two phenomena coincided was back in 1638."

"Is that so?"

"Yes. Back then, certain primitive societies actually believed that eclipses meant the moon was being swallowed by some sort of giant creature. A large snake or maybe a kind of outer space whale. There's a tradition in Iraq to that effect."

"Remarkable," Allenby replied, bored but glad Leland had done his homework. "And I see that the moon is still a kind of orangish hue. Could you explain why that is?"

"Well, Bill, you see, the red-orange color is the result of sunlight being filtered through our planet's pretty dusty atmosphere."

"Fascinating," Allenby remarked, just barely trying to sound sincere.

Several moments of more scientific elucidation followed, until, as the clock struck 9:37, the final bit of shadow lifted off the moon, leaving it once again whole and near to its familiar gray-white color.

"Wow! So that's it?" Allenby asked, staring up at the moon.

"Yep, that's the whole show!" Leland replied. "And I sure hope you invite me back for the next one in 2094. Actually, in *A*

Little More Space, there's a section that, though it doesn't relate directly—"

While normally Allenby might have been annoyed by Leland's sudden stab at self-promotion, he was at this moment distracted by something in the sky.

"Dr. Leland," he interrupted, his eyes on the moon. "Sorry, but that sort of green speck on the moon where the shadow had just been—what's that?"

(And it is here, at this question, that most versions of Bill Allenby's second and much more famous viral video begin.)

Leland looked up, squinted. The green speck that Allenby had pointed out appeared to be moving. The physicist watched a little longer, then shook his head. "No, that's not on the moon. Much closer. Maybe an airplane."

But it wasn't an airplane.

Lloyd Bruno, a cameraman with the show for over eight years, had little understanding of the fancy piece of machinery he was operating that night. Because of union regulations, the naval officers had been barred from operating the Astral HDR-8K themselves, and Lloyd had done his best to learn on the fly. Later, he would tell people that he at first thought the green dot that seemed to be getting larger and larger in the background was some kind of trick of the camera, a play of light, maybe a lens flare.

In interviews for years to come, he would describe how Bill Allenby and the crew had fled from the spot as quickly as their legs could carry them, while Dr. Leland had just stood there, frozen as though in shock, staring up and out at the oncoming light.

He would describe how he, himself, forty-eight years old with a wife and two kids, had ultimately decided to run, how he had grabbed the hand of Maureen Cruz, a panicked young makeup artist, and how they had rushed down a trail of cragged rock and dirt, not looking back, while most others around them did the same.

Bruno would be correct to say that Bill Allenby initially fled.

But unlike Bruno, Allenby didn't actually leave the scene. Rather, as he would later detail at lectures and fund-raisers and countless media award ceremonies, he, along with several of the naval officers and some brave members of his crew, crouched behind a production tent and did his best to watch from there. It is hard to know what Allenby or these other eyewitness accounts would have amounted to had Lloyd Bruno not left the Astral running. As it stands, their testimony serves mainly to verify the authenticity of the images that were captured by that camera and witnessed by the public.

The image of Leland, standing still, facing the expansive view and staring up at the stars. The image of the strange and brightly lit green structure moving over the mountains in the distance and toward the cliff side, toward Leland, with breathtaking speed. Of Leland being lifted up into the air by some unseen force and over the edge of the cliff, surrounded on all sides by a haze of green coruscating light.

Finally, the last bit of footage captured by the Astral camera and watched by 1.6 million residents of Los Angeles that night and over 150 million people in the next two weeks and billions more over the next several years, the image of Dr. Andrew Leland, washed-up celebrity physicist, rising higher and higher into the night sky.

CHAPTER 2

Shawn Ferris, twenty-four years old, too thin, found himself standing some fifty-five feet below Columbia University's Morningside Heights campus, staring at the remains of a legendary and notorious machine. In decades past, the machine had played a role in altering the course of human history, had indirectly led to countless lives lost and perhaps countless more saved. Now, it was threatening to unleash itself once again, this time on Shawn Ferris's future career.

But right now, he couldn't care less.

"Will you just take the damn picture?" Ricardo stammered.

Shawn readjusted the focus on his Olympus Stylus, but when he raised his eyes again to the giant mass of iron and steel assembled before him, he just continued to stare.

At eight feet high and twelve feet wide, its massive silver electromagnets suspended from its stately iron arch, the cyclotron was every bit the great behemoth he'd envisioned. Almost since his first day on campus, Shawn had been hearing stories about the legendary particle accelerator. Built by Columbia physicist John Dunning in 1936, the machine had been the first to split an atom on U.S. soil, initiating the government's infamous Manhattan Project and ushering in the nuclear era.

But by the mid-1960s, with bigger, badder atom smashers already on the scene, the cyclotron had been decommissioned and left to gather dust in a basement lab in Pupin Hall, home of the university's physics department. Once there, its mythic stature only grew, as it became a point of pilgrimage for students and professors alike. Finally, in 1987, access to its lair was officially sealed off after Ken Hechtman, an undergraduate with an anarchist streak, snuck in one night and made off with discarded tubes of uranium-238 (Hechtman would go on to achieve further notoriety in 2002, when, working as a reporter in Afghanistan, he was captured by the Taliban and tried as an alleged American spy).

Shawn had heard these tales and had seen old photos of the cyclotron, but being in the actual presence of its sixty-five tons, seeing its Start switch and WARNING stickers with his own eyes, was an overwhelming experience for which he hadn't been prepared. Standing in the great machine's path, he could swear he felt gamma rays penetrating his skin, though more likely, the energy and tension he was sensing was Ricardo's rising resentment for having been talked into joining him tonight.

"Just take the fucking picture, you jackass!" Ricardo exclaimed.

Ricardo, often nervous, wasn't wrong to be nervous tonight. Ken Hechtman had been expelled for his antics, and Shawn and Ricardo were both graduate students with prestigious fellowships. They had plenty to lose if they got caught, something Shawn had fully understood going in but that Ricardo seemed to be only realizing now.

Shawn quickly snapped three photos of the cyclotron's front, then moved around to its side and snapped three more. Then he turned his camera on some of the less-conspicuous artifacts littering the room. The rusted file cabinets lining the chipped walls, the large open closet that revealed a clunky ancient-looking computer, the open cardboard boxes filled to the brim with crinkly yellow files and fraying documents. All of this was history, and it was apparently being treated by the university as just that.

"All right! Enough!" Ricardo insisted.

"One more sec," Shawn responded as he carefully snapped two photos of what appeared to be old induction coils. "Okay."

They stepped out of the lab and back into the eerily abandoned Pupin basement. There, using a half-broken folding chair, they hoisted themselves up, one at a time, back into the air duct from which they'd emerged. After several minutes of crawling through the darkness, they dropped back down into Columbia's vast network of underground tunnels.

"Which way did we come?" Shawn asked, wiping dirt and rust off his cargo pants.

Ricardo, flashlight in tow, consulted the crumpled map he'd printed out from a Web site three nights before.

"Well, we *should* be somewhere under Chandler. Think we came from that way."

They turned left and proceeded down a long, dark corridor overhung with steam pipes and wires and lined at the sides by graffiti and rusted pieces of electrical machinery. The floor was covered with mud and what appeared to be the remnants of some sort of rail track.

"You see that?" Ricardo asked.

"What?"

"Huge-ass rat just ran right by us."

"Probably radioactive," Shawn mused. "Like Splinter."

Shawn had been kidding, but he wouldn't have been too shocked if there actually were radioactive vermin down there. In the '50s, the tunnels had been famously used to smuggle chemicals for the Manhattan Project, and who knew what might have spilled on these floors once upon a time?

As they turned another corner, they suddenly stopped short. Far in the distance, at the end of a long tunnel, something extremely bright was moving around on the wall. At first, they couldn't make out what it was. But when the movement abruptly stopped, they understood that it was a flashlight and that it was now being focused on them.

"You asshole," Ricardo muttered under his breath.

"No one forced you to come," Shawn shot back.

Despite the glare that now engulfed them, they could make out the shape of the short and stocky figure standing some forty yards down the tunnel, staring at them. It was the crown shape of his hat that gave his identity away. A university public safety officer. A campus cop.

So it's true, Shawn thought to himself. *The tunnels* are *under surveillance.*

"Hey, dickwads!" the campus cop called out to them.

Classy.

They stood still. Shawn turned to Ricardo. It was Shawn who had really gotten them into this, so he was going to let Ricardo decide their next move. If they surrendered now, they probably faced trouble, but who knew how much? If they ran and got away, they were probably golden—even if they'd been caught on camera, the odds that it could pick up their faces in this light were slim. If they ran and got caught, they were absolutely, positively, 100 percent screwed.

Ricardo took a deep breath. "Let's go."

With that, they spun around and shot off running in the direction from which they'd come.

"Right!" Ricardo called as they neared a corner, operating on instinct alone, and they turned right.

"Left!" he called as they neared another turn, and they moved left.

Soon enough, flashlights beaming forward like headlights,

they could see in the distance the stairwell leading back up to the first floor of Havemeyer. It was getting closer and closer. But if there was any feeling of relief, it evaporated instantly with the sound of footsteps coming up behind them. The campus cop was hot on their heels. He must have darted out from an intersecting tunnel, and he was getting much too close. Their legs aching like all hell, they raced up the stairs and into Havemeyer and right out the door.

Once outside, they sprinted across the shadowy, moonlit campus, the cop chasing and cursing from behind all the while. As they ran, flying past the Mathematics building and Earl Hall, barreling down the great stone steps of Low Library, Shawn thought of the many nightmares he'd had over the years where he was being chased. Always in those dreams, there had been intense feelings of panic and dread, of black death encroaching from behind. Now, all he felt was pure exhilaration. He couldn't explain it, and there wasn't time for reflection, anyway.

Reaching College Walk, Shawn and Ricardo made a hard right onto its redbrick path and bolted toward the campus's tall iron gate. As the opening got closer and closer, revealing Broadway and the downhill slope toward Riverside Park in the distance, they could hear the cop slowing down behind them, finally giving up.

Minutes later, they were out on the street, several blocks away, leaning against the side of a closed Starbucks, panting, wheezing, coughing their lungs out.

Sometime later that night, settling in at his desk in his cramped 110th Street apartment, Shawn plugged his camera into his laptop and began uploading the pictures of the cyclotron to his hard drive. When he was finished, he logged on to Schrödinger's Rat, the underground physics forum where he was known only as "Orpheus-Jack," and started to post them. "Eat your heart out, Buggers81," he typed as the caption for the first, addressing the user whose half-serious dare had been the impetus for tonight's adventure.

The high that he'd felt from the chase at Columbia had worn

off after he'd noticed, a little while after coming back, that his student ID was missing. He normally kept it in his back pocket. While he had no real reason to assume that he had lost it during his and Ricardo's escapade, he was left unsettled just the same. Still, there being nothing he could do about it, and he did his best to put it out of his mind. *C'est la vie.*

To kill time while he waited for responses to the photos, he headed over to the open Q&A boards, where users traditionally asked each other questions or solicited advice, typically related to academic research they were involved in.

Someone had just posted: "If you're working with a diverging lens whose focal length is 20 cm, where should you place the object to get a virtual image that's one-third the object's size?"

Shawn had already started typing the answer before he'd finished reading the question. This was typical. On any given night, he could spend hours like this, breezily fielding curveballs on subjects ranging from as general as Einstein's theory of relativity to as obscure as topological geometrodynamics.

After twenty minutes or so, Shawn was ready to check to see whether anyone had commented on his photos. The images were bound to make a strong impression, and Shawn was excited to see what people had to say. But just as he was about to hit the Back key, something suddenly caught his eye: a new private message was awaiting him in his on-site in-box.

Shawn clicked on the message. It was from AmberQ, which both surprised and intrigued him. Nobody knew exactly who AmberQ was, but most of the users assumed she (if she *was* a she) worked for the news media or possibly, though far less likely, the government. AmberQ posted almost exclusively in the Leland section, and nearly all her posts were fairly impressive scoops relating to alleged sightings or new biographical information that wouldn't hit mainstream news sites until hours—sometimes days—later. AmberQ and Shawn had corresponded several times before, but always in the forum, never via private message, and AmberQ hadn't posted anything in so long, Shawn had assumed she'd retired from the site.

The subject line read, "A to your Q." Shawn had no recollection of having asked AmberQ a question, certainly not recently. He opened up the message and squinted at the screen and tried to make sense of what he saw.

The message contained one line only:

"123 Bay Berry Drive, Emington, MN 56464."

Shawn ran his fingers through his dark, wavy hair. When had he asked AmberQ for an address? Had he asked someone else? An address for what? He leaned forward, rested his elbows on his desk and his chin in his palms, staring intently at the screen, racking his brain for any clue as to what this might pertain to.

When it finally hit him, much later than it should have, he felt a chill rush up his spine, and all thoughts of his missing student ID card, the photos of the cyclotron, and the cyclotron itself drifted off into the ether like forgotten dreams.

CHAPTER 3

When Shawn Ferris was in high school, he wanted to be an archeologist. Like the rest of the world, that changed after Andrew Leland.

Shawn could still remember the strange, exhilarating feeling, huddled with fellow students around his English teacher's laptop, as they watched the video for the first time. It was the feeling of endless possibility, and it was a feeling that was shared simultaneously by billions across the globe.

Of course, there was dissent in some circles in the beginning, allegations of a massive government hoax. But for the first time anyone could remember, it was the skeptics who sounded like lunatics and who were being laughed off the talk shows. Even popular debunker websites like MythKill and Decoder could find no obvious flaws with the footage, no evidence of CGI or composite imagery or that the video had not actually been broadcast live.

Besides, the event had been witnessed at the scene by multiple and unrelated individuals, not to mention the several hundred people from surrounding areas who had reported a strange object in the night sky and the dozens of cell phone videos that emerged in the following days, most taken by teenagers from Fontana and Rialto, which corroborated the footage from the Astral HDR-8K.

Yes, the crazies had far-fetched explanations for all of this, but for everyone else, the verdict was in.

Meanwhile, the world went on, but it was a different place. Changes in the scientific community were among the most palpable, as one of its biggest questions had now been seemingly answered or, at the very least, modified from a question of *if* to one of *who* or *what*. Closely related to this, many First World governments immediately shifted their priorities. For instance, both the U.S. and British governments infused billions in capital into scientific research institutes that had scarcely a clue as to what to do with so much money. Defense spending also skyrocketed around the world, as many analysts had predicted it would.

Pop culture was of course transformed, as well. Among the more obvious changes was a sudden influx of alien invasion films, notwithstanding outcries from some that the topic was now tasteless. Actually, the effect on pop culture echoed in many ways the era that had coincided with the first manned spaceflights, a period that had produced such television series as *Doctor Who* and *Star Trek* and films like *2001: A Space Odyssey*.

Overall, the mood in society was one of excitement and hope, though there was apprehension, as well. After all, kidnapping wasn't exactly anyone's idea of *coming in peace*, and nobody knew whether Leland had been eaten on the spot or crowned king in some faraway land (the latter possibility inspired at least one comic book series).

As far as religion went, many people abandoned their faiths, while many others found new reason to reembrace theirs.

One area where changes were subtler, but no less significant, was academia. According to a study conducted by the Quinnipiac University Poll, within a year of the events at Bernasconi Hills, physics majors had outnumbered those of all other subjects by three to one. Astronomy and astrophysics majors came in second and third.

When he had enrolled at Brown, Shawn Ferris initially wanted to study astronomy. Later on, though, on the insistence of one of his professors, he switched to physics during his junior year.

He was hard at work on an experiment in one of the university's newly renovated labs when his lab partner, Carl, burst into the room one day, looking ghostly white and out of breath.

"What's going on?" Shawn asked, looking up from an electroscope.

"You haven't heard?"

"Heard what?"

Carl took a second to take in some more air. "Leland. He's back."

At first, the news reports were tentative. A thin, bearded American had been picked up wandering in the southern portion of the Sonoran Desert, dazed and dehydrated. While several Mexican officials had noticed a striking resemblance to Andrew Leland, nothing could be certain until the man was properly identified. After he was brought back to the States and the correct tests were administered, his identity was confirmed, via a live press conference by Los Angeles County Sheriff Randy Phillips: exactly six years, seven months, and twenty-two days from the date of his disappearance, Andrew Leland had returned from the sky.

The twenty-four-hour news cycle went into overdrive. TV screens the world over were flooded with images of the emaciated-looking Leland, his long beard scraggly and unkempt, his eyes eerily vacant. However, if people had been expecting answers, they were in for a rude awakening. In a move that shocked and outraged the world, Leland refused to grant even a single interview request. More alarming, several media outlets reported that he was not cooperating with government agencies or scientists, either, instead insisting that he had been living in Mexico for the past six years, retired from scientific research, and working as a farmhand, and had no idea what all the fuss was about.

When he finally agreed to meet with his old colleague Dr. Kazuo Murata, the latter, after spending nearly two hours with Leland, told the press that it seemed to him that Leland genuinely had no recollection of the event that had made him world famous. Leland's ex-wife, Nancy Scott, who met with him briefly to discuss some financial matters, concurred.

These claims, however, did little to quell the rising anger, and there were even calls to have Leland imprisoned for "treason against the human race," as several pundits and politicians put it. But at the end of the day, there was no one who could force Leland to talk, and eventually, some three months after his reemergence, he disappeared once again. Not into the sky this time, but into the deep woods of the Blue Ridge Mountains or the dark hills of West Virginia or the swampy marshlands of Florida's Everglades, depending on who your sources were.

But if Andrew Leland thought becoming an old-fashioned hermit would make people forget about him, he couldn't have been more wrong. Not since J. D. Salinger had picked up and moved to Cornish, New Hampshire, had any recluse inspired so much world-wide fascination. All across the globe, Andrew Leland "societies" sprang up, formal groups devoted to the study of the man and the mystery. There were even one or two cults, which built elaborate mythologies around Leland and worshiped him as a kind of religious figure. And of course, there were the endless alleged sightings, many of them reported early by AmberQ on Schrödinger's Rat and feasted upon by the likes of Shawn Ferris, whose fascination with Leland had grown, over the course of four years in college, into a full-blown obsession.

It was in response to one of AmberQ's posts that Shawn, already at Columbia, had responded one night, "Up to here with this

torture already—stop trolling and just tell us where the hell he is!"
Shawn had of course meant it entirely as a joke. He had posted it
on the board and not given it a second thought. Now, a month and
a half later, she had apparently complied with his request.

The next day, Shawn couldn't focus in any of his classes. Ricardo,
meanwhile, wanted nothing to do with him anymore.

"'Cause unlike you, I actually give a shit about my future," he
quietly explained during their quantum mechanics seminar as their
professor droned on in front of a whiteboard.

While Shawn was less than happy to hear this, he didn't have
room in his brain to worry too much about it right now. He was
utterly consumed by AmberQ's message. *Could she possibly be telling the truth?* he asked himself. If she really did have access to that
kind of information, why would she ever provide it to a random
stranger online? That part definitely didn't add up. At the same
time, she'd been posting ostensibly secretive information for years.
Also, what motive would she have to lie? He couldn't think of
any, but the whole thing seemed ridiculously far-fetched just the
same. Still, whether the address was authentic or not, it was all he
had right now and more than he'd ever had before.

The last class of the day couldn't end soon enough. When
he finally got out, Shawn rushed back to his apartment, switched on
his computer, opened up his word processor, and stared at the blank
screen.

The challenge that lay before him was enormous. He was going
to try to enter into direct correspondence with a man who clearly
wanted nothing to do with anyone. Even more problematic, the
questions Shawn so desperately wanted answered concerned a topic
that this man claimed to know absolutely nothing about, an event
that he insisted never took place.

Shawn would not be deterred. He would have to be creative, he
decided. He would have to think entirely outside of the box.

He would have to lie through his teeth.

After several moments of deep thought, Shawn got to work and typed out the following letter:

Dear Dr. Leland,

My name is Shawn Ferris, and I am a William Godfrey Fellow in Columbia University's physics program. I am writing to you today because, though I understand the chances for a response are slim, I feel that I have no other choice. Certain information has recently been entrusted to me and, while said information has little bearing on me, it affects you greatly. In fact, it is little exaggeration to say that you must be made aware of it at once.

I understand that you may very well be telling the truth when you state that you have no recollection of the fantastical event that reportedly took place in Bernasconi Hills, California, and that it is certainly possible that all the time you were believed to be missing, you were actually living on a farm in Mexico. However, there is also a chance you have chosen to feign ignorance about what happened to you for reasons only you know. Either way, it is imperative that we meet and that I share with you the information I have. After all this time, you must finally know the truth!

I will be traveling to Rochester, Minnesota, in two weeks to visit my ailing uncle. Please let me know whether you will have time to meet for an hour or so. I promise you that afterward, I will not bother you again. Furthermore, if you do not have time to meet, but can only talk by phone, please call me at (636) 555-0113. Alternatively, you can e-mail me at SFerris15@columbia.edu. I look forward to hearing from you.

Best regards,
Shawn Ferris

After reading the letter back to himself, Shawn wondered whether he should delete his phone number. What if Leland called him and wanted to be told the information right away? Would he be able to make up some excuse on the spot? Then again, he could just respond that he wasn't able to speak about the matter over the phone. In the end, he opted to include it.

Shawn had misgivings about the approach he had chosen. It was risky and obviously unethical. But he reminded himself that Leland was being no less honest himself with all his bullshit about having amnesia and living in Mexico. Leland had no right to hide the truth about his experiences from the rest of the world. And given its importance, any means for extracting that truth had to be necessarily just.

Shawn mailed off the letter the next day. When two weeks went by and he hadn't received any response, he began to get antsy. After six weeks had gone by, his impatience had reached its limit. Figuring he had nothing to lose, he wrote another letter. This time, he abandoned his earlier tact and left out the part about having special information for Leland, supposing Leland may have seen through it the first time around and been turned off. In the new letter, Shawn instead opted for honesty and explained just how much he felt Leland owed it to civilization at large to share what he had experienced and owed it to people like Shawn in particular. He mailed this out, and again, his letter was met with no reply. Some four weeks later, Shawn mailed another one. Two weeks after that, he mailed another.

It would be a full ten months and fourteen letters later, long after he had been expelled from his program (his student ID card had been found at the foot of the cyclotron) that Shawn would finally receive some form of response.

CHAPTER 4

Downtown Alicante's sights and sounds—the vendors hawking trinkets and their rowdy, haggling customers, the children playing after-breakfast poison tag in the street, the throngs of tourists and the overall hustle and bustle of the San Blas district—seemed to stream in through Rafael's bedroom window all at once as his radio alarm blasted "Demente," the pop song that had been hijacking Valencian airwaves since May. Rafael turned to his left, but Maria, his young wife, wasn't there. He was surprised she would be up so early on a Sunday morning, but then again, he had no idea when she normally rose on weekends since he usually got up first or else slept until noon.

Not today, though.

Rafael shut off the alarm and rolled out of bed. He showered and shaved and climbed into his civilian attire of denim blazer, polo shirt, and corduroy pants, which Maria always said made him look like an Andalusian schoolboy. He approached the night table and stopped and stared for a moment.

He reminded himself that he didn't have to do this. Then he

reminded himself that that was precisely the point, that he was *choosing* to do this.

He took a breath and opened the drawer and removed its contents: his Star 30M pistol, which he secured in the shoulder holster under his jacket, and then the folded piece of paper he'd placed in there the day before. He unfolded the paper, stared at it for a long moment, then refolded it and placed it inside his left breast pocket.

Maria, frying something sweet and cinnamony at the stove, smiled warmly as Rafael entered the kitchen.

"Good morning, *amorcito*. Churros for the road?"

"No thank you, *corazón*," he answered in his Castilian Spanish, a stark contrast from Maria's Murcian dialect. "Running late."

"How many Sundays in a row are they going to throw at you? It's getting ridiculous, no?"

"I'm not going to the station today."

"No? So where are you running off to, then?"

"It's Sunday, isn't it, *mi cielo*? I'm going to church."

She gave him a quizzical look, but he only smiled and kissed her softly on the mouth before turning and heading out the low door of their cramped, one-bedroom apartment.

Anglada Parish lay in the hills just beyond Marina Alta, and with his car turning up A-7/E-15, Rafael could already hear the music. Brass bands playing *jota,* no doubt accompanied by men and women dancing the Fandango of Albaido, or the Brlea. *Dulzaina* players blasting ancient Spanish melodies over the countryside below. It was the first day of the Hogueras de San Juan, or Bonfires of Saint John festival, and the parish would be packed with locals, parishioners, and tourists all making merry. Mass had probably just ended, and, for a moment, Rafael wished he hadn't missed it.

He glanced at the small copper crucifix hanging on the dashboard, a gift from Father Ortega when he was eighteen. Since moving to Alicante in November, he'd been to church exactly twice, once on Christmas in his own neighborhood and once for a cousin's wedding at Anglada in April. Whatever his recent lapses in the religious department, however, today would go a long way toward making up for them. He reached into his jacket pocket and grasped the folded paper in his fingers. There was no way he could have left it behind—he clearly remembered removing it from the drawer—but he wanted to feel it now, to make everything more real.

After parking his car in the lot by the rectory, Rafael joined the crowds that were making their way over to an area outside the library where a makeshift podium had been erected. The music had ceased, and the dancers had stopped dancing, and Father Arroyo now strode through the crowd, making his way toward the platform. Humble and down to earth, at seventy-four, Father Arroyo still exuded the easygoing charisma that had made him so popular in Alicante. He ascended the platform and smiled warmly at the assembly before him.

"Dear brothers and sisters, venerable fellow priests," he began as the crowd quieted. "We live in a confusing age. Even Saint Arialdus or the martyrs of Cardera in their own times of darkness could not have foreseen the supreme challenges to our faith that we witness today. A time when so much is possible that too much is possible. A time when science is worshiped and religion is a subject of academic intrigue. When a new worldwide obsession with the stars and the heavens has replaced fear of heaven."

Standing off to the side, a little beyond the crowd, Rafael could see Father Arroyo's two assistant priests, a tall blind man with shaved head, sunglasses, and walking stick, and a thick redheaded man with a wide smirk. Rafael had met these two priests several months prior at his cousin's wedding. The blind man, he knew, was a recent émigré from Ireland, while the redheaded man was from the United States.

He stared at them for several moments, hoping that they wouldn't notice or recognize him, then turned his attention back to Father Arroyo.

"John the Baptist," the padre continued, "is described in the gospel as a man 'sent from God to bear witness to the light so that through him everyone might believe.' How we could use him now, my friends, how we could use him now. But in his absence, we, each and every one of us, must resolve to ourselves to be such witnesses, witnesses of the light, the luminescent, ever-enveloping light of God, in order that through us, our faltering brethren may believe anew.

"So on Saint John's Eve, when we bring our discarded tables and chairs and sofas and we throw them into the embers to create the always majestical and glorious bonfires of Saint John, fires that make the handiwork of our competing brothers and sisters in Santa Pola and Almoradi look like pilot lights, we must recall the true light to which we bear witness. And when we burn our old and useless furniture, we must also burn the useless, wasteful parts of ourselves, the doubt, the fear, the illusions, the vanity. We are sons and daughters of Alicante, we are children of Saint John, and we are first and foremost cherished children of the Lord! Amen!"

"Amen!" answered the crowd, which then applauded with much enthusiasm, even if Father Arroyo's sermon was noticeably similar to that from the previous year. As the padre descended from the platform, the jota music and dancing started up anew, and members of his flock encircled him to wish him well and exchange pleasantries.

Still standing off to the side, Father Reese, the heavyset, red-headed American priest, watched, while his companion, the quiet man with the sunglasses, Father McCord, stood listening to the music, soaking up the scene. As often happened when the two were together, Father Reese swiftly assumed the role of narrator.

"Francisco Guerra is shaking hands with the padre," he said in English. "Very enthusiastically."

"All right," McCord replied, with little interest.

"Guerra never gave the padre the time of day, you know. When the church needed access to the *emergencia* funds, Guerra wouldn't even return his calls. Now he's his best friend? Carlos Bartrina, he's also there, apple-polishing no less shamelessly."

"So what's changed?"

"What's changed? The word has obviously gotten around."

"And what would that be?"

"Oh, come on, Father McCord. You love to pretend to be above any gossip, but I know your hearing is 20 percent more powerful than the rest of ours, isn't it?"

Father McCord just smirked, and Father Reese continued, "Bishop Sabartes is moving to Toledo to become archbishop. That you'll admit to knowing, I'm sure. The very same weekend that was announced, Father Arroyo is suddenly called away to meet with the Presbyteral Council in Seville. A coincidence?"

"You think Father Arroyo will be appointed to take the bishop's place."

"Praised be He who grants you such discernment, Father McCord."

Over by the podium, Father Arroyo conversed briefly with several other revelers, then strode over to greet his two assistant priests.

"*Benedictus qi venit!*" Father Reese exclaimed in Latin as Arroyo arrived. "Glorious and inspiring, as always," he added in Spanish.

"I know, I recycled from last year," Father Arroyo said with a self-deprecating smile. "But with all the sangria flowing, I assumed it was safe."

"Ha, yes! Of course!" Father Reese agreed.

Father Arroyo turned to Reese's colleague. "How are you this morning, Father McCord?"

"I can't see any cause for complaint."

"Very cute, Father McCord. Well, I'm off to take confession now. If you two gentlemen would be generous enough to hold down the fort for a few hours, make sure nothing gets out of hand, it would be most appreciated. We'd rather not have Oswaldo hosing down vomit like last year."

"Of course, Padre," answered Father Reese. Then, when Father Arroyo had walked on, he leaned in closely to Father McCord.

"Notice the distance in his voice?" he muttered. "Subtle, but you could hear it. In his mind, he's already gone!"

As Father Arroyo moved down the path leading to the church, past the children carrying cardboard effigies on sticks and the ladies in bridal gowns handing out tuna-and-fig pies, revelers smiled, nodded, waved. As he rounded the corner by the old greenhouse, which Father Reese was supposedly renovating, he paused and admired the breathtaking view of Marina Alta below and the shimmering Mediterranean stretching beyond it toward the horizon. He had gazed upon this very same view thousands of times before, but this time his doing so was accompanied by a new and bittersweet feeling: nostalgia.

"What do you mean *retire*?" Bishop Alonso had exclaimed two days prior, eyes wide with shock, as a half dozen other bishops and priests sat uncomfortably, watching the drama unfold around a small table in a windowed room overlooking Seville's city center.

"I simply feel the time has come," Father Arroyo replied softly.

"And what time is that, Padre?" Alonso shot back. "A time when faith is cowering in the corner, when a man can be sucked into outer space on the evening news? Is that the time of which you speak, the time you feel is ripe for abandoning the Church?"

"My intention isn't to abandon anything," Father Arroyo replied.

"I'm sure it can't be any secret to you," Bishop Alonso continued, "that you were under serious consideration to assume Bishop Sabartes's former appointment. Now, we'll need to fill that position in Valencia and your own at Anglada Parish!"

Father Arroyo made no response.

"Why?" Bishop Alonso continued. "I'm afraid I simply don't understand."

"I can't explain it," Father Arroyo replied, but that was a lie. He didn't *want* to explain it. He knew exactly why he wished to retire: plainly and simply, he didn't have it in him anymore. Despite all outward appearances, his health was beginning to fail, as was his passion, if he was being perfectly honest with himself. More than anything, however, it was the weight, the tremendous gravity of his position that was doing him in. He had spent untold years absorbing other people's maladies—physical, spiritual, practical, personal—like a sponge. He had listened to their fears and nightmares, waded into the darkest corners of their souls, and calmly reassured them, attempted to give them strength. But despite his brave face, it had all taken something out of him, he could feel that, and he wanted desperately to preserve whatever was still left. In short, Father Arroyo wanted, for the final years of his life, to relax.

"Enough dissension," Cardinal Falero cut in, causing everyone to stop and turn to the head of the conference table. At ninety-three, Cardinal Falero often looked like he was asleep when he wasn't speaking. He was never asleep.

"If the padre wishes to retire, let him retire," Cardinal Falero declared, his voice hoarse and shaky. "And may God be with you, Padre Arroyo."

Brushing off the memory of that unpleasant discussion, the padre now stepped away from the vista overlooking Marina Alta, wound his way around the greenhouse, and turned in to the church, a tall Gothic structure that had withstood several disasters, including an infamous fire in 1849 in which dozens of worshipers assembled for midnight Mass had perished.

There were about twenty-five minutes to go before the first scheduled confession. The padre brought a copy of *Summa Theologica* into the confessional, where he read from it for several minutes, admiring the crisp logic of Aquinas's arguments. When the appointed time came, he set the book down and tapped his fingers against the mahogany of his armrest, an old enduring habit. After a moment or so, he heard the front door swing open and the confessor enter the church and settle into the small booth on the other side of the partition. Father Arroyo waited for the man to speak, but he didn't. This was probably his first time.

"Speak, my son," the padre invited.

There was a deep breath on the other side of the curtain and then the voice of a man who could have been anywhere between twenty and forty.

"Bless me, Padre, for I have sinned," the man said. "It's been . . . six years since my last confession. And my sin was confessed about then."

"You haven't sinned since then?" Father Arroyo asked.

"I sin every day, Padre, like everyone. But not like then. And sinning is not what brings me here today."

"So what brings you, my son?"

"A debt, I guess."

"To whom?"

"The Church, perhaps. Or maybe to God. I'm not even certain."

"Go on."

The man began to speak, then stopped, then started again. "Do you remember, Padre, back in 1999, a case involving a girl, a theater actress, who was badly disfigured in a robbery in a pawn shop?"

"In Almoradi?"

"Yes, exactly."

"Two teenage boys attacked her."

There was silence for a moment. Then, the voice continued. "We were twelve years old. Loners, both of us. I was quiet, tried to do what was expected of me, but Roberto—I'll call him Roberto— he was a visionary. Many of us, if we're not Roberto ourselves, we have a friend like him. Charismatic and up to no good, and we get pulled along like a mutt on a leash. In this particular adventure, far riskier than anything we'd ever attempted before, no one was supposed to get hurt. Roberto had assured me of this. He had scoped everything out, planned, made arrangements. It was going to be quick and easy and like it never even happened, except that we'd have the kind of *dinero* we hadn't before.

"But when the girl showed up, we panicked. Roberto held his butterfly knife to her face only to scare her, but when she screamed, thrashed about, he lost control. He swore it was an accident later on, and maybe it was. No one can ever know but him."

"But the robbery itself was not an accident," Father Arroyo interjected.

"No. No, it wasn't. They sent us to Santa Leticia. Not the worst place, not as bad as some of the youth centers you'll find in Malaga or Madrid, but you could have put me anywhere and I would have been in hell either way. I saw her face at night, the jagged red line running along her cheek like the pathways in a maze, the look of sheer terror in her eyes. I dreamed about her acting on the stage, the blood still running from her face, the audience shrinking in disgust. I died, Padre, and I would have remained dead were it not for a young chaplain, a man named Luis Ortega. Are you familiar with Padre Ortega?"

"No. No, I can't say I am."

"He taught me scripture, about purification and transformation and how there is always a way to be forgiven. Always, without exception. Even the unpardonable sin could really be pardoned according to Padre Ortega. Were it not for Padre Ortega, I know I never would have made it out with my soul intact. He brought me back to life.

"When I left Santa Leticia at fourteen, I wanted to be as removed from a juvenile delinquent as humanly possible, so I enrolled at the police academy in El Puerto and became a detective. Meanwhile, I lost track of Roberto. We hadn't remained close in Santa Leticia. I heard rumors that he'd gone to America, but I didn't truly know what had become of him—that is, not until a month ago when he showed up at our station in Dolores. Slick and clean cut, but with that same unmistakable Cheshire cat grin he'd had as a boy. He was somehow stranger, edgier than I'd remembered him, and he belonged now to some sort of intelligence unit, supposedly connected to Interpol, but probably not really. In the police force, we call such units *los misterios*. We never know for certain exactly what they are. We play host to them from time to time, by order of the CNP. We allow them use of our office spaces, even grant them access to our resources when necessary. Most importantly, we don't ask questions.

"Roberto's group has been working out of Dolores for three weeks now. The mission, as I understand it, involves an American fugitive, a terrorist who is believed to be hiding out somewhere in Alicante. From what I gather, he's considered extremely dangerous and guilty of unspeakable crimes. We haven't been told very much, but when I asked Roberto why he believed this man was in Alicante, he told me his photograph had been taken here, a picture that showed him walking with another man through La Explanada de España.

"This photograph was of course not shown to me. But we do share an office, and even among the most discreet operators, you will find that a certain sloppiness can develop. It's only natural in an office environment where people are working round the clock, barely eating or sleeping. Words are spoken too loudly. Documents are left out in the open longer than they should be. Other things, too."

At that point, Father Arroyo heard a slight rustling of fabric from the other side of the partition, and then a small, folded piece of paper was gently passed through the bars of the grille. With some hesitation, he retrieved the paper.

"Open it up," the voice instructed.

Father Arroyo slowly unfolded the paper.

"I bring this to you, Padre," the voice continued, "because I believe you will do what is right. I do not know what is right, only that the Church once saved my life and that I believe strongly in the power and reality of redemption. That a man can return from anything, anywhere, no matter what or who he once was and that his past is between him and God. Should you wish to speak to me again, my mobile number is written on the back of the paper. In the meantime, I leave this matter at your discretion."

Father Arroyo said nothing. He just continued to stare at the paper in his hands, at the grainy black-and-white photograph depicting two figures walking through La Explanada de España, the city's palm tree–lined main promenade. Their clothing was washed out by light, but their faces were relatively discernible. The man on the left, holding a cane and wearing sunglasses, bore a strong and obvious resemblance to Father Arroyo's Irish assistant priest, Father McCord, though his head was in the process of turning, and it was therefore difficult to identify him for certain. The man on the right, grinning widely, lifting one hand to shield his eyes from the sunlight, was without a shadow of doubt Father Reese.

CHAPTER 5

Shawn stopped the music and removed his earbuds as the bus driver announced their arrival in Emington, Minnesota. The trip had not been comfortable, had involved three buses, plus a night spent in a Chicago terminal, where Shawn was nearly robbed as he tried to sleep, propped up against an information kiosk. But now, as he strapped on his overstuffed backpack and disembarked from the bus, he felt a surge of adrenaline. The street on which he found himself was drab, lined with ranch houses and maple trees, pure middle-of-nowhere Americana, but for Shawn, it was Mecca, Eden, and the Emerald City all rolled into one. This was where he and the object of his obsession would finally unite.

Over the past four months, Shawn and Andrew Leland had exchanged no less than thirteen letters. Leland had made it clear early on in his first response that although he might conceivably enjoy exchanging ideas with a like-minded young physicsphile, he would under no circumstances discuss anything to do with his alleged abduction. Shawn had thus changed tactics and instead engaged him regarding his work. Several years earlier, Shawn had become an expert in some of Leland's early, more obscure work, particularly his much-ignored efforts to combine *Alcubierre drives* and *Krasnikov tubes*, two separate and well-known theories regarding warp drive, into one unified formula for achieving faster-than-light travel.

In his letters to Leland, Shawn questioned the scientist about the practical implications of his theories on these subjects, while also engaging him in a variety of other topics, such as cosmic inflation and quantum nonlocality. Leland, in his responses (always typed out in Helvetica font on recycled stationery) seemed impressed by the young man's grasp of the material and his eagerness to learn. He responded directly to some of Shawn's questions, though more often than not would meet a question with a question, teasing Shawn, encouraging him to find the answers on his own.

Shawn, for his part, was thrilled on multiple levels to be in close correspondence with the world's most elusive man. It was like a strange dream, something no one would ever have believed had he told anyone, which he didn't. Shawn also observed that Leland, in his willingness to correspond with such regularity, actually appeared to fit the stereotype of a recluse quite well: deep down, it seemed, he had been yearning for human contact all along.

But Shawn wasn't content with this type of relationship for long. As fascinating and enlightening as these exchanges were and as *cool* as it was to be in any kind of contact with Andrew Leland at all, neither contact nor friendship was what he truly wanted. What Shawn wanted was what everyone wanted: the truth.

"I think I mentioned to you previously that I have an uncle who lives in Rochester, MN," Shawn wrote one day, after having been in contact with Leland for four months. "I'll be visiting him again in several weeks. If there's any chance we could meet in person, I would greatly appreciate it. There are several issues relating to Lambda-CDM that I still can't quite wrap my mind around, and I think a longer discussion in real time would be extremely helpful. It would also, needless to say, be a tremendous honor to meet you in person, considering the profound impact your work has had on me. I would, of course, respect your wishes not to discuss subject matters which you've already previously indicated are off limits."

This last part was a blatant lie. Those "subject matters" were the only things he wanted to discuss. However, Shawn knew for certain that Leland would never agree to talk about his abduction in advance and that a face-to-face was the only way he could force the subject without fear of being ignored or hung up on.

Shawn waited for a response to his letter, but none came. Weeks went by, and Shawn wrote again, this time dropping the issue for now and asking some fairly trivial questions about black holes. But he received no response to this letter, either. When a third letter went unanswered, it became clear enough to Shawn that his correspondence with Andrew Leland had come to an end.

Which meant, of course, that he now had nothing left to lose.

Leland, Shawn felt, had been hoarding a treasure trove of revelations he had no right to hide. Fate had for some reason chosen him to be the first point of contact between humanity and an alien world, and to treat the experience like a private, personal matter when it in fact had implications for everyone was unequivocally wrong. So Shawn had made a decision: he would travel to Emington, confront Leland in person, and wouldn't leave without some answers.

Shawn sat down on the bus stop's bench, pulled out his phone and retrieved the image he'd found on Google Street View of 123 Bay Berry Drive. The house, though blurry in the picture, appeared to be a beige Cape Cod, simple and nondescript. According to his phone, the location was only about twenty minutes away, walking distance, so Shawn figured he'd head over on foot.

As he walked, since he'd already rehearsed everything he would say to Leland countless times over the past few days, Shawn just took in the scenery. Lots of simple-looking houses, a large colonial-style post office, a bland, concrete Wells Fargo. This was where Leland had made his home, possibly for as long as the past three years. It was incredible that someone so notorious and sought after, an individual of global significance, could have been hiding in plain sight among such ordinariness. Shawn wondered if anyone in the town might possibly know him, if anyone had ever recognized or perhaps even befriended him. Maybe it was even an open secret. Maybe lots of people knew who was living among them but kept it under wraps out of loyalty or protectiveness or some sort of midwestern code.

Shawn reached Bay Berry Drive and soon after, judging from the house numbers, the actual block where Leland lived. It was a quiet stretch, consisting of more ranch houses and, in the center of the block, a construction site, where men in hard hats were laying bricks, while others cleared out debris from a ditch using excavators and backhoe loaders. Shawn examined the house numbers on each side of the site and felt his knees turn to jelly.

No, he thought to himself. *It can't be.*

Trying to keep himself together, he approached one of the workers, who appeared to be inputting information into a tablet.

"What are you guys building here?" Shawn asked, trying to sound calm.

"School," the man replied, his eyes still on the screen.

"What happened to the house that was here before?"

"Torn down, what do you think?"

"How long ago?"

"About eight months, maybe," the man replied. "Why?"

Shawn had to prevent himself from gasping.

"Who lived there?" he barely managed to get out.

The construction worker looked up and gave Shawn a once-over and didn't like what he saw.

"Hey, who the fuck are you, anyway?"

Shawn staggered away and moved back onto the sidewalk. His heart was racing, and he felt nauseous. He struggled to make sense of it all. Was he in the wrong place? Could that explain it? He called up the image on Street View again. It was definitely the same address and, based on the water tower visible in the background, the same location, as well. But, he now realized, the image capture date on the corner of the screen was actually from three years ago!

This left only one thing that still didn't make sense: How could Shawn have been exchanging letters with someone for the past four months who lived in a house that had been torn down eight months ago?

There was an old-fashioned rail car–style diner several blocks away, and Shawn wandered in and settled into a booth, hoping to gather his thoughts. After ordering a plate of chocolate chip pancakes and a cup of coffee, he pulled out a stack of papers from his bag, all of the letters he'd exchanged with Leland, and began to pore over them, hoping for any kind of clue that might help him make sense of the situation.

He decided to go back to the beginning, to Leland's first letter. "Dear Mr. Ferris," it had begun, "I didn't want to respond to you up until this point out of a reasonable concern that you, like many others, were attempting to trick or exploit me. If that were the case, responding and thereby confirming that you have my address correct would put my privacy and potentially my person in serious jeopardy. I have made it clear on several occasions that I *do not recall* the events said to have taken place in Southern California, that as far as I'm concerned, *they did not occur at all*, and I will under no circumstances discuss that matter further. However, it does seem to me from your most recent letter, that you have an impressive . . ."

Shawn put the letter down as the waitress brought over his food. She was a pretty girl, probably in her late teens, and wore a faded Taylor Swift T-shirt. As she set down his pancakes and coffee, Shawn looked up at her and was struck with a sudden idea.

"Hey, can I ask you a question?" he said.

"Sure," she responded, smiling hospitably.

Shawn leaned forward a little and lowered his voice. "The rumors about this town. They true?"

"What rumors?"

"You know. That somebody very famous lives here."

The girl gave him a confused look. "Not that I've ever heard."

"Hey, I'm not a reporter or anything. You can trust me."

"I don't know anything about anyone famous living here or any rumors," the girl said. "Randy Williams from the Vikings used to live in Wadena County, but he moved out last year. Is that who you mean?"

Shawn shook his head.

"Then I don't think I can help you. Sorry."

The girl went away from the table, and Shawn reflected that if the letters hadn't actually been coming from Bay Berry Drive, who's to say they'd been coming from anywhere in Emington—or anywhere in Minnesota, for that matter? He turned his attention back to Leland's first letter. He would go through each letter, one by one, he decided. He wasn't sure what he was looking for, but he hoped maybe he would know when he found it, even if that meant sitting in that diner all day. Fortunately, he was only into the fourth letter when something caught his eye.

In his third letter to Leland, Shawn had asked a fairly straightforward question regarding the scientist's support for the *quantum consciousness* hypothesis, which theorizes that quantum mechanics might play an important role in understanding how human consciousness works. He wanted to know why Leland supported this controversial view, which seemed to actually contradict several of his other positions. Leland had responded with a detailed account of how his mentorship under Nobel Prize–winning physicist and prominent champion of quantum consciousness Eugene Wigner had led him in this direction.

The problem, though, was that Leland had never supported this view and had in fact been vocal in his opposition to it. For some odd reason, Shawn had been confused on this point, an error he only became aware of when he chanced upon a 2002 paper by Leland arguing that Wigner, genius as he was, had been all wrong about this particular subject. By the time Shawn discovered this paper, it was several months since his exchange with Leland on quantum consciousness, and he had forgotten the matter had ever come up.

Why, he now wondered, sitting there in the diner, would Leland have given him an account of how he came to support a theory that he not only never supported but had openly criticized? It was understandable that Shawn might have confused Leland's views, but how could Leland himself have done so?

There was an obvious answer: if the person Shawn had been corresponding with was not really Andrew Leland.

The thought was both mortifying to Shawn and plausible. All the time, his correspondence with Leland had seemed like a fantasy, too mind-blowing and incredible to be true. Maybe it was. But if Leland hadn't been writing the letters, who had? And what did he or she want with Shawn?

There were other questions, too. Shawn had been tipped off to Leland's supposed address by the mysterious poster on Schrödinger's Rat called AmberQ. Who was she really? Why had she given him that particular address? And how could Shawn's letters have been met with a response if they were actually being mailed to a construction site? This last question, Shawn thought, he might be able to guess an answer for. He had generally not used a mailbox but instead had given the letters to his building's mailman, which meant the letters could have conceivably been intercepted somewhere along the line, even if that seemed like a big stretch. Finally, Shawn wondered, why would anyone who wasn't Leland have amassed such an in-depth knowledge of Leland's early and more obscure research to the extent that he or she could fool someone as obsessed with Leland's work as Shawn?

Shawn felt like his head was spinning, and he stared straight ahead at the tiled wall near the diner's exit, trying to focus, to center himself. His quest for inner calm, however, was swiftly interrupted by a sudden vibration in his left pocket.

Shawn pulled out his phone. There was a text message on the screen from a number he didn't recognize, containing a simple, two-word instruction:

Go outside.

Shawn took a deep breath. He stuffed Leland's letters into his backpack and stood up. His eyes zeroed in on the exit, and as he walked toward the door, he felt as if he were in a dream, the door getting closer and closer, some unknown fate awaiting him on the other side. He thought he could hear the waitress calling out to him, but he couldn't focus on what she was saying.

He stepped outside. A dark gray SUV was waiting at the curb. He received another text:

Get in the van.

Now, Shawn had a decision to make. The person in the van might be Andrew Leland. More likely, it was whoever had been lying to him for four months. Either way, he would be at their mercy. Yes, the mystery in which he had become engulfed would probably be cleared up very quickly, but the risk was great.

Too great.

Shawn took a step forward, as though intending to advance, then did a sudden about-face, ready to run the opposite way, but someone had snuck up from behind and had been ready. In a blur of movement, he felt his legs get swept out from underneath him, and the next thing he knew, he hit the ground hard and was lying on his back, staring up, wincing from the pain. The last thing Shawn remembered seeing before the world suddenly turned black was the face of a young woman bent over him, injecting a needle into his arm, her hair dangling over his face, shiny and jet black with deep amber highlights.

CHAPTER 6

A miniature Mount Vesuvius, baking soda and vinegar lava erupting out of its crater. A red balloon attached to a test tube, inflating by itself. Cups of Coke, Sunkist, and Poland Spring, each containing human teeth.

These are some of the experiments Shawn is up against at the Bridgewater Elementary School annual science fair. His own project is far less flashy. No models, no props, just a large piece of oak tag covered in diagrams, sketches, and handwritten text. But if you pay close attention and follow through on Shawn's detailed instructions, you'll find yourself having built a nifty self-driving car that not only operates flawlessly but is cheaper and more efficient than most previous designs.

The other kids don't bother trying to understand it, while the adults gather round, some studying the poster board in a vain effort to follow the science, some asking Shawn informed questions, some just smiling, proud and amused that a twelve-year-old in their own town could be so ambitious and precocious.

Shawn's science teacher, Mr. Wilcox, however, seems decidedly unimpressed, possibly even disturbed.

"Hadn't we discussed metamorphic rocks?" he asks.

"I started on that, but I got bored."

"Come with me."

Twenty minutes later, Shawn is sitting in the principal's office, being asked the same basic question for the third time, as his father and Mr. Wilcox look on.

"Shawn, we're all very impressed by your project," Principal Davis asserts, "but we know the design itself isn't yours. So whose is it?"

This time, Shawn just stares at him.

"Shawn?"

"I have a question. If you don't know whose it is, how can you know it's not mine?"

Principal Davis glances at Mr. Wilcox, who turns to Shawn and smiles.

"Shawn, you're the smartest student in my class by a country mile. We both know you're good. We both also know you're not *that* good."

Shawn can't believe this. He'd awoken that morning full of excitement. He was going to make everyone so proud. What a joke that turned out to be.

He turns to his father, who's staring out the window, obviously wishing he was anywhere else.

"Dad, you *saw* me make this. You know how hard I've been working on this project!" he exclaims.

His father nods.

"Yes, you did put a lot of work in," he answers in a soft voice. "But I can't say who came up with what."

And then his father smiles, a sweet, sympathetic smile that just makes everything that much shittier.

"Shawn, I'm not going to punish you. Don't be afraid. You can be honest."

That's it. He's had it. He can't sit there another second. In fact, he physically can't; he's sick to his stomach, needs to hurl right away, and he sure as hell can't do that in the principal's office. That would really make him look guilty.

But when he tries to stand up, he can't. It's as though he's glued to his seat. He keeps pushing down on the armrest to lift off, but his butt won't move.

Principal Davis starts to laugh. Shawn looks up at him and can't believe what he sees. His principal's eyes have taken on a bright red hue, and his irises have become thin and catlike. As he laughs, a long, serpentine tongue protrudes from his mouth.

Shawn turns quickly to Mr. Wilcox and then to his father. They, too, have undergone the same transformation. Panic rising, Shawn desperately tries to get out of his seat, but it's no use. He's completely stuck, trapped, as the three men or whatever they've become continue to laugh their horribly shrill laughs with more and more glee and more and more menace . . .

Shawn awoke with a start. For a second, the only thing that registered was a powerful throbbing in his head, like how he always imagined a hangover might feel if he drank. Then, as the pain began to clear, he sat up and took in his surroundings, which didn't really amount to much. The room he was in was mostly bare, except for a ceiling fan, a folding chair (onto which his outer clothes had been draped), some random-looking pieces of tape on the wall, and the cot on which he lay. There was a window near the edge of the bed, though, and it seemed to be dark outside. Shawn swung his feet onto the floor to get a better look when the door of the room suddenly opened.

A short, bald man with fleshy features and wearing a swanky three-piece suit stood in the doorway.

"Good. You're up," he said in a soft, childlike voice. "Rachel wants to see you."

"Where am I?"

The bald man gestured to Shawn's clothes. "Get dressed."

A few minutes later, the man led Shawn down a corridor. As they walked, they passed several large windows, through which Shawn could barely make out what looked like a college campus, though it was too dark outside to be sure of anything. The building they were in also seemed to be a dormitory—or a former dormitory, at any rate. That might explain the tape on the wall of that room, which may have once been used for posters.

The man led Shawn into a small office at the end of the hall, where a young woman seated at a desk was waiting for him. Once Shawn was inside, the man exited, closing the door behind him, leaving Shawn and the young woman alone. Shawn recognized her at once. The last time he had seen her face, she'd struck him with a needle.

"Have a seat," she instructed.

After a moment's hesitation, he sat down across from her. The office was spare, probably a former dorm office and, most likely, Shawn sensed, not the woman's actual office.

"Do you know who I am?" she asked.

"You're AmberQ," he answered.

"Very good."

She looked to be around his age, maybe a few years older but under thirty. Her eyes were large and rectangular like an anime character's. Her hair was black and shoulder length with amber highlights that had no doubt inspired her online alias. There was something about her overall appearance that struck Shawn as not only beautiful but familiar, though he couldn't tell if that was because he'd actually seen her before or because she reminded him of someone else.

"My name is Rachel," she said. Her speech had just the slightest trace of an accent, possibly Australian or New Zealand.

"Why did you bring me here?"

"We didn't want to. We weren't ready for you to make a move yet. But once you did, we decided to make the best of it."

"It was you all along, all those letters from Leland. Am I right?"

She nodded.

"Who are you?"

"Shawn, do you like conspiracy theories?"

He didn't answer.

"Many people believe that we didn't really land on the moon in 1969," she continued. "They're half-right. We landed there in 1951. The first time, at least. By 1969, we'd been there at least four times already."

She paused, and he realized she was waiting for some kind of reaction.

"And I'm supposed to just believe that."

"You're not supposed to anything. You can believe me or you can believe what you thought before, what everyone else thinks. It's up to you."

Okay, he could play along.

"So, what, are you saying there were earlier moon landings and NASA kept them a secret?"

She shook her head.

"NASA never knew. NASA had nothing to do with them."

"How could NASA have had nothing to do with them? Who did?"

"We did. Ambius."

"Okay, so what's Ambius?"

"The real NASA. Or, to put it another way, Ambius is everything NASA doesn't know it's missing."

Shawn shook his head in frustration.

"I can't follow. You're not giving this straight. And what does this have to do with Leland? Where is he really?"

"We're coming to that. And I'm sorry, I'll try to be more clear.

Ambius is a multinational space program. In all the ways that matter, it's the only space program. It was started in 1939, a good nineteen years before NASA, when Earth first made contact with intelligent extraterrestrial life. We never could have found them ourselves, but they found us. The first communication came from a planet in the Epsilon Eridani system, but once contact had been established, we essentially joined the larger community. We were in the intergalactic phone book, so to speak. Meanwhile, we were exposed to incredible technology, things that helped Ambius advance rapidly beyond what we ever could have accomplished on our own. NASA was established shortly thereafter, a parallel program that emerged from the Committee for Aeronautics, which would exist completely independently from us, with no knowledge that contact had already been made, and which could act as the public face of space exploration."

"A front."

"Exactly. A front. Otherwise, there'd be no way to advance scientifically without alerting the world to the fact that intelligent extraterrestrial civilizations exist. And that could not happen. The evolution of the human race needed to proceed unimpeded by mass hysteria, politics, or religious interventions. Do you understand?"

He didn't respond. He didn't want her to think he was accepting her story, even if in spite of himself he was becoming very interested.

After a brief pause, she continued, "Just like the nations of our world, the different populations of the universe vary in their dispositions. Ten years ago, our intelligence sources learned that a certain planet was planning to attack us. We're still not entirely sure why, but there were some indications it had to do with our natural resources. You may have heard in the course of your academic career that Earth, because of its size, distribution of elements, and its perfect distance from its star, is fairly unique in the universe. This is true. We're the subject of great envy, Shawn. At any rate, we weren't going to sit and wait for this attack to happen, so we implemented an advanced plan to build a kind of protective barrier, a large cosmic shield comprised of exotic matter that could essentially trap any object trying to pass through it and redirect it thousands of years into the past."

"That's impossible."

She only smiled.

"So, what, you had some kind of alien technology at your disposal to be able to build something like that?"

"Not for this. We had a plain old regular human scientist at our disposal. A well-known theoretical physicist who had been secretly working with us for years and who, in the early part of his career, had conducted groundbreaking research on ways of integrating the Alcubierre drive with the Krasnikov tube. More recently, he had postulated a theory that the two could be effectively combined to create a kind of wall or screen of curved space-time."

The terms *Alcubierre drive* and *Krasnikov tube* blindsided him and rang in his ears. It couldn't be. Or could it? Rachel saw the look on his face, and she nodded.

"But how could he have worked for you?" Shawn stammered. "He was a hack who hadn't contributed anything to science in decades!"

"So it would seem. But if you were working for the most covert organization in the world, what would *you* want people to think?"

He shook his head. "I don't believe it."

"Like I said, you don't have to."

Shawn closed his eyes. This was all so much to take in. He opened them again. "So did he build your shield?"

"No."

"What happened?"

"You know what happened. Everyone knows what happened."

"Bernasconi Hills."

She nodded. "Leland hadn't even gotten a chance to begin

adapting his old research for the project. They knew, and they took him."

"And what did they do to him?"

"We don't know."

"What do you mean you don't know? He came back! What did he say happened?"

"He said what you already know he said. That he didn't even remember being abducted in the first place. That the whole thing never happened."

"But what did he say *to you*?"

"He didn't say anything to us."

"What? What do you mean?"

She took a deep breath.

"When Leland came back, we had no idea why, just like we had no idea why we hadn't been attacked in the time he'd been gone. We wanted the answers to these questions. Why did they keep him alive? Was he telling the truth about not remembering anything? As soon as he was picked up in Mexico, right after the first round of the media circus, we requested he be brought to a facility in Texas for immediate questioning. But the feds got to him first. They certainly didn't buy his spiel about having no memory, and they wanted more time with him. They continued to question him, eventually resorting to enhanced interrogation techniques. Nothing too unorthodox, probably not even as bad as what they use in Guantanamo. Problem was, traveling upward of eleven light-years is apparently not the healthiest thing for a person's heart. They pushed just a little too hard, and that was it."

Shawn stared at her in shock.

"So all those rumors about him living in the woods or the hills . . ."

"Stories that serve everyone's interests, including ours."

Shawn sat there in stunned silence as Rachel gave him a moment to process it all. Then she continued, "We'll probably never know the truth about what he experienced in space or why he came back. Just as we'll never know why he claimed to have no memories, whether his mind had actually been wiped clean or whether it was all part of some master plan. What we do know is that the threat is still very real. We can't say why they haven't attacked yet, but ten years isn't much time between two planets separated by trillions of miles of space, and we have no reason to think the attack has been called off. On the contrary, we have every reason to believe it's imminent. Meanwhile, in the time since Bernasconi Hills, we've made dozens of attempts at building Leland's cosmic shield, and every single one has failed spectacularly. My colleagues think there's no one on Earth who understands Leland's theories well enough to finish what he started. I disagree."

Shawn, who'd been staring at the floor, looked up at her. He knew where this was going and couldn't believe she could possibly be serious.

"Let me get this straight," he said. "You're asking a grad school dropout to build a giant shield made out of time travel. Is there a punch line coming, or is that it?"

"You sell yourself short, and you know it. We read your posts on gravitational singularity and superluminal tunnels on Schrödinger's Rat, and we've been spitballing with you by mail for months. We know you're not 'smart'—you're one in a fucking million. And grad school dropout or not, you understand Leland's work better than anyone else alive. Is that not the case? Don't misunderstand, we're not asking you to do this yourself. We're asking you to do this with us."

Shawn was quiet a minute.

"Okay, let's imagine for argument's sake that I really do understand Leland's work better than anybody. Still, why would I help some shady secret government outfit that tricked me, kidnapped me, and, if you're not totally full of it, has been lying to the whole planet for almost a century?"

Rachel smiled. "Because you wouldn't just be helping some shady secret government outfit. You'd also be saving the world." She leaned forward, her anime eyes staring imploringly into his own. "Please, Shawn. Will you help us?"

Some hours later, lying in a slightly more comfortable bed in a more furnished room in the same building, Shawn couldn't sleep. A ceiling fan circled above him, and his eyes absently followed the blades. He had a big orientation in the morning, would get situated and meet the other scientists he'd be working with. For now, though, his mind was back on his elementary school science fair and what had really transpired after he'd been accused of cheating.

Even though Principal Davis and Mr. Wilcox couldn't prove that he'd stolen his design for the car, they disqualified his project, anyway, and suspended him from school for a week. They also let the word get out among his teachers and peers that Shawn had plagiarized his project, turning everyone's jealousy into disdain. But Shawn knew the design was his. No one believed him because they just couldn't accept that he was better and smarter than they were.

One day, things would be different, he'd promised himself then. Someday, people wouldn't hate him for being smarter than they were.

Someday, they would thank him.

CHAPTER 7

On June 24, at the stroke of midnight, Father Arroyo ambled over to a massive pile of discarded furniture and papier-mâché statues and lit the whole thing aflame, exclaiming, *"Deus lux mea!"* as hundreds of spectators broke into wild applause, punctuated by the sound of fireworks and blasting trumpets. The statues, giant effigies of local celebrities and politicians, burned one by one along the cliff side as the crowd danced before them with an exuberance that rivaled the larger festivities taking place at the same time on El Postiguet Beach. La Crema, the climax of the Bonfires of Saint John festival, had commenced.

As revelers watched to see which statue would go the longest without becoming consumed, Father Arroyo noticed Father Reese and Father McCord standing off to the side, away from all the action. The moment Father Reese stepped away to chat with someone else, Father Arroyo approached Father McCord.

"Padre, might you have some time tomorrow evening to stop by my office?"

"Of course, Padre."

"Great. Thank you."

As Father Arroyo walked away, he glanced over his shoulder once more at Father McCord. The assistant priest stood alone, motionless, his dark sunglasses brilliantly reflecting the flames he couldn't see. Father Arroyo couldn't trust him, he knew that. But he couldn't trust himself, either.

The next morning, at the crack of dawn, Father McCord rose from a fitful slumber and could still hear her voice. It was the third time he'd dreamed about her that month, and once again, her voice had been a soft and sweet whisper; different, he knew, from how it had been in life. Putting on his cassock and collar, he marveled at how his conscious memories always seemed to complicate things, while his dreams seemed to understand.

In the afternoon, he read aloud to a group of students from Salinas, whom he'd been teaching from the beginning of the month. One of the students asked him, "Padre, what's it like to be blind?"—a surprising question only in that it was being asked so late by this particular group.

"Imagine what you would see," he replied, "if your head fell straight off."

Children gravitated to Father McCord for much the same reason many adults found him distant and aloof: he didn't try too hard to be your friend. He was congenial, but there was also something closed off about him, not unlike his good friend at the parish, Father Reese. While on the surface Father Reese seemed much more an open book, he wasn't; though intrusive and gossip prone when it came to others, he was remarkably private and defensive when it came to himself.

Sometime after dinner, at the direction of Josep, the aging parish secretary, Father McCord took a seat in the antechamber to Father Arroyo's office. After a few moments, Father Arroyo opened his door and invited Father McCord to enter.

"How do you do, Padre?" Arroyo asked as Father McCord took a seat.

"Fine, thank you."

Father Arroyo gathered some papers into a pile and shoved them in a drawer, wondering as he did why he felt the need to make a show of tidying up for someone who couldn't see the mess nor the show. He leaned back in his chair and exhaled, making a soft whistling sound.

"Padre," he said, "have you heard the name 'Salvador Quintana'?"

"No, I can't say I have."

"He's a scientist, apparently something called a 'medicinal chemist.' Develops new drugs and medicines for pharmaceutical companies. I lunched with him and his wife last week; they want me to officiate at their daughter's wedding. Nice people. Over the course of a lovely and respectful conversation, Dr. Quintana suddenly asks me, 'How, Padre, can you continue to believe in all this crazy *tonterías*? Heaven is within reach! One man has even been there and back! Soon enough, we'll all be going there, and it won't be Jesus who will take us—it will be science! It will be progress and forward thinking and intelligence, everything to which your precious church stands in total opposition!' Mind you, his manner and tone remained entirely pleasant, even as he was telling me that my church opposes intelligence."

"And what did you say?"

"I conceded that yes, science might take our physical selves to spectacular places, even out to the farthest reaches of the heavens. But our souls, our true selves, will remain fixed on the ground until we accept that real transformation occurs only in the infinite space inside of us. The *Great Infinity Within*, as I like to call it. And that it is only through faith in our Lord and Savior that we will obtain true heaven, true spiritual salvation, true discovery, and adventure! A spacecraft can take you very far geographically, but only real faith can bring you to that wondrous place, that magical dimension where you can feel all of existence moving within and without you, where you are everything combined with everything and your heart and the rhythm of the universe beat as one."

There was a moment of silence as Father McCord waited to be sure the padre was finished speaking.

"Sounds like a perfectly fine response," he said.

Arroyo smiled.

"Oh, I do believe I'll miss you, Father McCord."

"Are you going somewhere, Padre?"

"Indeed I am. Though that's just between you and me."

"Valencia?"

"No, no. I'm retiring, Father McCord. What made you say Valencia?"

"Father Reese was convinced you were taking over Bishop Sabartes's position."

"Is that what he said?"

"He speculated."

"Well, that does bring me to the reason I asked you to come see me. Padre, I have an important matter to discuss. Something I cannot speak about with anyone else and something that requires the utmost discretion."

"Certainly, Padre."

"Father McCord, do you remember last year when you located the nine hundred euros that had been missing from the sacrament fund?"

"Yes."

"You found it in a cupboard in the rectory kitchenette, if I recall. Is that right?"

Father McCord nodded. He didn't like where this was going.

"Well, I'm not going to question the likelihood of that money being discovered by you of all people. Especially because from what I gather, your blindness has never represented any kind of impediment. But it might not surprise you if I said I've always known you didn't just stumble upon it. I'm not certain how you did retrieve it, but I have a fairly good idea of how it went missing. You're a fine friend to Father Reese, and I'm sure you do what you can to protect him, but his gambling problems and the occasional thievery that accompanies them predate your arrival here by several years. Random items of value have been going missing since he first arrived from Seminario de Málaga. I'm certain there are parish priests who would have sent him packing long ago, perhaps even reported him to the authorities, but I have always chosen to overlook such things, provided they're kept under relative control. Unfortunately, I now have some reason to believe that Father Reese's problems may run deeper than mere vice."

Father McCord was silent for a few moments, unsure how to respond. "What do you mean?" he finally asked.

"There is a good chance I'm wrong. But in the meantime, I need for you to be entirely open and up front with me, even more so than I can be with you. There is much at stake here, Padre. For everyone and especially Father Reese. I need you to not hold back, and as I said, I need to be certain that anything I say to you will be kept in confidence. Your friendship and proven loyalty to Father Reese make you the last person I should be speaking to about this, but they also make you the first. I believe I can trust you, but it would be very reassuring to hear you concur."

"Of course, Padre. I won't repeat a word."

"Good, Padre." Father Arroyo leaned forward and spoke in a low voice. "I have reason to suspect that Father Reese may not be who he claims to be."

"What? Who might he be?"

"*That* I can't discuss at this time. Meanwhile, is there anything you can tell me about his past, from before his arrival in Spain?"

"Past?"

"Yes."

Father McCord took a moment to think. "Not really. I know about as much as anyone else, I suppose. Worked as a schoolteacher in Michigan. Decided to become a priest sometime thereafter or maybe at the time. He's not generally forthcoming about his past, as you already know."

"Do you think there's any potential you could possibly find out more?"

"Well, I can try."

"I'll be leaving to Burgos for several days. Preliminary discussions with the search committee for my replacement. While I'm gone, if there is any way you can try to gather any kind of information that might be pertinent, even if you suspect it could be false, it would be most helpful."

"Yes, I'll certainly try."

"Try hard, but not too hard, if you gather my meaning. It is *crucial* you don't arouse suspicion. Not only would that undermine things, it could potentially put you in danger."

"I don't fear harm from his hand."

"Padre, if the suspicions about Father Reese are correct, then we don't really know him at all. You must play this very carefully, do you understand?"

Father McCord nodded.

"Good. And please don't misunderstand, Padre. I am not trying to determine that there is anything sordid in his past. On the contrary, I am trying to determine that there *isn't*."

"Yes, Padre."

"I thank you for your help."

Father McCord left Father Arroyo's office and made his way to the library. He had but twenty pages left of *The Dialogue of Saint Catherine of Siena* and wanted to finish it. He understood now, after his discussion with Father Arroyo, that there were far more pressing matters at hand, but he was nevertheless determined to finish.

He removed the book from his special section of the shelf and sat down with it at the small reading table where he'd spent countless hours over the past two years running his fingers through ancient and modern writings late into the night. He had only gotten a few pages in when his mind began to wander. Not to his discussion with Father Arroyo but to his dream from the previous night. He reached into his pocket and pulled out a small black leather pouch, from which he removed a jewel about the size of a large strawberry. Though it resembled a ruby, its color was closer to crimson than blood, and its surface was far softer than a ruby's, more like talc or gypsum. He rubbed his fingers along its side, his mind drifting further and further away from Saint Catherine's writings, when he sensed a sudden presence in the doorway.

"Good evening, Father Reese," he said.

Reese smiled and walked into the room.

"Good evening, Father McCord," he replied, pulling up a chair and taking a seat across from him. "I was looking for you earlier. I wanted to go over some notes for my confirmation class, but Josep informed me you were in some sort of meeting with the padre?"

"That's correct."

"Special occasion?"

"Just a general progress evaluation."

"Really! I wonder why he hasn't asked to meet with me, too. The padre and I haven't had a real heart-to-heart since February."

Father McCord shrugged and tried to return his attention to his book while Father Reese sat there in silence.

"All right, Father McCord," he said finally. "You don't need to share with your good friend the true nature of your conversation with the padre. I already know everything."

"You do?"

"Indeed I do. And if the padre considers you a worthy replacement upon his leave for Valencia, who am I to disagree?"

"I'm sure if I could see your face," McCord replied, "I would see your smile and know you were kidding. As is, I can only hope."

"It makes sense, I guess," Reese continued. "Or not really, but at least on the surface. You'd been an assistant police chaplain in Dublin, not exactly shepherding a great flock, but I have virtually nothing that could make me remotely suitable."

"You don't think being a schoolteacher has certain things in common?"

Father Reese laughed. "Well, perhaps in some ways."

"Where was that, in Michigan?"

"Yes."

"And what about before that?"

"Before what?"

"Before you were a teacher."

"You mean, what was I doing before I was a teacher?"

"Yes."

Father Reese paused, looked at Father McCord. McCord was sitting still, his chin raised, his right index finger resting on a page in his book.

"Different things, Padre."

"Very specific answer."

"My history is my concern, Father McCord, just as your history is your concern. You know me by now. I don't inquire into your doings in Ireland, nor should I. I don't ask you about why you left or about the one you left behind, either, the one whose name you dare not speak or, dear Lord, the heavens will come crashing down on Chicken Little. The one who I assume gave you that beautiful little gem you're always carrying around. You know, I've never really gotten a good look at it like this. It's quite spectacular to behold."

"I wouldn't know."

"It has a beautiful red color, and the surface looks almost silky. Forgive me, I realize I may as well be speaking Greek. But it's really something else. If you're ever hard up and feeling unsentimental, I'm sure it could fetch you a nice sum in Plaza de la Santa Faz!"

Father McCord instinctively returned the jewel to its pouch and the pouch to his pocket.

Father Reese sat there for several more moments in silence, then sighed wearily.

"Well, the matter is surely not up to either of us, but if you do wind up being handed the keys to the kingdom, please remember that I always thought you were a very handsome priest."

"May I return to my reading," Father McCord asked, "or are you planning to keep up this nonsense all night?"

Father Reese rose from his seat.

"*Buenas noches*, Padre."

"Good night, Father Reese."

The American priest took several steps toward the door, then paused.

"Oh, I nearly forgot. I've finished my work on the old greenhouse, if you can believe it. Perhaps you'd like to visit sometime tomorrow afternoon. I'd love to show you around. So to speak."

"I'm not entirely sure what the point would be, but I suppose it would be my pleasure nonetheless."

"Terrific! *Ciao*."

Father Reese left the room, and Father McCord sat there for another hour or so, reading Saint Catherine's *Dialogue*, but not really. From the time he had taught himself Braille, he couldn't imagine wanting to read any other way. Physical books were sensual experiences to begin with, but absorbing the words and ideas through the medium of touch made them so much more so.

Tonight, however, his mind kept drifting, and the wind whistling through the church's spires didn't help matters any. The church was over three hundred years old, and with that kind of age came a symphony of various noises, which, in this case, peaked in the cool early hours of the morning. There was a legend, often repeated by children who grew up in the parish, that if you listened hard enough, you could sometimes hear the shrill cries of the worshipers and priests who had burned alive in the fire of 1849.

Why? Father McCord asked himself. Why was she still haunting him like this? Why was she entering his dreams at night and refusing to leave even after he'd awoken? Why couldn't he just forget?

CHAPTER 8

It was 4:00 P.M., and Shawn's eyes were hurting badly. The only source of light in the old library was the sun streaming through the small Victorian windows and a pocket flashlight that Ravi had lent him. The words in the dictionary-sized tome he'd been crouching over since ten, the first in a three-volume set called *Textures of Hyperspace* and the last in human history not available digitally, appeared to have been printed in an eight-point font. But the pain wouldn't matter soon because if Shawn continued to inhale that musky air any longer, he'd pass out, anyway. He was allergic to dust, and the building seemed to have been built from it.

Shawn finally closed the book and left it there on the table. This was a ghost library, and books didn't need to be put away. The entire campus, in fact, was a ghost campus, and as Shawn exited the building and proceeded down the gravel path leading to the student center, he felt like he'd entered one of those recurring dreams where you're suddenly back in college except everything feels somehow off.

In this case, Minnesota's former Dellwood College, years after shutting down, had been repurposed as an Ambius satellite facility, operating largely out of the former student center and physics buildings, which were several of the only ones on campus still functioning. There were other satellite bases, Shawn suspected, though no one had confirmed this for him, nor had he been told anything about the location of Ambius's main headquarters, assuming a main headquarters even existed.

In fact, in the six weeks since Shawn had been initiated into the Dellwood operation, dedicated exclusively to warding off the aliens' impending attack, there was very little that he had learned about Ambius's wider operations or the larger universe it had discovered. How many countries were members of Ambius, and who were they? With how many different planets was Earth in contact? Did Ambius train astronauts like NASA, and if yes, had they been to other planets, and if yes, how many? What were aliens (*any* of them) really like? Everything was a mystery.

The team at Dellwood operated with laserlike focus on its specific scientific goals, much like a special forces unit that knows details of its own mission but is totally in the dark about that mission's larger significance. However, Rachel, who was team leader and several levels higher than the rest on the Ambius food chain, clearly knew much more than she was willing to disclose, and Shawn sensed that this was to a lesser degree true of the dozen or so other scientists living on the campus, as well.

As the superstar prodigy among the group, Shawn received lots of attention, and the other scientists would often pepper him with questions, quizzing him about string theory over beers for shits and giggles, but his own questions to them would go unanswered. If he asked who within the U.S. government knew about Ambius—the president? Congress?—or what was the name of the alien race that had kidnapped Leland and was currently threatening them, they would respond evasively, insisting they had no idea, that such information was classified and off limits to anyone, and so on. He never believed them.

On some level, he could understand. Ambius's entire existence was top secret, and all the other recruits had been involved in it for years, while Shawn had joined the project only weeks ago. How could he expect to be at the same level of clearance as the rest of them? Why should they trust him? He would need to prove himself, he figured. But understanding that didn't make him feel any less isolated.

Still sneezing sporadically from the dust of thousands of neglected books, Shawn entered the dining hall, where Pat, the in-house cook, had whipped up an Italian dinner. He joined Ravi and his wife, Megan, at a table in the corner.

"Make any headway with *Textures*?" asked Ravi, shoving a forkful of pasta into his mouth. Ravi was a few years older than Shawn and had emigrated from Bangalore when he was nine. He'd met Megan at Dartmouth, where they'd been graduate students in geophysics and astrophysics, respectively.

"Sort of," answered Shawn. "Really just slogging through right now. I'm guessing he'll get to the juicier stuff in volume three, but I'll be lost if I don't go through all the other crap first."

"You do know Rosen has it all on his Kindle, right? Scanned that whole motherfucker last year."

Shawn stared at him. "You're shitting me."

Ravi shook his head.

"So you knew I was trekking to the library and marinating in mothballs every day, while all this was already on Rosen's Kindle."

Ravi shrugged. "Hey, man, I thought you enjoyed the scenery!"

Megan, who was cool and liked to dress like she wasn't (she seemed to model her personal style on Velma from *Scooby Doo*) laughed hard. Shawn laughed, too, in spite of himself.

Ravi and Megan had been near the end of their programs at

Dartmouth when Ambius recruited them. Rachel had shown up unannounced at their offices one day and invited them to a conference at nearby Colby-Sawyer. However, when the car that was supposed to take them arrived, it took them to Minnesota instead.

(Had they not been drugged, they may have objected to this sudden change of plans.)

If that seemed unorthodox, it was nowhere near as extreme or elaborate as the operation behind Shawn's own recruitment. Shawn still didn't know the full details, but apparently the faked correspondence with Leland had been a vetting process, a way for Ambius to test not only Shawn's knowledge but his critical-thinking skills, his modes of problem solving, and, crucially, his ability to workshop ideas with others. But when Shawn suggested a face-to-face meeting, the Ambius scientists became concerned he might be onto them. They decided to wait and see what would happen next. When he finally showed up in Emington looking for Leland, they seized the moment and seized him.

It was Rachel who had actually composed most of the letters, and it was she who had championed Shawn to her mysterious higher-ups, she who had believed that he may hold the key to completing the gaps in Leland's published research and could potentially take Leland's theories on warp drive from the realm of the theoretical to the practical.

After dinner with Ravi and Megan, Shawn made his way over to Laboratory B in the lower level of the old physics building, where he gave Rachel and Lyle, a lean, fortysomething astrophysicist from Oklahoma, a rundown of his findings from the previous night. After several minutes of explication using a marker and whiteboard, Shawn stepped to the side and let Rachel and Lyle study his calculations and figures.

After a few moments, Lyle shook his head. "It's dead in the water."

Shawn looked at him. "Excuse me?"

"Well, maybe. You're building this whole thing on the foundation that tachyons are *real things*. But if they turn out not to be, we'll be shit out of luck."

"It's not dependent on tachyons."

"Sure it is."

"No, it isn't."

Lyle laughed like he expected this kind of resistance. "Look at the sign of the mass terms!"

"*You* look at them!"

"It's not dependent on tachyons," Rachel said softly, her eyes fixed on the board. "They're required where space-time is flat from the outset, but in Shawn's model, or at least how it's formulated here, it doesn't have to be."

"Exactly!" Shawn exclaimed, glaring at Lyle. "I actually thought you might object on naked singularity grounds. Guess you're not familiar with that argument."

Lyle glared back at him. "All right, Professor. So if your space-time can be flat, then there's no problem with Leland's original synthesis proposal in the first place, and we're just wasting our time studying discrepancies that aren't discrepancies."

"Yes," Shawn replied, "if you misinterpret the whole paradigm, sure, that's a reasonable conclusion. But for the rest of us, how he jumps from parallels to synthesis is a pretty big fucking mystery."

Lyle stood there in silence for a moment. Finally, he smiled. "Well, good luck with that, Sherlock. I'm hitting the sack. You two have a blast."

Lyle walked off, and Rachel turned to Shawn.

"There a problem?" she asked.

"No problem," he answered.

"This isn't Schrödinger's Crap dot-com. You know what's at stake here. This is bigger than all of us, and no one's going to put up with anyone's bullshit. Egos have to be checked at the door."

"Or what? You guys will throw me out of here? I bet I couldn't even leave if I wanted to. I 'know too much.' Which is ironic considering I know next to nothing."

"You know as much as we can tell you at this point. And that's better for you."

"Better for me how? You want me to help you save the whole planet, and you won't even tell me who we're saving it from."

Rachel sighed. "I know you're frustrated, Shawn. I was frustrated, too, when I first came on board, but like I've told you from the beginning, for right now, you need to trust me."

"Trust you. Trust you when I don't even know who you are. You spent months stalking me, and I don't know anything about you, where you come from, how you got recruited, not even your last name, probably not even your real first name. But me, I'm supposed to give you everything freely. Lie to my father about where I am, stay in this prison working my fucking ass off, whoring out everything I am for some faceless shadow group that might not even exist and just 'trust' you. Sounds like a great deal."

Rachel took a step toward him. "If you want to leave, leave. No one will stop you. I promise."

He stared back at her. "I need sleep."

Back at his room, Shawn couldn't actually sleep, so he reread some of Andrew Leland's first book, *The Order of Chaos*, in bed. It couldn't shed any light on the issues Shawn was wrestling with now, but he didn't expect it to. What he hoped was that somehow the act of engaging with Leland's mind might spark an epiphany that would open everything up for him. After forty-five minutes of nothing happening, he shut the book and flipped it around. A thirtysomething Leland smiled at him from the back cover. If pictures could speak, Leland could just tell him everything right then and there, explain how the various theories reconciled with one another—and then leave all that boring technobabble behind and tell him where he was taken to from Bernasconi Hills that night and who took him and how he helped them and why he eventually came back.

Since pictures don't speak, Andrew Leland just continued to smile that cocksure grin, as though his happiness was in fact directly rooted in knowing so much that Shawn didn't.

"Fuck you, too," Shawn muttered.

There was a knock at the door.

"It's open," he called out.

The handle turned, and the door opened to reveal Rachel, standing there in a light windbreaker.

"Can't sleep?" she asked.

"Nope."

"Interested in going for a walk?"

Under a crescent moon, they made their way through the darkness of the woods that surrounded the campus, neither saying much. Rachel led Shawn along a narrow gravelly path. In addition to animal noises and the crushing of leaves and thistles underfoot, he could hear rushing water in the distance. Soon, they had exited the woods and were standing at the edge of a canyon carved by a wide, swiftly moving river some seventy or eighty feet below. The stars above had to be some of the largest and most luminescent Shawn had ever seen. The river glistened in the moonlight, and Shawn wondered what would happen if he jumped, whether the current would just carry him along or whether the rocks in the water would break him into dozens of pieces.

Rachel rested her elbows on the small wire railing that had been erected at the edge of the cliff and stared out at the nighttime view.

"I can't tell you what you don't absolutely need to know," she said. "After six weeks, you don't get that kind of clearance, and if that sucks, I'm sorry. But I will tell you something no one else here knows. Not because it's a secret but just because it's none of anyone's damn business. Rachel is my real name. But when I was growing up, people called me Roach."

She didn't need to tell him her last name. At the word *Roach*, everything clicked. The tiny trace of an Australian accent. The way she had seemed vaguely familiar from the start.

"No shit," he said.

She nodded.

"I watched you on *Brain Freeze* every day."

"You and ten million others."

Shawn had been just nine when the twelve-year-old wunderkind known as Roach Chalmers, a charming and lively transplant from Down Under, had wowed audiences across the United States with her scientific prowess. She had lasted fourteen weeks on the popular quiz show, at that time a record, before being eventually displaced by a librarian from Brooklyn. For a kid like Shawn, whose intelligence had often made him an outcast, seeing this confident young Aussie use her giant brain as a source of empowerment, rather than alienation, was nothing short of a revelation.

"It's a pretty big high to be a TV star when you're still in your training bra," she said, her eyes following the current below. "Not so much fun to be an ex-TV star forever after. When I got to high school, I rebelled against what everyone expected from me. I knew I couldn't live up to it, anyway, so why bother being looked at like a freak? I stopped wearing tweed skirts, dropped my *Rocko's Modern Life* accent. Stopped reading books about nanochemistry and Galileo and started doing what other girls my age did, spending Sundays at the mall or the movies instead of the library, trying to be just like them. And what do you know, it worked. I eventually *stopped being smart*. People don't think that can happen, but they're wrong. When I got to college, I took a physics course just to fill a requirement. My professor saw something in me and brought something out in me. Something I thought was dead because it mostly was. And then, after the monster had been fully reawakened, he told me about a little extra work he did on the side."

Rachel turned away from the river and looked at Shawn.

"I didn't want to be special anymore, Shawn. But I *am* special, and so are you. I said before that we have to check our egos at the door, that what we're doing here is not about us, that it's about something much bigger. That's bullshit. At the end of the day, *we* were called upon to do this because *we* are the only ones who can. And you know what that makes us?"

He shook his head.

"Fucking badass."

Shawn smiled, but Rachel's expression remained dead serious.

Later, when he returned to his room, the Leland book was still resting on his pillow. Shawn placed it on the night table and got into bed. The industrial ceiling fan whirred away above him. As usual, he watched it spin for several rotations until eventually his eyes closed. For the first time in as long as he could remember, he was thinking about someone other than Andrew Leland as he drifted off to sleep.

CHAPTER 9

Father Arroyo's fingers tapped nervously on his armrest as the train pulled away from the station in Madrid and on toward Villena, the last stop before Alicante. He had been tapping like this on and off throughout the journey. From time to time, the irritated mustachioed man sitting across the aisle would glance at him, then quickly look away, unwilling to reproach a priest. The padre would stop, then resume a little while later without even realizing.

He tried to distract himself by staring out the window at the green meadows and wheat fields rolling by, the lush Valencian countryside, but it was no use. He had been antsy the entire trip, but especially so since his phone call to America two days prior, and now that he was only moments away from returning to Alicante, his anxiety had reached fever pitch.

Father Arroyo hadn't originally intended on calling the American school where Father Reese claimed to have worked. The idea had occurred to him sometime during dinner, while Father Bayarri was pontificating about art history or classical composers; had he not been so preoccupied with thoughts of Father Reese throughout the meal and the whole trip, in fact, he might have remembered the topic. He dismissed the notion of calling the school at first, worried that his inquiries might somehow get back to Reese, but later, sitting in his hotel room in downtown Burgos, he changed his mind. It took only minutes of Googling in the downstairs business suite to track down the number.

"Who did you say you were again?" a man identifying himself as the school's vice principal had asked, after Father Arroyo inquired about Reese's time at the school.

"My name is Father Alberto Arroyo."

"Yeah, but, I mean, who are you?"

"I'm the head of Anglada Parish in Alicante, Spain."

A brief pause.

"Leon Reese never worked at this school."

"I'm sorry?"

"I remember who he is. He interviewed here about six years ago, maybe seven, but we didn't take him."

"Why not?"

"What's your connection to him, if I might ask?"

Father Arroyo cleared his throat. "He's one of my assistant priests at the parish."

"How well do you know him?"

"Fairly well."

Another pause.

"I'm going to level with you, Father," the vice principal said. "Mr. Reese gave a fine interview, charming, smart guy. Then we did a background check and found out he had a record."

"You mean . . . an *arrest* record?"

"Yep."

"My God. For what?"

"No idea. We never reviewed the file. Frankly, we didn't care."

"You mean you weren't going to hire him once you knew he'd been arrested."

"No, Father, I didn't say that. That would be discriminatory and illegal. Let's just say we found a more qualified candidate sometime afterward."

"I see. Thank you for your time."

"Bless you, Father."

The call had shaken Father Arroyo up, though he wasn't sure what it all meant or what to do next. He wasn't certain he could investigate further without rattling cages and didn't know where to begin, anyway. But now that he'd confirmed Father Reese had lied about his past and in fact had a criminal record, he realized the chances of Father McCord coaxing any useful information out of him, let alone *reassuring* information, were nil. He also wondered if he might not have put Father McCord in grave danger by getting him involved in all this.

However, if Father Reese had been arrested for anything to do with being a wanted and dangerous terrorist, why would he have been let out of prison? And once released, would he have then applied for a job at a school and, later on, fled to Spain and entered the seminary without ever bothering to change his name?

Something didn't add up, and Father Arroyo, being no great sleuth, wondered whether he should just call the detective from the confession booth already. However, that still seemed premature. Yes, it turned out Father Reese had an arrest record, and yes, he had lied about his work history, but what did that really amount to? After all, it wasn't like he thought Father Reese was a saint to begin with. He already knew he was at the very least a gambler and a thief, both of which might very well tie in neatly to his having a criminal record in America.

When Father Arroyo's train arrived at the Alicante terminal, Josep picked him up in an old, beat-up Lincoln and drove him back to the parish.

"Would you know if Father McCord happens to be in his room?" the padre asked as Josep helped carry his bags into his quarters in the rectory. "I must speak with him rather urgently."

Josep gave a confused look.

"Padre McCord is more likely sitting in a hotel room, enjoying a view of the Sierra Nevada, I should think."

"What do you mean?"

"He's at a conference in Granada. You didn't know?"

"Not at all. He told you he was going to a conference in Granada?"

"No, the fat one told me, after Father McCord had already gone."

Father Arroyo tried to hide his panic. "Father Reese told you?"

Josep nodded, and Father Arroyo pulled out his cell phone and dialed McCord's number, which went straight to voice mail. This wasn't surprising given that cell phone usage at the parish was virtually nonexistent, thanks in large part to policies the padre himself had put in place. He turned to Josep.

"I know of no papal conference taking place in Granada or anywhere else in the country this week. Where is Father Reese right now?"

"He's usually in the greenhouse right about now. Padre, what's going on?"

"I'll be back soon."

Father Arroyo's heart raced along with his feet as he made his way to the greenhouse. Why, he asked himself, had he ever involved Father McCord? Ostensibly, it was for help in determining the truth about Father Reese, but in reality, he always knew Father McCord wouldn't be able to find anything out. The real reason why he had gotten McCord involved, if he was being honest with himself, was because he needed to unload, to share the burden. How, he wondered now, could he ever have been so selfish and so stupid?

Upon arriving at the greenhouse, a short and wide structure built from tempered glass and wood, he stepped inside and was momentarily stunned by its transformation. Father Reese had outdone himself. The spruced-up greenhouse was now fully functioning, with new exhaust fans and sprinklers and was lined, wall to wall, with blossoming vegetation. The American priest stood in the corner, spraying some noxious chemical onto a batch of ripening Spanish bluebells. He looked up with surprise and smiled.

"Padre, this is most unexpected! I trust you had a pleasant time in Burgos. Do you like what I've done with the place?"

Father Arroyo just stared, and Father Reese continued, "Now the children can have someplace else to visit on holidays besides the Benidorm Zoo. Plants can provide a good model for children, I think. While it's our human nature to occasionally stray, a plant moves unfailingly toward the light."

Occasionally stray. Some of us on more occasions than others, thought Father Arroyo.

"Where is our friend Father McCord?" he asked, an unmistakable iciness in his voice.

Reese blinked in confusion, a gesture that struck the padre as a bit too obvious.

"Where is Father McCord?" Father Arroyo repeated, this time a demand more than a question.

"In Granada, as far as I know. Said he was attending a conference on the writings of Thomas à Kempis."

"When did he tell you this?"

"Yesterday evening. Right here in the greenhouse, as a matter of fact."

"Father Reese, you and I both know very well there is no conference on Thomas à Kempis taking place in Granada."

"Padre, with all due respect, I know this fact not well or unwell. And I have no idea what you mean to suggest, but this tone is very unlike you. If there's something else you wish to say, by all means, say it straight out."

Father Arroyo wanted to just let Reese have it, to tell him he knew he was a liar and a criminal, knew he had stolen the sacrament money from the parish, knew he had a criminal record in America, and then to demand the whereabouts of Father McCord at once.

Instead, he smiled sheepishly. "I'm sorry, Father Reese. I've had a rough go of traveling and was a little concerned that Father McCord would leave for a conference without discussing the matter with me first."

"I can understand that, Padre. I can certainly understand, and I accept your apology. I don't think there's any cause for concern, however. He probably meant to tell you and forgot."

"Yes, I'm sure you're correct. Happy planting, Father Reese. You've done a most terrific job here, despite my early skepticism. Magnificent."

"Thank you very much."

Father Arroyo left the greenhouse. Father Reese stared after him for a moment, then returned his attention to his bluebells.

Back at the rectory, Father Arroyo went up to his room and closed the door behind himself. He approached his spare wooden dresser and stopped and stared for a moment. His heart pounding, he opened up the top drawer and removed the black-and-white photograph of Father Reese and Father McCord that he had received from the police detective in the confession booth days before. He turned the paper over, where the detective's phone number had been scrawled. He took his cell phone out of his pocket and dialed.

CHAPTER 10

There's an old idea that great theorists make for terrible experimentalists. When Nobel Prize–winning theoretical physicist Wolfgang Pauli was a young professor in Switzerland, his colleagues took note of a mysterious phenomenon. It seemed to them that every time Pauli would enter a laboratory, experiments being conducted therein would suddenly self-destruct. Lab instruments or machinery, witnesses insisted, would either spontaneously fall apart or else just plain stop working. While there were those who laughed at the suggestion that Pauli's mere presence could bring about such mishaps, others, such as German physicist James Franck, lent the "Pauli effect" serious credence. When Franck was working on an experiment at the University of Göttingen and a sophisticated device suddenly and inexplicably exploded, he wrote to Pauli telling him he wished he had been there so he could have blamed him for the mess. Pauli subsequently informed Franck that he had actually been changing trains in Göttingen at the time the incident took place, en route from Zurich to Copenhagen.

The belief in Pauli's magical tendency to wreak havoc was so pervasive that one time, a group of his colleagues decided to parody the phenomenon by rigging a chandelier to crash from the ceiling as soon as he entered a conference room. When he entered the room, the rigging mechanism malfunctioned.

Shawn, at his core, was definitely more theorist than experimentalist, and so these old stories about Wolfgang Pauli were very much on his mind as he and Rachel, standing before two suspended aluminum plates and a basin of ethanol, attempted to simulate the Casimir effect in Dellwood College's Laboratory B. This famous experiment, in which two uncharged objects in a vacuum appear to attract one another, involves what may be the only real-world example of negative energy, a kind of "exotic matter" that was to be the essential building block of Leland's planned cosmic shield. It was only through vast amounts of exotic matter, the belief went, that the negative energy density required for warping space-time could be achieved. It was only through exotic matter that the cosmic shield would be able to send any object that tried to penetrate it back thousands of years into the past.

At Shawn's signal, Rachel submerged the lower halves of the hanging plates into the ethanol, and then Shawn turned a switch and activated the shake table upon which the basin rested. Small waves began to form on the ethanol's surface, and soon the two plates were moving closer and closer together.

"So what's new here?" Rachel asked, her eyes on the plates.

"Nothing yet," answered Shawn. "But if you keep watching, the plates are gonna start making out."

Rachel didn't respond or even smile, just kept staring at the plates. In the little over a month since their nighttime walk to the river, their relationship had not progressed as Shawn had expected it to. If there had been any change at all, as far as he could tell, it had been solely on his end. He was now all but consumed by her, while she treated him with pretty much the same aloofness as before. If anything, she had become even colder in recent weeks. He was mystified by this and just a little bit crushed.

"I don't get it," she said, turning away from the metal plates to Shawn. "Are we just running through a typical Casimir analog?"

"That was the plan."

"What for?"

"I thought it was a good place to start before we move on to the next step."

"You mean the next ten steps? You already know that our last team was knee deep into CPA lasers and magnetic fields when they failed to produce a billionth of the EM we would need."

"Well, we'll be going in another direction, won't we?"

"Not if we can't find one. What do you have for me, Shawn? What can you give us to work with here?"

Shawn turned off the shake table and let the plates drift back to their default positions. "I've gone over my moving mirror theories with you."

"And I've told you that they're good for turning powder into sea monkeys. We're trying to build Jurassic Park."

"I'm working as hard and as fast as I can, but this isn't gonna happen overnight."

"Maybe it won't happen at all."

"What does that mean?"

She paused, looked at him. "I still have faith in you, Shawn. But the shadows above me aren't sure the work you've been doing is leading anywhere."

"So, what, they're going to send me home?"

"I don't know."

"No, of course they won't. With what I know, they would never let me leave here alive. We both know that."

Rachel didn't answer. Shawn left the lab and walked back to his dorm alone. In the hall, as he made his way to his room, he heard what sounded like a party coming out of one of the other rooms. The door was open a crack, and he peeked in and saw Ravi, Megan, and several other of the younger scientists involved in a lively round of *cottabus*, an ancient Athenian drinking game where players attempt to fling masses of wine from goblets into small bowls without the liquid losing its bulk in the process.

"Care to join us?" Rosen, an astronomer from MIT, called out.

"No, thanks. Gonna hit the hay early."

But lying in bed, Shawn struggled to fall asleep. When he closed his eyes, all he saw were equations. What was being required of him was pure alchemy. He needed to find some way to produce exotic matter from thin air and to create enough of it to yield an actual *warping* of the space-time continuum when the most exotic matter anyone had ever produced, outside of the Casimir effect, was exactly none. Even a promising theory he had recently been exploring, that negative energy could be achieved via a rapidly accelerating mirror, had severe limitations. Though Rachel was receptive to the idea, he hadn't the faintest clue of how to create a system that could accelerate a mirror fast enough to create any exotic matter, let alone the quantities required here.

He opened his eyes and stared at the industrial ceiling fan spinning above him. Only a few months ago, he had been a graduate student at Columbia, kicking back in its storied lecture halls by day and sneaking through its even more storied underground tunnels by night, like on the night of his ill-fated pilgrimage to the famed cyclotron. The ceiling fan actually kind of reminded him of that spectacular machine. Just barely, if he looked at it the right way. In the wide, cylindrical motor above the blades, he could see the cyclotron's similarly shaped, gleaming electromagnets. In the down rod that connected the fan to the ceiling, he saw the thin iron poles affixed to the cyclotron's arch. And in the fan's overall spin, he saw the swiftly spiraling charged particles within the cyclotron's vacuum chamber, accelerating to ridiculous, unimaginable speeds . . .

He bolted upright, his heart racing.

Was it possible?

He jumped out of bed, threw on a T-shirt and pair of shorts, and dashed off to the physics lab.

It was some three hours later when he knocked on Rachel's door. After a few minutes, she answered, looking as out of it as she got, which wasn't much at all.

"What?"

"Come with me."

Twenty minutes later, they were standing in the physics lab before a whiteboard, onto which had been scribbled thousands of barely legible equations and diagrams and rough sketches.

"What am I looking at?" she asked.

"You asked me to give you something to work with. Here you go."

She stepped up to the board and stared at it for a few minutes. Then she began to move around, zeroing in on certain parts. After about fifteen minutes of careful examination, she walked back over to where Shawn was standing. He looked at her expectantly.

"Well?"

She turned to him. "How long have you been down here?"

"Since about one."

"You take any uppers?"

"What?"

"Speed, ice, meth."

"Jesus, no. I don't use any of that stuff."

"Three hours is nothing for the output on this board. And from all the chicken scratch and smudge marks, I'd have thought you spent even less time. Shawn, did you look at this even once before coming to get me? Did you check any of it over, make sure there were no contradictions or incorrect substitutions or other random mistakes before coming to my room, dragging my ass out of bed at four in the morning, and showing me all this?"

Shawn opened his mouth to answer, but she stepped closer to him and put her finger to his lips.

"Of course not," she said. "You didn't have to. Because you're a fucking genius."

She smiled, probably the first real smile since he'd met her, and before he had any idea what was happening, she grabbed his face, pulled him in, and kissed him long and hard on the mouth.

CHAPTER 11

The Gothic old church house stood high and imposing in the moon-light, its bat-like gargoyles peering out watchfully from the roof and the wind whistling softly through the bells as two shiny black Volkswagens pulled up outside of it. Diego Sala, dressed in a stylish velvet blazer and jeans, was the first to get out, followed by six men in dark suits. Diego rolled his shoulders a few times as though trying to rid himself of a back itch, then felt inside his inner jacket pocket for his pistol. He turned to his companions and smiled his wide, unmistakable Cheshire cat grin.

"How we feeling tonight, *mis hermanos*?" he asked, in his Castilian-accented Spanish.

"Like stallions," they answered in unison.

"Remember. The stories you heard from Norway and South Africa may or may not be true. If they make you afraid, consider them bullshit. If they light a fire under your asses, believe them with all your hearts and souls. *Ándale!*"

Inside the church house, in the dimly lit dining room, a meal of *caparrones*, a bean and sausage stew, was under way. Father Arroyo sat at the first table with Father Reese, Josep, and several deacons, while the rest of the staff and clergy sat at two other tables. Fathers Arroyo and Reese each did their best to pretend as though the day's earlier tension was completely forgotten.

"So what happens if you've got something that just won't grow?" Father Arroyo asked, doing his best impersonation of someone who cares even a little about gardening.

"Well, it depends," Father Reese answered. "You can try adding fertilizer. Often, you might have to dig the whole thing up and—"

Reese was interrupted as the doors to the room suddenly flew open and Diego and his men burst in, 9mm submachine guns in tow. With loud and gruff demands that nobody move, they aimed their weapons directly at the priests, deacons, and staff members, all of whom stifled their instincts to immediately rise from their seats.

"Where's the lights?" Diego asked.

No one answered.

"Where's the lights?" he asked again, louder.

"The lights are on," Father Arroyo answered.

"Can't see shit in here," Diego muttered. He turned to his men. "Round them up. Bring them into the chapel."

"May I ask what this is all about?" Father Arroyo asked, unsure himself whether his question was genuine. On the one hand, he knew exactly why these men were here. On the other, machine guns and barked orders were hardly what he'd been expecting.

"You may and you just did, Padre," Diego answered with a friendly smile. "Don't again."

When the clergy and staff had been brought into the chapel, Diego had them cluster together in front of the stage and the altar. He stared them over for a few seconds, looking at each of their faces individually before finally addressing them as a group.

"Which one of my holy saints here is Father Arroyo?" he asked.

"I am Arroyo," the padre answered.

"Come forward," Diego said, beckoning theatrically with his hand like a king to a subject.

Arroyo stepped out from the group.

"Where is the American priest?" Diego asked him.

Father Arroyo hesitated to answer. He had been expecting normal police officers to arrive tonight, men with badges and formality and civility. These men, if they were police at all, were unlike any he'd come across before. He wished now that he had never made the call.

"Detective Bustelo said you'd told him on the phone the American priest was here. So where is he?"

"I'm sorry," Father Arroyo replied, struggling to find his voice. "I believe I must have been confused."

"Confused?"

The padre nodded. "We don't have any Americans at the parish."

He hoped and prayed none of the others would contradict him, that they would have faith in his judgment even if they couldn't know why he was lying. He also wondered how Father Reese was reacting to all this, but knew that a glance in his direction would surely give him away.

Diego, instead of getting angry, smiled warmly at Father Arroyo. A nearby statute of Saint Francis caught his eye, and he walked over to it, looked it up and down approvingly. He took a few steps back, stared at it again, and drew in a deep breath of satisfaction.

"Detective Bustelo," he said, turning back to Father Arroyo, "has a deep reverence for the church. You see, when we were in juvie together, back in Santa Leticia, there was a priest with whom he was very close. Father Ortega. He had a major impact on him. Inspired him to change his whole life. Me, I only knew him as the *maricón* who liked to give it to me up the ass every night after lights out. I suppose it's my dumb luck to be so much more attractive than Detective Bustelo."

Diego turned back to the statue and, with a swift release of his foot, sent it toppling over and shattering into pieces on the hard wooden floor. He turned back to Father Arroyo, removed his pistol from his jacket, and aimed it squarely at the padre.

"Where is the American priest? If I have to ask again, you'll be answering without your face."

Father Reese suddenly stepped forward.

"My good señor, I am the American priest," he said, his voice just the slightest bit shaky. "My name is Father Reese. Leon Reese. I am the man whom you seek."

Diego looked at him, snorted, and turned right back to Father Arroyo. "Not this *gordo*," he said. "The bald man. With the dark glasses and the stick."

Father Arroyo peered at him with confusion. "Father McCord? He's not American, he's Irish!"

Diego smiled. "Of course. And he's blind, too, right?" He turned to his men. "You see, *mis hermanos*? This is why the Church is so backward. They're all a bunch of fucking idiots!"

He turned back to Father Arroyo. "Where is this 'Father McCord'?"

"Father McCord is gone."

"Gone? How long?"

"Since yesterday."

"To where?"

"Nobody knows."

"What do you mean nobody knows? You're the head priest, aren't you? You don't make it your business to know the whereabouts of your clergy?"

Father Arroyo cleared his throat. "Father McCord had said he was going to a conference in Granada. But there is no conference in Granada."

Diego stared down at the floor, disgusted. He looked back up. "Where's his room?"

"It's the third one down on the left in the rectory."

Diego turned to two of his men, Jordi and Santiago. "Search the room. Tell me what you find."

The men went off, and everyone else waited in silence as Diego paced around in circles, occasionally rolling his shoulders again, like a pent-up bull with no outlet for his energy. Father Arroyo didn't know what to expect and wondered if there was anything he could say to somehow calm the situation. He was deeply out of his depths and knew it. *Silence at the proper season is wisdom*, he reflected.

About Father McCord, the padre thought nothing. It was a subject beyond his grasp.

Jordi and Santiago returned.

"Gone," Santiago confirmed. "No clothes, no belongings. Just a wooden cross in the dresser drawer and a small book written in Braille. Bible, I think."

Diego nodded. "Well, no need to remind you all of the new policy. Time to enforce it."

The men hesitated.

"Yes, even with men of God, *mis hermanos*. He has to know what happens when he makes friends, what happens to anyone who helps him, anyone who shelters him. He's alone in this world, *mis hermanos*. He needs to always remember that."

Diego turned to Father Arroyo. "Dearest Padre, you clearly tipped him off somehow. So what happens now is really your own doing. But don't worry, you won't lose any sleep over it. Quite the contrary."

He aimed his pistol at Father Arroyo's heart.

In his last few seconds, the padre wondered if there was time to perform last rites, if only mentally and if only to himself.

But there was time only to wonder.

Diego smiled. "*Perdóname*, Padre."

He fired two rounds, sending Father Arroyo flying backward into the others. Several of the priests, including Father Reese, caught him by the shoulders, but the blood was already pouring out of him, and his eyes were closed.

Diego looked at his men, nodded, and they trained their machine guns on the rest of the priests and deacons and staff and began to fire away. When they were finished, the bodies of the victims lay collapsed before the stage in a sickening heap. The men stood there for several moments staring, shaken and disgusted by what they had just done.

Diego pulled out a cigarette lighter and walked over to the stage. He bent down and lit the corner of the top step. Soon enough, all four rows of steps were on fire, and flames were riding up the sides of the altar, as well.

"A second fire in Anglada Parish," he mused. "Some churches have no luck."

He stepped back and watched as the flames engulfed the entire stage. Then he walked over to the priest's chair and lit that aflame, as well. He then lit the pulpit and the lectern on fire, too.

"All right, my stallions. Let's vamoose before someone in the area calls the fire department. Or we die."

Jordi tossed McCord's discarded cross and Bible into the flames. "You think he'll get the message?" he asked.

Diego shrugged. "If he's still in Spain, probably. If he's gone, doubtful. Once he moves on, he moves on. He'll turn up soon enough somewhere else, as someone else, no doubt about that. *Ándale!*"

The men turned toward the exit and froze in place. Standing in the doorway, walking stick in tow, was the priest Father Arroyo had called McCord. He glanced at the small mountain of corpses in front of the stage, but if he had any reaction, it was concealed behind his dark sunglasses. He turned to Diego's men, who, along with Diego himself, now had their weapons trained on him.

Diego smiled and addressed the new arrival in English.

"Welcome, Andrew. You can breathe easy. Your days of running are finally over. Our orders have changed, and you're no longer wanted alive. We have someone else, you see, smarter than you ever were. He'll help us, and you can finally have the peace you deserve." He turned to his men. *"Apunten, listos, fuego!"*

The men unleashed a storm of firepower. Amid the unrelenting spray of bullets, the priest raced across the far wall, dove behind the large pipe organ in the corner, and knocked it on its side, walling himself in behind it. The men trained their firepower onto the organ and moved in on it, blasting round after round of ammunition through its mahogany body and lead piping, creating a horrifying music in the process—until the whole instrument suddenly came flying out at them from the corner. Those who didn't scramble out of the way quickly enough were knocked to the ground and, in at least one case, fatally crushed. The priest leaped out from behind it and, with several fierce sweeps of his walking stick, knocked out the weapons from the hands of those few bewildered men still left standing.

Jordi, who had been knocked to the ground by the edge of the organ, stared up at the priest and for the first time took in what he was seeing. The man's clothing was riddled with bullet holes but absent of any blood. He had run through a haze of firepower and remained not only unscathed but strong enough to knock a pipe organ on its side and then hurl it across the room.

The stories, Jordi reflected, were true.

One of the men came at the priest with a large combat knife. Exceptionally trained, he danced around the priest with the grace of a ballerina, moving in and out, making various slashing motions with the knife, foreplay for the kill. The priest extended his stick and, with the same motion with which one might swing a tennis racket, took off the man's head.

He then turned to another man who had started to rise and

kicked him hard in the chest, putting a hole through it. The dead man collapsed back to the ground.

Jordi, still on the floor, scrambled for his submachine gun, lying a few feet away, and the priest spun around and, using his foot, pinned down Jordi's arm. With his other foot, he stomped Jordi's skull, ending him.

The priest looked around. All his assailants were down. He turned his attention to the pile of corpses in front of the stage, some of which had already caught fire. He walked over to them and lifted up Father Arroyo and moved him aside to get to the body underneath him: Father Reese.

Just then, he felt something small and light hit the back of his head. He turned around, but didn't see anyone behind him.

At that moment, beneath the back row of pews, Diego scrambled forward on his stomach, out of breath, pistol in hand. He had just sent a bullet to the back of the man's head, and he could swear it had simply bounced off. Diego could see the exit of the chapel, just twenty feet from where the pews ended. He stayed down another few seconds, then rose to a crouch and raced toward it. He had only been exposed several seconds when he felt something pierce through him. He collapsed on his side, convulsing, clutching the front of the bloodied walking stick, which now ran through his belly like a spear. The priest stared at him for barely a second from across the room, then turned his attention back to Reese's corpse. He sifted through Reese's two pants pockets. Nothing. Then, in the left pocket of Reese's cassock, he removed the object he had been looking for, the reason why he'd come back.

He raised the crimson jewel up and watched as it reflected and refracted the surrounding flames. He wrapped his fingers around it, clutched it tightly, and then deposited it in the pocket of his own cassock.

Diego lay near the exit, coughing up blood, still clutching the front end of the stick. The priest walked over to him and pulled the stick halfway out of his stomach, while with his foot, he turned Diego onto his back. He stared down at him.

"You said you had someone else now. Who?"

Diego coughed up more blood. "I'm dead already. I won't tell you anything."

The priest took hold of the top of the staff protruding from Diego's body. "Actually, you're going to tell me everything."

He twisted the staff. Diego screamed.

About five minutes later, the door to the church house swung open, and the priest formerly known as Father McCord emerged. He could hear sirens somewhere in the distance. He mounted the stolen Bultaco motorcycle he'd parked outside, revved it up, and rode off.

As he sped through the darkness of the N-332 highway, along the coast of the black Mediterranean and past the ancient castle ruins of Mount Benacantil, he could feel his identity as Father McCord slipping away, everything being blown off him by the wind and left behind in the road. The same thing had happened before with previous personas, and it was fine by him. He'd never really been any of them to begin with, except for Andrew Leland, and he hadn't been him in so long, he could hardly remember what that felt like. Identity, personhood, these were liabilities he'd dispensed with long ago. To be no one, to be nothing, was so much better.

This was, of course, the exact opposite of what the rest of the world believed.

CHAPTER 12

Shawn stared at the homes, churches, and factories of Rockford, Illinois, as they whizzed by. He had been riding in the car for over seven hours, past cities and towns and farms and forests, and everything he saw was incredible to him, though nothing more so than that fact itself, that after months of being cooped up in the old abandoned college campus, the ordinary could be quite this exhilarating.

"And Evanston comes after Rockford?" he asked.

"After Elgin, which is after Rockford," answered Rachel, at the wheel.

Shawn looked back out the window. Between two buildings, he could see the shimmering blue of the Rock River, a tributary of the Mississippi. About an hour and a half to go, he figured.

"Now don't get all gushy when you meet him," Rachel warned.

"Course not," he replied, though he wasn't so sure. The "him" to whom Rachel had been referring was Dr. Roland Burke, a legend in theoretical physics and one of Shawn's all-time heroes. Like Shawn, Burke had studied both astronomy and physics at Brown

University, before moving on to Stanford, where he received his Ph.D. in astrophysics and cosmology, and then to the Perimeter Institute in Ontario, where, together with a small band of some of the world's greatest minds in the field, he had developed a theory for detecting dark matter. This little achievement, among other things, had landed him the revered Sakurai Prize in 2002.

He was also, as Shawn had just recently learned, one of Ambius's primary scientific overseers. Burke and several peers had reviewed Shawn's supposed "mirror breakthrough" and felt it just might be the real deal. Burke wanted to meet with him, so with Rachel driving, they had set out that morning from the campus in Dellwood to Northwestern University, where Burke was professor emeritus.

"Motherfucker," Rachel growled.

Shawn looked and saw that a PT Cruiser had cut them off in traffic. Rachel grimaced at it, and Shawn smiled and returned his gaze to the window. Over the past seven hours, the two hadn't talked much, but that was okay. And if they hadn't kissed since that one unforgettable time in the lab two weeks earlier, that was okay, too, at least for now. Their relationship had undeniably, fundamentally changed. If they weren't exactly an item, there was a real connection nonetheless. Whatever else they were or might become, they were close.

As Rachel pulled into Northwestern's visitors' lot on Sheridan Road, Shawn felt a surge of adrenaline. For the past three months, he'd been working in close quarters and near total isolation in a surreal, almost dreamlike environment. Though he'd been told repeatedly about the vast implications of the work he was doing, he had never truly accepted them. How could he? Totally cut off from reality, it was as though someone had said that if he didn't button his shirt correctly, the universe might explode. Now, however, as he and Rachel got out of the car and set foot onto Northwestern's Evanston campus, a scenic mix of modern and Gothic architecture nestled along the shoreline of Lake Michigan, on their way to meet one of the most important scientists in the world, it all suddenly felt so real.

"Yes, Dr. Burke is expecting you," a smiling department secretary informed them before instructing Shawn and Rachel to have a seat in a small lounge area adjacent to the faculty offices.

A poster on the wall proclaimed in bold letters: "Students, unlike string theory, can be tested."

After several minutes of waiting, Dr. Burke emerged from his office, a burly man with a bushy gray beard and small rectangular glasses that made him look just a little too much like Santa Claus.

"Kyle and Natasha!" the great scientist exclaimed, using the same names Rachel had given the secretary. "Always a pleasure when former students drop by!"

He embraced them lightly and hustled them into his office, closing the door behind them. Inside, Shawn and Rachel took seats across from Burke's desk, and Shawn marveled inwardly at the adornments on the wall, the degrees and awards, the framed photos of Burke with other leading lights, plus the awesome knickknacks on Burke's desk, including an anthropomorphic toy Higgs boson particle with a smiley face and arms and legs.

"So, the boy wonder himself," Burke said with a wry smile. "My little Roach here has been hyping you up for some time."

Roach. So here was the physics professor who'd brought Rachel's inner genius back to life.

"It's a great honor to meet you, sir," Shawn said. "I've been reading your work for as long as I've been studying physics."

"Please, the honor's mine. My colleagues and I have spent the past three weeks poring over your theory. Accelerating mirrors using electromagnets. Impressive. *More than* impressive. It seems obvious in retrospect, like so many good solutions, but it was never obvious, was it? Congratulations on a job well done."

Shawn tried hard to restrain his enthusiasm. "Thank you, sir."

"So, a Brown Bear, like myself. And then Columbia's Leder-man program? Is McDowell still stewing in his juices, working on his 'theory of anything'?"

Shawn laughed and nodded.

"Where are you from originally?"

"Newton, Mass."

"Parents still live there?"

"My father does. My mother passed away when I was a kid."

"Terribly sorry to hear that."

Shawn murmured an awkward thanks, and Burke turned to a small cooler at the side of his desk and pulled out three Heinekens.

"Brewskies?"

"Sure."

He popped them open and handed two to Shawn and Rachel and took a long, savory sip of his own. He then put it down on his desk and let out a deep, satisfied sigh. He looked at Shawn.

"The theory you propose has some pretty big implications be-yond Leland's cosmic shield. You realize that, don't you?"

"Yes. I mean, I was focusing on the immediate objective, but yeah, I guess there are all kinds of implications one could draw out."

"And how do you feel about those implications being 'drawn out,' as you say? Tested and explored, down the line."

"I mean, once we're done with this, I would say, let's go all the way. Why not, right?"

"Why not? How about ethical considerations, for one thing? You start messing around with the space-time continuum, and pretty soon you're facing all kinds of dilemmas. Who gets to use this technology? What might happen if it's proliferated? And don't forget, our little group is not exactly regulated by any outside body. Sure, at the highest levels, there's some knowledge and coordi-nation, but they don't really understand what we do. We barely do, ourselves! And we certainly don't have to answer to any public interests, no more than the Easter Bunny or the Tooth Fairy do.

So how does that make you feel? So much immense power and zero accountability?"

Shawn thought about it for a few moments, Burke waiting patiently for his response. He could feel Rachel staring at him, but he didn't look at her.

"I think," he said, speaking slowly and deliberately, "that we need to trust ourselves. And if we can do that, there's nothing to be afraid of and we should move ahead with any ideas we might have. I mean, yeah, it could be that whatever we do, working in these new frontiers, there will inevitably be some element of recklessness. But we can be *responsibly* reckless. We just have to fully commit to not doing any harm to our world or to any other. That's the balance, I think. We need to be ambitious, but also humble. As long as we can stick to that, I say we should move full speed ahead."

Burke nodded and smiled. "Ambitious, but humble. Well said, Shawn Ferris. Now, if you don't mind giving Roach and me a few moments alone, we need to speak about you behind your back."

"Sure," Shawn replied with a smile, and he rose and exited the office.

Shawn returned to his seat in the lounge. Two students—it wasn't clear if they were grads or undergrads—were standing by the cappuccino machine, engaged in a heated debate about the likelihood of there being water on the newly discovered world of Kepler-186f. Imagine, Shawn thought, knowing what he knew, the banality of debating about Kepler-186f. Later, they'd probably go to some required lecture on string theory or quantum mechanics and then spend the rest of the afternoon idling away in the library or some campus coffee shop or, most likely of all, on Facebook. Not long ago, he'd been just like them. Just a few months back in another universe, one that wasn't hanging in the balance, one that he, Shawn Ferris, hadn't been called on by some secret society to rescue from oblivion.

Shawn didn't ask Rachel what she'd discussed with Burke

when they got back in the car to leave Northwestern. And when they crossed from Illinois into Wisconsin, he didn't ask her then, either, nor when they crossed from Wisconsin into Minnesota. He felt he wasn't supposed to, that it was somehow understood that he wouldn't. But when the temptation got to be too much and it started to feel like a game of how long he could hold out and he felt ridiculous, he abruptly cut off their present conversation about midwestern drivers and asked her exactly what Burke had said in his absence.

"Six hours into the ride and now you want to know what he said?"

"Just tell me," Shawn said, suddenly anxious.

Rachel hesitated a moment, and then smiled. "He wants you to come join him at the Docks."

"The 'Docks'?"

"Our main headquarters. He wants you to be involved, hands on, with the next phase of the project."

He stared at her. "You're serious?"

"You must have made a good impression. What with finding the key to the whole shield and everything."

"I was pretty sure that's where my contributions ended. Like, 'Good work, thanks, and so long.'"

"Nope."

Shawn looked out the window. It was nighttime now, and they were coming into Minneapolis. The day had been surreal already, but this news, that he would be collaborating with Roland Burke and who knows whom else, felt impossible to process.

He turned back to Rachel with a sudden look of concern. "Wait, but does that mean . . . that it's good-bye for you and me? If I'm moving out of the campus?"

She shook her head. "You're smart, kid, but I'm not exactly Homer Simpson myself. And they'll need me to keep your arrogant ass in line, anyway. I'm coming, too."

Shawn smiled and then quickly turned to face the window

again. It was the second time that day he'd had to cover up bursting enthusiasm. He'd get to have his cake and eat it, too.

That night, with all the delirious excitement of the past day, Shawn struggled to fall asleep. Finally, somewhere around 1:00 A.M., he drifted off, a contented smile on his face.

About an hour later, something woke him. Before he opened his eyes, he could sense a nearby presence and, moreover, could hear breathing. He opened his eyes and was startled to find Rachel sitting at the edge of his bed.

"I'm sorry," she whispered. "I should have knocked."

"What are you doing here?" he asked, his voice weak from having just woken up.

She gave a playful smile and shrugged. Shawn lifted himself to a sitting position and stared at her. Dressed in just sweatpants and a T-shirt, she looked more beautiful than ever. She stared back at him, and they sat there like that for several seconds, not saying anything. Then Shawn leaned in and put his arms around her, and they started to kiss.

"Shawn," she interrupted a few minutes later. By now, they were deep into a full-on make-out session, and Shawn wasn't exactly keen on taking a break.

"Yes?"

"I want to ask you something."

"Yeah?" He kissed her again.

"You said today we need to be ambitious, but also . . . *humble*. What do you mean by humble?"

"I don't know," he answered and moved in to kiss her again, but she pulled away.

"What do you mean by humble?" she repeated. He stopped to look at her. She wanted an answer.

"I guess I mean that we have to know our place. You know,

we're just one planet in a really big universe. Whatever we do, we shouldn't harm anyone else."

"So what about the planet that wants to destroy us? We can't harm them?"

"That's different; they want to kill us. Anyway, can we talk about this a little later?"

He moved in to kiss her, and she resisted again.

"But what if they didn't? Or what if there was some other planet that wasn't trying to kill us but was just in our way? Maybe preventing us from getting something we wanted or needed or maybe just vying with us for the same precious resource and there's not enough of it to go around. How humble are we supposed to be in a situation like that?"

"I'm not sure I get what you're asking."

"I'm asking you what happens, Shawn, when it's us or them?"

There was an urgency in her eyes and in her voice that made him uncomfortable. Feeling the need to escape her intense gaze, he glanced over her shoulder at the door to his room and noticed that she'd left it slightly ajar when she'd entered.

Through the crack, he could see the empty window display in the hall.

"What do we choose, Shawn?" Rachel asked. She was breathing heavily, even more than she'd been when they were kissing.

"We choose us," he answered.

"Even if that means being less than humble? Even if it means not always being so nice?"

"Yes."

She eyed him skeptically. "Are you *sure*?"

"I'm . . . is it hot in here?"

"What?"

He pulled away from her and swung his legs over the side of the bed.

"I just . . . I need to get some air in here. I feel like I can't breathe."

"Shawn?"

He had gotten to his feet and was moving toward the window. "I think I just need some air."

By the time she realized why he was opening the window, it was already too late to stop him.

The grass below rushed up at him, and Shawn spread his arms and legs out from their locked-in positions and landed with a hard roll. He could hear Rachel calling frantically to someone else, two stories above him, as he scrambled to his feet and broke into a panicked run.

While her sudden and bizarre questioning had unsettled him, it hadn't been that alone that had prompted his sudden flight from the window. Rather, it had been a reflection he'd caught in the empty display window outside his room, specifically of a short, bald man waiting patiently out in the hallway with a handgun. Shawn had seen the man before: it was he who had come into Shawn's room on his first night at the campus and brought him to Rachel. Though Shawn hadn't seen him since then, he now wondered whether the man might not have been there all along, always just out of sight. It was certainly plausible. Shawn had never really known too much about what this surreal place was or what they were all doing here, and now he understood that he'd known even less than he'd thought.

If there was one thing of which he was certain, however, it was that if he had stayed in that room any longer and answered Rachel with anything other than what she wanted to hear, he probably would have wound up dead.

As he ran toward the trees, he heard Rachel scream out words that he would never be able to unhear: "Shoot him!"

Shots rang out from somewhere behind him, probably the window from which he'd jumped. He didn't dare look back, and as he moved into the woods, he could hear a door swinging open somewhere behind him, followed by shouting and running feet. He went deeper into the trees and heard other sounds, more distant now. An engine revving up and, a few minutes later, what sounded an awful lot like a helicopter taking off somewhere in the distance. Was that possible? Who had a helicopter on the campus, and where had they been keeping it?

What the fuck was *this place?*

Shawn heard the sounds of rushing water and, before he knew it, found himself in the middle of a clearing. He recognized the spot right away, the old wire railing and behind it the cliff side overlooking the rushing river below, and he cursed his subconscious for having obviously led him there. Footsteps were coming up somewhere behind him. He moved toward the railing and peered down at the rushing water, as the footsteps grew louder and slower simultaneously. His pursuer, he knew, had exited the woods and was now right there in the clearing with him. Shawn didn't turn around; his eyes remained fixed on the water. If it was deep enough, he might not break any bones. If it wasn't, he'd probably splatter on impact.

Of course, it didn't matter. As he well knew, he had only two options right now: jump, or worry about it and *then* jump.

"Don't!" a voice called out, but Shawn swung himself over the barrier and leaped out into the open air. For a fraction of a second, it felt as though he were suspended midair, the Minnesotan nighttime frozen all around him, and then he was suddenly hurtling straight down toward the black water below, once again doing his best to keep his feet tucked in under himself. With a tremendous splash, he landed in the water, went under, and then broke the surface, gasping, a fiery pain shooting through his entire body. He screamed as he realized that in addition to being bent or broken, he was also badly cut. He tried to swim, but it was nearly impossible; both his right arm and left ankle were in excruciating pain. Water rushing at him from all sides, he went under again, then broke the surface once more, gasping, barely registering that, out of the corner of his eye, something else was now plummeting from above.

There was another tremendous splash, and had Shawn been less focused on not being swept under by the waves, he would have been both horrified and shocked that his pursuer had apparently leaped into the river after him. Barely conscious at this point, Shawn felt himself suddenly grabbed by the arm and pulled in close. He shut his eyes, everything slipping away, and when next he opened them, he was lying on his back on the riverbank, expelling water from his lungs in violent bursts. When he was done coughing, he lay there panting and looked up at the figure staring down at him, a dark shape silhouetted by the moonlight, a tall and wiry man with a shaved head and no discernible expression, though Shawn could only just barely make out his face.

It was a face he would have known anywhere.

"How . . . ?" Shawn whispered, too weak to use his full voice. "You're dead."

The man moved his lips, but his response was drowned out by either the rushing river, the pounding in Shawn's head, or both. It all made sense now, Shawn realized. He had never even survived that fall from the cliff. What he was seeing, this impossible hallucination, was his final vision, an echo from his life reverberating just below the surface of his fading consciousness.

Or maybe it wasn't. Maybe what he was seeing was real, the ghost of Andrew Leland, his lifelong hero, come to welcome Shawn into the great beyond. Except why would it be Leland and not his own mother? He was still wondering when the darkness once again overtook him.

CHAPTER 13

Shawn woke to a musky smell and the sound of rain. He opened his eyes, but everything was black, and when he tried to lift his head, he found that the muscles in his neck were too weak. Gradually, his eyes adjusted. He was in a dark, wood-paneled room, a cabin or shack. He tried again to lift his head, this time with more success, and was able to make out a dim figure sitting in a chair by a small window not far from the bed.

"Don't try to move."

That voice.

"You're in bad shape," the man continued, "and we won't be able to stay here long."

"It's really you," Shawn whispered. "Jesus, there's so much I want to know."

"Right now, I ask the questions," Andrew Leland replied. "What did they tell you?"

"About what?"

"Everything."

Shawn took a deep breath. His head was still fuzzy and his

voice still weak, but he rallied whatever strength he had and did his best to explain. About how Rachel had lured him in with the fake letters supposedly written by him. About how she had told him about the history of Ambius and about Leland's supposed death and about the imminent threat Earth now faced from another world. About the cosmic shield that Leland had originally been brought in to build and about Shawn's own solution for generating enough exotic matter to build it and then about his escape out the dorm window once he'd realized that his life was in danger. When he was finished speaking, he was completely drained of energy and out of breath. He lay there, panting, waiting for Leland to respond.

After what felt like forever, Leland finally spoke.

"Your girl was smart. Fed you half-truths, reversals, and out-right lies. First off, Earth is alone. Others did help us out once upon a time and gave us technology, but they stopped once they got to know us. Save for a few hired mercenaries who mostly gather intelligence, no one has had anything to do with this planet for decades—we're the black sheep of space. Second, I never worked for Ambius, had never even heard of them before I was taken. But I was asked by someone else to build a protective shield, and I did. A cosmic wall made out of space-time curvature exactly like the one you described. Using magnetic fields like a particle accelerator, just like you guessed."

"I don't understand," Shawn said, fighting his weariness, trying to stay focused. "If you already built the wall, what did Ambius need me for?"

Though he wasn't looking at Leland and couldn't have seen his face even if he was, Shawn had a faint sense that, in the pause before his response, Leland was smiling at his stupidity.

"To help them tear it down," Leland answered. "You have no idea what you've done."

As Shawn tried to make sense of what Leland had just said, in his weakened state, it seemed too difficult to process.

Or maybe he knew exactly what Leland meant and wasn't ready to face it. He closed his eyes, willing himself back to sleep.

Leland watched him for a few moments. Then, when it was clear the boy was no longer conscious, he turned his attention to the window and to the star-filled night sky that could be glimpsed, beyond the treetops, from where he sat. In his right hand, he held Diego's loaded pistol and in his left, the strawberry-sized crimson jewel.

He gripped it tightly, shut his eyes. It was his only physical connection to her in this world, and though he hadn't dreamed about her since leaving Spain weeks earlier, it seemed to him that tonight, he could feel her more strongly than ever.

He stared out at the stars above, and for the first time in ages, no doubt triggered by listening to this kid's story, his mind was brought back to that fateful night nine years prior in Bernasconi Hills, the night the world learned it wasn't alone, the night that changed him and everything else forever.

CHAPTER 14

Andrew Leland tried to scream, but no sound came out. Minutes before, a dimwitted newscaster named Bill Allenby had been asking him about an expanding green dot in the sky, and now the twinkling lights of San Bernardino and Indio and Los Angeles were getting smaller and smaller underneath him as all of Southern California began to look increasingly like a map. He couldn't make anything out too well, though, his vision obscured by a surrounding prism of green light in the midst of which he was suspended and basically frozen. The air was cold and getting thinner, and soon breathing took priority over screaming until that too became impossible and he passed out.

When he awoke, he was lying in what seemed very much like a normal bed in what seemed very much like a normal bedroom, though one without any windows. Were it not for a constant vibration and a total lack of ambient noise, he might have thought he was emerging from another of the drunken one-night stands that had become routine since his split from Nancy.

He sat up and looked around. The walls, ceiling, and floor were off-white, blank, and utterly pristine. He noticed that he felt far too relaxed than he reasoned he should be, which he attributed either to shock or having possibly been drugged.

This is happening, he thought to himself, several times in a row. *This is happening* in real life, *and it's happening* to me. But what was happening? There was a closed door. He stared at it, and, as if on cue, it opened, and a man suddenly entered the room.

Or, if not a man, something that very much resembled a man. From across the street, he could pass for one, though if anyone glanced for more than a few seconds, he or she would probably notice the unnatural fluidity of body movement that Leland was noticing now. And there was something else that was off, too, beyond the man's movement, something vague and elusive but present nonetheless, a strange *otherness* that Leland could sense if he couldn't quite name.

The figure approached the edge of the bed and looked at him, and Leland involuntarily shuddered. It was like making eye contact with a statue; there was nothing but emptiness, like peering into two glass eyes.

"You're not real," Leland said without meaning to speak.

The figure nodded.

"What are you?" Leland asked.

"I'm a representative. An avatar of your hosts." Its voice was smooth and oddly casual sounding.

"Who are my hosts? Why am I talking to you and not them?"

"You're not built to see or hear them," the avatar responded. "If you experienced them directly, your senses would distort your perception, and communication wouldn't be possible."

"And they're from another planet?"

"Yes."

"Am I on some kind of a ship?"

"Yes."

For a moment, Leland felt the slightest sensation of panic

welling up from the pit of his stomach, but he took a breath and managed to calm himself.

"What do they want with me?"

"Your help."

"My help? With what?"

"Your world is more dangerous than you know. And now your hosts' world has become caught in your crosshairs. A secret collective of leaders and scientists on your planet has decided we have something they want, which they aim to take by force. While our civilization is far more advanced than yours, that is of limited utility in this case. For one thing, humanity's capacity for wreaking destruction has always been wildly disproportionate to its scientific progress. For another, we don't know how Earth might engage us, whether by a conventional attack, which could put our coveted possession in harm's way, or by some form of theft that we might not anticipate. What we want is to become completely inaccessible to Earth."

"And . . . how would you accomplish that?"

"A shield. Our engineers have been exploring the possibility of a special barricade, one that could warp the time and space surrounding our world so that any ship or weapon that tried to pass through would instead be redirected far into the distant past. This shield would therefore be not only physically impossible to penetrate but *logically* impossible. And we have lately become convinced, Andrew Leland, that it is your research and your mind that will provide the solution for making this idea become a reality."

Leland wasn't sure whether to laugh or cry. He knew to what research the avatar must be referring, and he had just barely gotten those mid-'90s papers on Alcubierre drives and Krasnikov tubes accepted by peer-reviewed journals. Meanwhile, some alien race had been huge fans?

But there was something else that confused him even more. "I don't get it," he said. "If your civilization is so much more advanced than my own, why would you need my help?"

And now, for the first time, the avatar smiled.

"You must understand that 'advanced' does not mean more intelligent or creative. To put it in terms you might appreciate, Mozart lived on your planet more than two centuries ago. Can anyone on your world today compose a symphony better than he could? Will anyone ever?

"We are not a race of artists or innovators. We are engineers. We've appropriated all our major innovations from other worlds, near and far. Your planet is not notably advanced, no, but your kind is remarkably creative, both for the good and the bad. And your work, Andrew Leland, is art. Your theories are the key to what we've been trying to achieve. We need you to build this barrier for us. We need you to compose our symphony."

Leland struggled to take this all in. The situation seemed so unlikely and so unreal that he couldn't really get his full bearings.

"You should know that you can't survive on our planet as you are," the avatar continued. "To help us, you have to become one of us. We can't force you; the choice has to be yours alone."

"Wait a minute," Leland said, leaning forward as the reality of the situation suddenly began to crystallize for him. "You're telling me you want me to come with you to your planet and live there and . . . work for you?"

"If you so choose, yes."

Leland stared at this thing, this *avatar*, as though seeing it for the first time. He climbed out of bed and walked right up to it, saying nothing, and the avatar didn't move or change its expression. He looked the machine over, circled it, examined it. It looked so much like a person but clearly wasn't one, yet it didn't look like a wax figure or a mannequin or a statue or anything else he'd ever seen. What struck him most of all was that strange *otherness*. It was almost as though it wasn't exactly three dimensional, yet wasn't less or more than that, either.

Could this all be a dream? he wondered.

No. You sometimes knew when you were dreaming, but you *always* knew when you weren't.

Leland shut his eyes and reflected on the past fifteen years. At one time, he had been a cutting-edge scientist, one of his generation's leading minds, a thinker at the forefront of new discoveries, of understanding and teaching others about how the universe truly works. Somehow, gradually and without consciously intending to do so, he'd receded from that identity and become something else with little resemblance to who he'd once been. And that was okay with him, most of the time. He liked going on TV, living in posh Silver Lake, bedding beautiful women . . . who wouldn't? He'd accepted that this was how he was going to end his career, and it wasn't a half-bad way to go out. In reality, that rush he used to get from scientific research, especially those rare eureka moments where you realize you've just made some new discovery or had some startling insight that could have major implications, that high was a thing of the past, had been almost entirely forgotten by him at this point.

Almost.

Leland opened his eyes and gazed again upon this strange and wondrous machine, this avatar that was beseeching his help on behalf of an entire world. And he smiled to himself. How ironic, he thought, that it should believe it was asking a favor of *him*. For in Andrew Leland's heart of hearts, he knew that this was not merely a chance to become a true scientist again. Nor could one accurately call it a great opportunity or even the opportunity of a lifetime.

This was, at the most conservative estimate, the opportunity of twenty lifetimes.

Leland gazed into the avatar's eyes and into the cool nothingness that lay behind them.

"I'll help you," he said.

The avatar smiled. It stepped closer and removed from a pocket some kind of tiny thumbtack-like object, which it swiftly and without warning pressed into the flesh of Leland's right arm. Immediately, Leland felt excruciating pain. His entire body started to burn and visibly whither, causing him to cry out.

Was he melting? Disintegrating? The pain was so enormous, so much more visceral and intense than any he'd ever known, he wondered if he had been tricked, if this was all some sort of trap. When would it stop? Would it *ever* stop?

"Don't be concerned for your body," the avatar said calmly. "You won't need it anymore."

Suddenly, the burning was replaced by something else, an entirely different sensation, incredible and pure, a feeling more exhilarating than any he'd ever experienced in his life. It was as though he could feel all of existence moving within and without himself. As though he was everything combined with everything.

As though his heart and the rhythm of the universe beat as one.

CHAPTER 15

The North Atlantic shimmered in the sunlight. Cecil, who seconds before had been laughingly insisting the water would look more turquoise once they were farther out from the beach, now bent forward, clutching his knee in agony, as Lopez and his fellow airmen looked on in shock.

"Don't ever fuck with my business again," Cecil's assailant, a shirtless, chiseled local with an outstretched bamboo stick, rasped from between the reeds. He had appeared out of nowhere, and now Lopez and the others waited to see what would happen next. Several of them were bona fide killing machines, but they were also on vacation with no interest in getting involved in whatever this was all about. Fortunately, after a few seconds, Cecil took a deep breath, straightened up, and silently led them onward, limping now, while the man with the stick only glared after and then disappeared back into the reeds.

The underside of paradise, Lopez reflected as a newly somber Cecil silently handed them over to a colleague, who distributed their life vests and led them into their rented banana boat.

That underside was something they'd all begun to notice in the past day or so since their arrival on the island. "Everybody here is selling something besides what they're selling," Valucci had observed the night before, over rum-and-pineapple concoctions on a hotel balcony overlooking the outdoor pool. "The cabbies are all club promoters, the Jet Ski guys are ganja dealers, the dealers in the casino, mark my words, half of them are pimps."

Jackson nodded sympathetically. "Lotta nerve these poor people have, ruining your tropical fantasy."

Lopez grinned and took a long sip of his Bahama Mama. At thirty-six, he was the oldest in their unit, but more important, he had the most impressive pedigree by a long shot, and so the others gave him a certain deference. Spending this month's block leave together had been his idea, though he hadn't pushed any specific locale, just so long as it had turquoise water, his one sticking point.

And Cecil had been right. As the banana boat moved farther out from the shore, the water took on that greenish hue he'd seen in brochures and on the hotel website. While the boat bounced upon the waves and his companions launched into a tasteless rendition of "Day-O" with faux Caribbean accents that the driver in the attached speedboat must have really loved, Lopez closed his eyes and let the hot sun beat down on his face. When he opened them again, sometime later, they were moving back toward the beach, and he could make out the entirety of the hotel, a grand, glitzy structure of pastel-colored towers that loomed over the whole island. But it was only after they'd disembarked from the boat, all the unpleasantness about Cecil and the man with the bamboo stick forgotten, as they made their way back up the beach toward the hotel, that he spotted *her*. Tall and voluptuous, with chocolate-colored skin and shiny black braids spiraling upward around her head like an African queen, she looked far too regal to be braiding some tourist's hair. But that's exactly what she was doing, her fingers threading through the tresses of some vapid-looking blonde sprawled out on a beach chair, sipping a martini. Lopez wished he could stop in his tracks and just stare. Instead, he kept his eyes on her as he passed and glanced over his shoulder once or twice after, and five years later, when the whole trip to the Bahamas would feel like centuries ago, he would still remember the way she looked that day on the beach. Here was a woman, he'd remember thinking, who could be worth giving it all up for.

Giving it all up? The idea had once been unthinkable. But then, hadn't doing the unthinkable marked his entire military career? Practically every move he'd made since basic training, they'd told him was not how it's done, ass-backward if not technically a violation of protocol, and he'd pushed ahead and *come out* ahead. The idea of riding out his contract and then leaving the whole life behind and settling down with a woman he loved was so counterintuitive, would be viewed as such a boneheaded move and colossal waste by his superiors and fellow operators, that it suddenly seemed like one of the most daring and thrilling operations he could ever perform. In other words, for the first time in ages, the thrill was back!

He realized, of course, that this woman could be some kind of mirage. In that moment, with the sun striking her in that heavenly way, she might have looked like an angel, but what did he really know about her, besides absolutely nothing? She might not be retirement-worthy, after all. Instead, she might be like those beautiful sirens from ancient Greek mythology who would lure naïve sailors to their doom on the rocky coasts. He would need to use the next few days to find out.

That night, Jenkins and Harris left the hotel for something called the "Booze Cruise," and he and Wang decided to hit up the Carnival, one of the hotel's two casinos. While Wang bled his spending money at the blackjack tables, Lopez opted to take a stroll around the room, and he nearly spilled his drink, stopping dead in his tracks, when he caught sight of her again, standing by the slot machines, decked out in a hotel uniform and holding a drinks tray.

She was alone. There'd be no better time to approach than right now. Really, this was perfect. He didn't even need an opener; he could just order a drink from her and take it from there. Could he order a drink from her *for* her? Would that work? Too cute? His whole pattern of thinking was becoming unfamiliar to him. He was a decisive man of action, not a neurotic; what was she doing to him? Now was clearly the time to act, and yet all he could do was stand there, utterly frozen, hoping she wouldn't catch him staring. What was he waiting for? *If you can recover control of a forty-five-thousand-pound Mudhen after losing eight thousand feet of altitude*, he chided himself, *you can talk to this lovely barmaid right now*. But he was paralyzed with fear. And he *liked* it.

"You're a soldier, aren't you?"

The voice, coming from behind, had a thick Australian accent. He turned around, and a young woman was standing there, jet-black hair with blond or maybe orange highlights. She'd seen him and the others around the hotel, she told him, and could tell from their crew cuts and body language they were military. Her ex-boyfriend had been a reservist with the Coast Guard, she explained. Glancing over his shoulder, Lopez could see that his African queen was gone. That was okay; he clearly wasn't ready yet. Next time, he'd somehow work up the cojones to talk to her, but in the meantime, he'd allow himself to take comfort in the easy interaction he was having with the Australian girl. Lauren, his consolation prize called herself. She was a grad student in chemical engineering at the University of Melbourne, having returned home after attending college in the United States.

"Ever been Down Under?" she asked.

Dewn Unda. He hadn't. She asked what kind of soldier he was, and he told her he was an airman in the air force, to keep things simple.

She invited him back to her room, where they sat at a table by the window, drinking Bacardi and getting to know one another.

Soon, he felt tipsy enough that he was almost tempted to go back down to the casino and try to talk to the beautiful drinks waitress again, but he realized he'd surely make an ass of himself now. Meanwhile, the girl told him about growing up in Perth and her experiences as the only white member of an Aboriginal dance troupe. But all the while, her body language told a different story. She wanted sex, and she wanted it now.

He waited in bed, checking e-mails on his phone, while she changed in the bathroom. Why did she have to change in there if he was going to be seeing her naked in a few minutes, anyway? *Life, how full of mystery you are!* When she emerged from the bathroom, she was still wearing her clothes. "Airman in the air force?" she asked. "Why so modest, Captain Lopez?"

How did she know his name? He wanted to ask her, but when he tried to speak, his jaw felt unbearably heavy. Actually, everything felt heavy, including his limbs. He couldn't move anything! He glanced at the bottle of rum and the empty glasses on the table.

Shit. What had she done to him?

"If I had your credentials," she continued, "I'd tell every girl I met. Navy SEALS, Force Recon, and, after all that, AFSOC? That's a pretty impressive set of experiences. Unique set of skills."

He passed out while she was still speaking, and when he came to, he was in an unfamiliar location, and the girl was asking him if he liked conspiracy theories. The conversation that followed would change his life forever.

Now, five years later, they were having another conversation, and Rachel was changing his life once again. They were sitting, just him and her, in a bungalow somewhere in the bowels of the Docks, Ambius's main headquarters and his home ever since that fateful trip to the Bahamas. Rachel was telling him that the hypothetical mission for which he'd been training these past three years was finally no longer hypothetical. They had figured out how the cosmic shield worked and, more important, how it could be removed. The technology had caught up. Of course, with Ambius, the technology never simply just "caught up," but the less you knew about how exactly shit went down, the better.

"So the shield has been taken down?" he asked.

"Not yet," she answered. "But it will be taken down before you get there."

"Okay."

"*Right* before."

Lopez's eyes widened. "Say what?"

"It has to go down right before you get there and go back up right after you leave. Otherwise, they'll be able to follow you."

Lopez furrowed his brow. "That even possible?"

"All the scientists and engineers say yes."

"So how much time will that give me?"

"Twenty relative minutes."

"Sounds awful tight."

"It is."

Lopez leaned back in his seat and looked out the window of the bungalow. Outside, an Ambius truck was wheeling what looked like a giant glass cocoon across a wide, empty lot. He turned back to Rachel.

"What will it look like?"

"What will what look like?"

"The main prize."

Rachel smiled. "Apparently, a lot like an oversized lotus."

"Lotus?"

"Like a big flower."

"Jesus fuck," he muttered. "So what are my odds?"

"Of mission success?"

"Of me *not dying*."

She looked at him funny. "You never asked that before."

"I'm asking now."

Rachel took a moment to think. "Well, there are a number of variables. As you know, the Phoenix 12 has failed to launch in two out of seven tests. It won't fail again, but statistically speaking, we should take it into account. If you survive that, and you *will*, you'll need to make it all the way to the target. Then, if we somehow fail to deactivate the shield, you won't know it, so you might suddenly find yourself anywhere from five minutes to five thousand years in the past. Otherwise, if everything has gone right and the shield is down, you'll need to remain undetected from entry to exit. Likewise, the shield's disablement will need to go unnoticed. Overall, I'd put your survival odds at 60 percent."

Lopez took a deep breath.

"But that's just on paper, Lopez," Rachel said. "The reality is you can *do* this. More importantly, you're the only one who can."

He nodded, but his mind was elsewhere. She had been so beautiful, he remembered, far too regal to be braiding some tourist's hair or serving drinks in some hotel casino. And he, the rising star of his unit, had been so brave so many times before, and, of course, at the moment he needed it most, his courage had totally deserted him. Things might have been so different today if he'd only acted. He might never have left Air Force Special Operations Command. His parents might know he was still alive. He might have been outside New Mexico more than twice in the past three years.

He had given everything up because they, and specifically Rachel, had convinced him this was his patriotic duty. Not to the United States of America but to mankind itself. So now he would be traveling nearly twelve light-years to steal some object whose power he had no conception of and for purposes that remained completely murky. From the beginning, the mission had been described to him in the loftiest terms. *Humanity needs you*, he'd been told. Lately, though, he'd begun to wonder if it was less about the survival of the human race and more about the same old ravenous

hunger for dominance and power that had driven so many histori-
cal conquests and discoveries.

Rachel was now reminding him of how important the mission
was, just how much was at stake, but he was only pretending to listen. And just as his mind couldn't focus on any of that right now, he
knew that in eight or nine weeks or whenever it would be, when he
would hear the numbers being counted down in his headset and
feel the g-forces pushing down on his chest, the fruition of five years
of rigorous training finally come at last, he would be thinking only
about the life he could have had if he'd just had the balls to talk to
the woman from the beach.

CHAPTER 16

Iraj paged through the latest issue of *Hyperion Starship*, sipping a melted Slush Puppie and deliberately losing track of time. The rain had started around ten, had increased at about midnight, and now was a full-on storm the likes of which he hadn't seen in New River since last November, when the local Dairy Land went halfway underwater and all you could see were its red gambrel roof and the top of a ceramic ice cream cone sticking out of the water. Iraj wondered whether he should go outside and sandbag the gas pumps, but he really didn't feel like moving, and with Mr. Shokof away, it was so much easier to just stay inside the store.

Iraj turned his attention back to his comic book, a shameless rip-off of *Star Hunters*, which itself had begun as a "tribute" to what happened in California. As he read, he found his mind was adding to the story, twisting it around, a sure sign that his earlier espresso had failed. He eyed the wall clock: 3:30 A.M. He looked out the window, at the lonely pumps being pummeled mercilessly by the rain. No cars had passed this way in hours. True, even in monsoon-like weather, you never knew when some poor soul might suddenly show up needing gas or a cup of coffee, but, as Iraj figured, there was a reason for the expression "Fuck it." He closed his comic and locked the store, then went into the adjoining storage room, where a dusty old mattress lay on the floor surrounded by Campbell's soup cans, and spread himself out and went to sleep.

Sometime later, a noise startled him awake. His eyes now open, he didn't move, just lay there listening. He couldn't see much through the cracked door of the storage room, but someone was definitely in the store. He could hear them moving. Walking through the aisle, no doubt swiping whatever their heart desired.

Mr. Shokof's Glock. It was in the drawer behind the register. Lot of good that would do. No less useless would be calling the police; he'd probably be heard making the call, and they wouldn't come, anyway, not tonight. Moving very slowly, he slid himself off the mattress and onto the floor, then, crawling on his side, inched his way over to the cracked door and peered into the store.

A thin young man with rumpled clothes and a short, untrimmed beard was taking cans of vegetables off the shelves and dropping them into a suitcase. Probably a runaway, Iraj thought, though a little older than the ones who usually passed through. This kid looked like he was already out of his teens, maybe somewhere around Iraj's own age of twenty-two. Most important, he looked harmless.

Iraj slowly got to his feet and regarded the sponge mop leaning against the wall. Not a baseball bat or a hockey stick, but it would have to do. The weapon itself hardly mattered, anyway, it was how you held it and the look in your eyes. He picked it up, spread it out between his hands like a ninja's *bō,* and, kicking the door all the way open, barged out into the middle of the store.

The young man with the beard looked up and froze.

Like a deer in headlights, thought Iraj.

"Fuck you think you're doing, kid?" he asked.

The young man just looked at him. Not a look of fear exactly, but of . . . what, expectation? Iraj couldn't quite understand it until he realized the kid wasn't looking at him but *past* him. Without moving, Iraj glanced up at the round security mirror in the corner of the ceiling. Sure enough, someone was standing right behind Iraj, a man with close-cropped hair who, despite sunglasses, seemed vaguely familiar. Someone he knew? Before he could turn around, there was a flash of movement from the man in the mirror, and Iraj was hit in the back of the head and knocked out cold.

"He'll be okay," Leland said, and he and Shawn went back to dropping items from the shelves into their suitcases.

Twenty minutes later, their stolen Honda Civic now loaded up with supplies from Iraj's convenience store, they pulled off Arizona's Interstate 17, Leland at the wheel, and onto the dirt road that led back to the abandoned farm. They arrived at the barn where they'd slept the past four days and got out of the car. The rain was still coming down in sheets.

"Should we unload?" Shawn asked, gesturing toward the trunk.

Leland shook his head. "No point. Assuming this lets up, we're out of here at dawn."

"But this is the best spot we've had in weeks!"

"When that kid wakes up, he'll call the cops, and the whole area will draw heat."

"Over a minimart? You don't think that's a little paranoid?"

Leland flashed Shawn a look that reminded him *paranoid* wasn't one of the words you used around the man.

Inside the barn, they removed their wet clothes and hung them on rusted hooks. The rest of their belongings lay strewn all about: clothing, blankets, maps, cans. The air was humid and smelled like rotted wood. Shawn climbed into one of two grimy sleeping bags that lay on the floor while Leland, hunched over on a low bench, sorted through a crumpled collection of maps. He had banned the use of smartphones or tablets, anything that might have a SIM card or GPS that could allow them to be tracked.

"Clarkdale, Sedona, Payson . . . ," Leland muttered to himself, while Shawn just stared at the black mold on the walls, small spiraling dots on the pale wooden boards that looked like Hubble shots of the Milky Way with the black and white reversed.

A sudden flash of light illuminated the room, followed by an impossibly loud crash that seemed inches away.

Shawn startled, while Leland acted like he hadn't noticed anything. Shawn watched him a moment. "Did they have lightning there?" he asked.

"Where?" Leland didn't look up.

"You know. *There.*"

Leland went on rustling papers and muttering as though Shawn hadn't said anything at all. Shawn was used to that, and he closed his eyes and listened to the sound of the rain beating down on the roof, interspersed with occasional cracks of thunder in the distance. They'd likely be heading out first thing in the morning, but there was still time to get some sleep. Leland, he was sure, wouldn't be going to bed anytime soon. In the month and a half since Shawn's escape from Dellwood College, he had never gone to sleep after Leland nor woken up before him.

Shawn adjusted his position several times and then closed his eyes and began to drift off, while Leland, sounding like some kind of madman or shaman, continued to mutter under his breath as the names of unfamiliar American towns floated in and out of Shawn's fading consciousness.

CHAPTER 17

What happened to Andrew Leland? The question had haunted Shawn ever since high school, and while he certainly had more information now than he ever did before, it had had never been truly answered and in fact had only morphed, taking on deeper, more psychological dimensions. Where once Shawn wondered merely about the basic facts of Leland's experiences in space, now the mystery encapsulated Leland's entire identity, as well.

As far as Shawn could tell, there were at least three Andrew Lelands. The first, and the one Shawn related to most, was the brilliant young scientist who had revolutionized the field with his early work in theoretical physics in the late '90s and early 2000s, whose first treatises were obscure and long winded, but whose writing eventually sharpened into articles and books so lucid and original that each time you read them, the depth and singularity of his brilliance struck you anew. Next, came the sellout Leland of the following years, a grinning, self-satisfied C-list celebrity who had seemingly made a conscious decision to dumb down his persona in order to make it lucrative, an ambitious goal for any physicist but one that had largely paid off, even if his reputation among his peers had steeply declined.

If those Andrew Lelands were accessible, easy to characterize, the third and present Andrew Leland was a mystery wrapped inside an enigma wrapped inside a very boring man. The antithesis of the former media-happy playboy, this Leland was silent, joyless, and intensely private, making him something of a less-than-ideal constant traveling companion. He also bore no real resemblance to the celebrated genius that had constituted his original incarnation. If his famous brain ever produced an interesting thought nowadays, something beyond which town or city would provide them with the best cover for the next few days, he evidently kept it to himself. He didn't talk physics, and he sure as hell didn't talk about anything that had happened to him in space.

Meanwhile, the limited information he was willing to disclose differed sharply from what Shawn had been told back at Dellwood College. On his first night there, Rachel had said that after having been discovered in Mexico, a bearded, haggard-looking Leland had been brought somewhere in Texas and interrogated by the federal government before Ambius could speak to him first. In truth, it had been Ambius itself that had interrogated Leland. What had he experienced in space? they demanded to know. Why had he come back now? Most urgently, what was the exact nature of the giant shield he had built for the other planet, and how could it be dismantled?

But in stark contrast to Rachel's account, instead of Leland's heart giving out under the stress of their inquisition, he had escaped. How he had done so, how he *could* have done so, he would not reveal, though Shawn had his own ideas. In the past month and a half of observing Leland day in and day out, he had come to suspect that, beyond the changes in his personality, Leland might have come back from space different in other ways, too. *Physical* ways. Several incidents, including Leland's initial rescue of Shawn from the river, hinted at this. If that were indeed the case, it might explain not only how Leland had escaped from Ambius in Texas but also how he had continued to elude capture ever since, even as Ambius had hunted him across the globe with trained teams of foot soldiers. In the Netherlands, South Africa, most recently in Spain, he had been confronted by Ambius hit squads again and again, and each time, he had somehow narrowly escaped. It didn't add up unless there was more Leland wasn't telling.

Spain had been different, though, in two notable ways:

First, they hadn't just gone after him this time; when they thought they'd missed him, they had murdered all those who'd been close to him, presumably as a warning that wherever he went, he would bring disaster to anyone he befriended. Second, when they found him, they didn't try to take him alive, as they'd done in the past, but actually tried to kill him. (According to Leland, he survived only because a fire suddenly broke out in the old church where he'd been cornered and he was able to escape under the cover of smoke.)

They didn't need Andrew Leland anymore. They had Shawn.

Rachel had told Shawn that a certain planet was planning a deadly attack on Earth and that Ambius needed him to complete Leland's work and help them build a giant shield in outer space for protection. This was a total inversion of the truth. In reality, it was *Earth*, and specifically Ambius, that had been planning to attack the other world. There was apparently some extremely valuable object or resource they possessed (Leland couldn't or wouldn't tell Shawn more about it), and Ambius was determined to steal it. The aliens became aware of Ambius's plans, and so they recruited Andrew Leland to build the cosmic shield to protect *them*. And once he had done so, a desperate Ambius had in turn recruited Shawn, a supposed expert on Leland's work, to figure out how to dismantle it (flipping the story, meanwhile, so Shawn thought he was helping them build it). Looking back now, Shawn realized he was probably the only person on the entire Dellwood campus who hadn't known the truth, who had believed they were all there to try to save the world.

The irony, though, was that the fake threat Ambius had concocted to lure Shawn in had become all too real—they just didn't know it. In the time since Leland had built the cosmic shield, the aliens' stance toward Earth had evolved. No longer was the shield deemed sufficient to counter the danger of such a reckless and destructive planet as Earth. The threat it posed needed to be permanently neutralized. Earth, it was concluded, had to be destroyed.

The one thing preventing that from happening, though, was the shield, whose existence blocked the aliens from attacking Earth as much as it blocked Earth from attacking them. And while Leland never said so directly, reading between the lines, Shawn understood that the only one on that world who could have effectively dismantled it for them was Leland himself. Presumably, he had refused to do so. What happened after that and how Leland wound up back on Earth were still missing pieces of the puzzle.

Now, thanks to Shawn's unwitting help, the aliens wouldn't need Leland to dismantle the shield because Ambius would do it, instead, totally unaware of the doom that would invite.

"Can't we just tell Ambius the truth?" Shawn had asked on an open highway somewhere between Minneapolis and Salt Lake City. "Shouldn't that do it? Just say, 'Hey, Ambius, that planet you want to attack? It's actually already planning to attack *us*, and that big shield you want to remove is actually the only thing preventing them from doing it'?"

Leland, at the wheel, shook his head.

"Why not?"

"One of two things would happen: they wouldn't believe it, or they'd think they can strike first."

"Why?"

"Arrogance. It's their defining trait."

Shawn considered that a moment. "Fine. Then screw Ambius. What about just telling everyone? We could expose Ambius, expose everything that's going on!"

"And who do you think would believe us?"

"Who would believe Andrew Leland if he came out of hiding and spoke openly and honestly to the world? Everybody."

Leland shook his head. "It would be too late. Ambius won't be stopped."

"You don't know that. Anyway, at least people would know what's coming. Even if they couldn't do anything about it, they'd be *prepared*. The world has a right to know."

Leland suddenly turned to him. "You don't get it. If the world knew it was going to be attacked and slaughtered by an advanced alien race, the world would destroy itself before the aliens ever got here."

Leland turned back to the road, and Shawn remained silent, though he didn't really buy what Leland was saying. The world hadn't destroyed itself when it had watched a man get snatched up into the sky on live TV. The world had adjusted. Either way, it wasn't Shawn's or Leland's or anyone else's place to protect humanity from itself. Shawn knew, however, that there was no point in arguing further. Leland's stubbornness on this issue, his perverse, fatalistic insistence on riding out the apocalypse instead of doing anything to prevent it, hardly seemed rooted in logic. It was almost as though on some level he wanted the confrontation to happen, though Shawn couldn't for the life of him imagine why.

In the meantime, the plan was to lie low and survive. The whole world was living on borrowed time. Ambius would take down the shield and the other planet would attack, and what happened after that was a burning bridge Shawn and Leland would cross when the time came. For now, they would remain focused on everyday concerns like where to find food, shelter, supplies, how to stay unrecognized, unknown. Shawn knew this passive approach of self-preservation was probably unconscionable, but he also knew that defying Leland wasn't an option.

"Why are you keeping me with you?" he'd asked him early on. "We both know you'd move faster without me."

"True. But you'd last about two hours without *me*."

Leland was probably right, but Shawn had trouble believing he actually cared much about him, just as he hadn't seemed particularly regretful when recounting the priests who'd been murdered on his account in Spain. The main reason Leland was keeping him around, he suspected, was exactly the same reason Shawn was wanted dead by Ambius: he knew too much and couldn't be trusted to keep that information to himself. It was the unspoken dynamic in their relationship, that whatever else Shawn was to Leland, he was also his prisoner.

Meanwhile, though Leland would occasionally recount things that happened during his time on the run, he never discussed his experiences in space. If Shawn even tried to bring up the subject, Leland would immediately shut down. When Shawn had been at the campus with Rachel and the other young recruits, he'd been kept in the dark about anything beyond their specific project. Though he had yearned to hear about other planets and the intelligent life they contained, as well as the advanced alien technologies that Ambius had come to possess, no one would tell him anything of substance, and it frustrated him to no end. Now, fate had brought him together with Andrew Leland, the *real* Andrew Leland, the man whom he had spent years obsessing over and longing to meet, and it was the same old shit all over again. His dream had come true and had turned out to be just another dead end.

CHAPTER 18

In the cool and misty morning, after rubbing down the surfaces of the barn with microfiber cloths to wipe out fingerprints, Shawn and Leland loaded up the Civic with everything they had, and, Leland commanding the wheel, they got back onto I-17, headed north toward Flagstaff. The idea was to lay over in Camp Verde for the next few days, unless by some chance they found a suitable hideout along the way.

They did.

It was Shawn who first spotted the old mansion, its witch-hat turret and weather vane jutting out from behind the honey locusts that dotted the side of the highway. The small portion of the structure visible from the road was striking in both its design and its dilapidation. It looked like a haunted house, which meant it looked like a deserted house.

Shawn alerted Leland, who pulled the car off the highway and onto a narrow wooded road that turned out to lead almost directly to the house itself. About sixty yards from it, he stopped the car, and Shawn got out. Being the far less conspicuous of the two,

Shawn would now approach on his own, scope out the scene, and if the house turned out to be as abandoned as it seemed, Leland would pull in round the back and they would unload their things.

As Shawn walked the overgrown driveway leading up to the entrance, the old mansion loomed over him. Tricolored in cream, pink, and lavender and comprising a host of cylindrical and triangular shapes, classy but asymmetrical dormers, chimneys, and balconies, it reminded him of some of the old Victorian manors he used to see on school trips in Massachusetts, but with a dash of Dr. Seuss or Disneyland thrown in. A plaque affixed to the front door read:

> The Atterbury House. Built by James Creighton in 1869, this gorgeous 21,000-square-foot Queen Anne Victorian was home to Dr. Timothy Atterbury, a 19th century oil heir and scholar of French literature. The interior includes eleven rooms, among them five bedrooms, a parlor, foyer, dining room, servants' quarters, and library. Today, the house is preserved as a historic museum.

But it was clearly no museum, at least not anymore. Its body paint was chipping all over, and about half of its decorative fish-scale shingles were missing. As Shawn ascended the balustrade staircase leading to the front door, he half expected to crash right through it. When he reached the entrance, he pressed the button on the brass doorbell, feeling a little absurd. After the anticipated interval of silence, he tried the doorknob. At first, it didn't budge, but once he'd put his back into it, the unlocked door cracked open, and Shawn stepped gingerly into a wide vestibule. Almost immediately, he began to cough as beams of natural light from the high windows illuminated thick columns of dust. Covering his nose and mouth, he did a quick trek through the house, which yielded no signs of *human* habitation, and then went back outside and gave Leland the all-clear.

Several hours later, after most of the windows had been opened and the house aired out, Shawn and Leland sat on the floor of an upstairs bedroom, eating a silent meal of instant lentil soup they'd cooked on a tiny portable butane stove. Despite the abundance of rooms, they had designated just a single one for eating, sleeping, and storing their belongings in. This was part of the Andrew Leland MO of survival. Always consolidate, so if you have to move out, you can move out now.

After dinner, as Leland busied himself with a crinkled atlas, Shawn set about exploring the old mansion in greater depth. The plaque outside had mentioned servants' quarters, but Shawn hadn't seen evidence of any yet, so he thought he might try to seek those out.

But there was one place he knew he wanted to check out first.

The Atterbury library, located on the mansion's first floor, was a wide, round room with rosewood paneling and arched, curtain-draped windows. In the center sat an antique red velvet settee and several leather armchairs resting upon what looked like a Moroccan rug, all of this overhung by an elegant crystal chandelier. But what really drew Shawn's attention were the hundreds, or likely thousands, of books lining the shelves floor to ceiling. Back at Dellwood College, the dusty old school library had felt oppressive and claustrophobic. Now, after six supremely boring weeks on the road, the sight of so many books made Shawn feel suddenly free and alive.

He took a step closer to one of the shelves and was delighted to find that, in addition to his interests in French literature, Dr. Atterbury must have also been something of a science geek. At least one section was full of books on anatomy and physiology. Shawn scanned the titles, names like *Physical Science and Sexuality* and *On Curing Intemperance*, works by authors now obscure, but who might have been greatly renowned in their own times. One book that sounded particularly intriguing was *Mind and Brain* by Thomas Laycock. Slowly and gently, Shawn pulled it out from the shelf and blew some dust off its ancient leather binding. But when he opened it and started to flip through, he squinted in confusion. The first twenty pages or so appeared to be blank. He flipped through some more and discovered that the whole book was blank!

"Braille," said a voice behind him, and Shawn nearly jumped out of his skin.

How long had Leland been standing there? Shawn breathed a sigh of relief and looked back down at the book and realized he was right. In the late afternoon light, he had totally missed the embossment that covered all the book's pages.

"Someone who lived here must have been blind," Leland said. "Maybe Dr. Atterbury himself, though probably not. Don't imagine there were enough Braille books in the nineteenth century for a Ph.D." Leland walked passed Shawn and pulled out a thick volume from another shelf. Shawn watched as he thumbed through the pages and then stopped at a certain spot and gently fingered the paper, a perceptible distance coming into his eyes.

Shawn observed him only a moment longer.

"How did you get past the shield?" Shawn asked, surprising himself. He'd wanted to ask the question for a long time, but only here and now, in the quietude and stillness of that majestic room, did he suddenly summon the courage.

A cloud passed over Leland's face, his trance broken. He looked at Shawn, frowned. Shawn swallowed, but pressed on. "The cosmic shield should have worked both ways," he said. "So how could you have made it through to get back here? Was it not as impenetrable as it was supposed to be?"

Leland stared at him a moment longer, then looked down at the book he was holding, blew some dust off the page, and closed the cover. "Let me ask you a question," he said. "You're in a spacecraft going ninety thousand miles per hour and you hit the shield. What happens?"

"You get shot back in time."

"How far?"

"Probably around six thousand years."

"Okay. Good. And if you're in a ship going thirty thousand miles per hour?"

"Around two thousand years. But *no* spacecraft could get you to a perfect speed with enough consistency that you could pass through the shield and wind up on the other side still in the present."

"No spacecraft you know. And it's not just about speed, is it? Are you hitting the shield at a twenty-degree angle? Fifty-degree?"

Shawn considered this.

"Even so," he said, "considering all the variables at play, to calculate everything just right and then to actually *execute* it that way would be virtually impossible."

"Yes."

Shawn waited for Leland to say more, but he didn't.

"Okay. All right. So if you were somehow able to just *pass through* the shield instead of taking it down first," Shawn asked, "does that mean Ambius could do the same thing from the other side?"

"Possibly. But they won't need to now, will they?"

Shawn didn't let that faze him. "Where's the ship you came back in? What happened to it?"

"You're asking a lot of questions."

"What happened to *you*?"

"Me?"

Shawn paused. He, himself, could barely believe where he'd taken the conversation, but by the same token, there was no backing down. It was now or never. The discussion wasn't going to be continued over breakfast the next morning. "You're not the same person anymore," Shawn said. "The way you jumped from eighty feet and rescued me from that river without a scratch. The way you've outrun Ambius all over the world. A normal human being would have been caught ages ago."

Leland returned the book to the shelf. "Guess I've had lots of luck," he said. "Don't push yours." With that, he turned away and walked out of the library, leaving Shawn by himself again.

Shawn spent a little more time in there, browsing the collection, which turned out to also contain fascinating, non-Braille tomes on anthropology, American history, and even some introductory—and severely outdated—textbooks on astronomy and physics. When the light began to dim further, he reached into his pocket for his small LED flashlight and, as he did, felt a stab of hunger, despite his lavish feast of instant soup, and he suddenly remembered something else he'd been intending to do.

Minutes later, Shawn clicked on the flashlight and scanned his new surroundings. A large freestanding cabinet structure stood to his left, a long tublike sink with two faucets to his right, and directly in front of him, an ancient-looking stove. As much as he loved canned vegetables and soup, he'd decided a working kitchen wouldn't be a terrible thing, though he had serious doubts about whether anything in here was still usable. The stove, for instance, was no doubt worthless, given that it had likely been decades since any gas company had serviced the house.

However, resting on the floor nearby, there appeared to be an even older type of stove, and this one didn't seem connected to, or dependent on, a gas line. The strange antique, which sort of resembled a small lamp, consisted of a wide single burner head jutting out from a fat metal cylinder, presumably some sort of fuel tank. If the tank wasn't empty, there might be some way to get the thing going, though Shawn would have to figure out how.

As he bent down to get a closer look, he couldn't help but smile. Once again, his world had turned inside out. A little over a month ago, he'd been trying to determine how two disparate theories of faster-than-light travel could combine to create a giant shield of space-time curvature. Now, he was trying to turn on a stove.

People sometimes describe an almost supernatural feeling of being watched, as though the hairs on the backs of their necks can somehow sense that another is observing them. Shawn knew perfectly well that there was absolutely nothing supernatural about this phenomenon, that the inexplicable "feeling" described was actually the result of a hardwired "gaze-detection system" in the brain. Our peripheral vision is extremely sensitive to the eyes of others and so alerts us when the position of someone's iris relative to his or her sclera indicates we're being looked at. However, at this particular moment, the only things in Shawn's field of vision were the front and sides of the kitchen. So how to explain that he was having that mysterious feeling right now?

Shawn turned immediately to the point on the smaller stove that was reflecting his flashlight, and sure enough, he could barely make out the image of a short, shadowy figure standing behind him, just beyond the kitchen, and he could make out the eyes, glowing out of the darkness, that he'd felt watching him. Shawn spun around and aimed his flashlight directly at his observer, who instantly took off running. "Hey!" Shawn called out and, without missing a beat, raced after in pursuit, flashlight shining forward. For a moment, he thought he'd lost the person, but then, turning a sharp corner, he caught sight of them at the far end of the hallway, running through a low doorway Shawn hadn't previously noticed. Shawn followed through the door and almost lost his balance before grabbing onto a railing. He was at the top of a creaky wooden staircase that led down into total darkness. The elusive servants' quarters, he realized! Footsteps barreled down the stairs below him, followed by a sudden crash, thud, and piercing scream. Shawn quickly swiveled his flashlight downward. The last two steps of the no-doubt rotten wooden staircase had given out, and a teenage boy lay writhing in pain on the stone basement floor. Shawn was about to call out and ask if he was all right when Andrew Leland suddenly brushed past him from above, practically flying down the stairs. Leland leaped over the missing space at the bottom like he'd already anticipated it, landed hard next to the kid, and pulled out a pistol Shawn never knew he had.

"When I count to three," Leland said, aiming the gun right at the kid's head, "you're going to tell me who I am. One, two, three . . ."

CHAPTER 19

The kid winced in pain. "Too tight," he groaned as Leland yanked another layer of duct tape across the instep of his left foot. The kid had sprained his ankle pretty badly and was lying on his back on a dirty air mattress with his foot elevated over Leland's knee while the latter fashioned a makeshift compression wrap. Shawn stood off to the side, looking on as a small battery-operated desk lamp glowed from a wooden table in the corner of the room. The kid had shown him how to turn the lamp on, and it illuminated the cigarette boxes and comic books that populated the table.

"You some kinda doctor?" the kid asked Leland.

"Nope."

"So how do I know you know what you're doin'?"

Leland shrugged.

"Christ."

Though he'd told Leland and Shawn he was twenty-one, the kid looked closer to seventeen, and with his long, messy red hair, torn clothes, and small patch of raw, fleshy scarring on his left cheek, he gave off a hard and scruffy vibe that was somewhat offset by his youth. Despite the pistol being aimed at his head, he had not told Leland who Leland was, just to go fuck himself, which surprised both Leland and Shawn and made Shawn wonder if he might be crazy. But while they couldn't know for sure, they didn't think he recognized Leland. Several times in the course of their travels, they had run up against people who seemed like they did, and there was always a discernible look of recognition and amazement, even reverence. This kid displayed none of that, not even at first.

"Y'all gonna be stayin' awhile?" he asked.

Leland shrugged. "If we feel like it."

"Well, see, this here is kinda my place."

"Your place?" asked Shawn with a smirk. "You look a little young to be Timothy Atterbury."

"I didn't say y'all gotta leave."

"And we didn't say you could stay," answered Leland.

The kid looked angry for an instant, but seemed to calm himself quickly and prevent himself from reacting. For a few moments, he said nothing at all, just stared at the floor, looking somewhat perturbed. Finally, he looked back to Leland. "You said yourself I can't walk," he said. "Maybe how 'bout this? How 'bout we all stay? I don't ask you what you're doin' holin' up in some old mansion, you don't ask me what I'm doin' holin' up in some old mansion. I give you access to my food and supplies, and no, I ain't livin' off Lucky Strikes; I got a whole stash of canned food, bottled water, batteries, toilet paper, you name it." He turned to Shawn. "I'll also teach you how to fire up that li'l kerosene stove if you like. Then, when the supplies run out, y'all will restock with enough stuff so that if and when you wanna move on, I'll be able to get by just long enough till I can get back on my feet. Seems like an equitable arrangement to me. Whaddaya say?"

Leland stared at him for a few seconds, then looked to Shawn. It occurred to Shawn that this was probably the first time Leland had ever really sought his opinion. He shrugged, genuinely unsure what to do. On the one hand, part of him welcomed the idea of a companion besides Leland. On the other, his experiences with Ambius had made him far less trusting than he once was.

Leland turned back to the kid. "What kind of phone you have?"

"Galaxy."

"Can I see it?"

The kid hesitated, shook his head. Leland pulled out the pistol and aimed it at him. "Give me your fucking phone."

The kid retrieved it from his pocket and handed it to him. Leland popped open the back and pulled out the SIM card. He handed the phone back to the kid. "You got yourself a deal."

"I really don't get it," said Shawn later that evening when he and Leland were back in their room. "How can he not recognize you? He saw your whole face *up close*."

"We'll have to watch him carefully. Don't forget, I've been under the radar the past few years, and he was only a kid back when I was big news. Not everybody is completely obsessed with me."

Shawn ignored the dig. "What do you think he's running from?"

"You saw that burn mark on his cheek."

"What? Abuse?"

Leland shrugged.

"Okay, but why's he hiding out here?"

"Why not?"

"I don't know. I mean, if I had run away from home, I'd probably go for a big city, someplace I could disappear, start over. This isn't any kind of life for anyone. I mean, well, besides us."

"Maybe he's scared of getting caught, sent back. Or maybe he's planning to *go back*. This could be just a break."

"What, like a vacation?"

"Who knows?"

"Did you have to shove that gun in his face?"

"Yes."

Shawn sighed. "Well, I guess you're right; we'll just have to watch him close. I feel like it doesn't add up."

"Things sometimes don't. People don't always do what you expect."

"That's for sure," said Shawn, gingerly settling into an old Windsor chair by the window. "Like for instance, say some guy goes on a trip somewhere special that no one else has ever been. You'd think when he got back, he would tell at least some people what it was like. All the amazing things he saw. All the incredible people or, you know, *creatures* he encountered. You'd never imagine he'd just keep it all to himself, not tell a soul, act like he didn't even remember it."

Leland hadn't been looking at him, and for a moment, Shawn assumed he would just ignore him.

"What if he *didn't* remember it?" Leland suddenly asked, turning to him.

"You told me you helped them build the shield," Shawn said. "And that afterward, they decided to attack Earth and that the shield is the only thing stopping them from doing it. How could you know all that if you don't remember anything?"

"There's a big difference between knowing and remembering," said Leland. "I wouldn't have lasted in that atmosphere for five minutes. Even if I could have, my senses wouldn't have been able to assimilate anything. In order to exist on that world, I had to become something else. And that something else is gone now, along with everything it experienced. This body you see here never went anywhere, and these eyes never saw anything. This body experienced nothing but the ride there and the ride back. All I have are bare-bones facts—that's it. If you want to know what anything was actually like, what *anyone* was like, your guess is as good as mine."

Shawn shook his head. "You must remember something."

"I don't."

It rained all through the night. In the morning, Shawn descended the stairs to the basement (carefully hopping over the missing portion), carrying a bowl of instant oatmeal he'd cooked up with his and Leland's electric kettle. The kid lay on his back on the mattress, tapping furiously at his phone screen as some tinny video game theme played from the speaker.

"Thought you might want breakfast," Shawn said.

The kid looked up, smiled, and turned off the game. "Thank you kindly," he said, taking the bowl from Shawn.

Shawn watched as he hungrily devoured the oatmeal. He ate with such abandon that Shawn wondered if he hadn't been exaggerating about the food and supplies he would supposedly be sharing with them.

"So," Shawn said when the boy had finished, "you say you know something about old stoves."

In the kitchen upstairs, Shawn carefully released a few drops of denatured alcohol into a small round cup situated just below the burner of the smaller stove.

"Okay, good," the kid said, looking on from a short wooden folding chair. "Now light her up."

Shawn struck a match and lit the alcohol aflame.

"Once it burns out, close the air valve and start pumpin'."

Shawn waited for the flame to drop off, and then he shut the air valve. He took hold of the small, silver handle protruding from the side of the tank and began to pump, carefully moving it back and forth, in and out of the tank. Soon enough, a blue, sootless flame had materialized in the center of the burner.

The kid smiled. "Voilà!"

Shawn watched the flame, then turned to the kid. "How'd you figure all this out?"

"Not much to figure out. Works about the same as a modern Primus. My family's been using those on camping trips for years. So what's with you and the old man?"

"What? What do you mean?"

"Well, not sure how to put it politely. Are you his son or his bitch?"

This took Shawn aback. "Neither!"

"Right. Okay. Well, he ain't exactly Mr. Warm and Fuzzy, is he?"

"What happened to not asking each other questions?"

"Think I was pretty clear on what questions we was and wasn't to be askin'."

Shawn considered this. "Okay. No, he's not warm and fuzzy. Where are you from?"

The kid laughed. "Well played, partner. Small town in Texas you ain't ever heard of, and pretty soon I won't remember it, either. Old man calls all the shots, huh?"

"What makes you say that?"

The kid snorted. "Don't gotta be no rocket scientist to see it."

There was no glint in his eye as he spoke, no knowing smile, but the words *rocket scientist* still made Shawn uncomfortable.

"Where are you headed?" Shawn asked.

The kid shook his head. "Uh-uh. Wrong kinda question. I mean, you ain't gonna tell me where y'all are headed, right?"

"I don't know where we're headed."

This was the truth, but the kid rolled his eyes. "Wherever it is," he said, "I reckon you'll be tethered to your buddy. Maybe you're better for it. Me, I couldn't stand being on anybody else's leash all the time."

"I'm not on any leash."

"So you say. We're all on some kinda leash. Somebody's leash, somebody's code, someone's way of life. Until we decide to cut our-selves loose."

Shawn smiled. "You're a lone ranger, huh?"

"I am now." He gestured to the stove. "Very important—when you pump, if it seems clogged or anything, don't ever try to force it."

"What happens?"

The kid smiled and leaned in a little. "See this nasty scar on my face?"

At around noon, having sorted through the kid's supplies with Le-land and then having spent a few hours in the library, Shawn deci-ded to get out of the house a bit. Though he had far from exhausted his explorations of the mansion, he'd been indoors too long, and the combined energies of Leland and the kid were starting to rattle his nerves. He needed air, and the dewy, juniper-scented breeze of forest fresh after a rainstorm certainly fit the bill.

Stepping outside, he could see and hear distant cars roaring down the highway through the tall trees. He headed in the opposite direction, circling around to the back of the house and then onward up a narrow wooded path. He knew Leland preferred to keep him close, so he hadn't mentioned anything about going. Like he'd told the kid before, he wasn't on anyone's leash. Andrew Leland didn't need to know his every move.

As he pushed farther into the woods, he became mindful of a familiar sound coming from somewhere up ahead. He kept walk-ing, the sound getting closer and closer until at last he'd reached just the sort of picturesque scene he'd been anticipating: a narrow brook, shaded by tall pine trees and snaking its way downhill through large and craggy moss-covered rocks. It was beautiful, like something out of a nature video, but Shawn could barely look at it. When he did, he was transported right back to the magical night Rachel had led him through the woods at Dellwood to the river. It had only been a few months back, but it felt like a lifetime ago. As they'd watched the water rushing beneath them, illuminated by the moon, she had told him about how special they both were. That although they'd been initiated into something greater than themselves, they were nonetheless great themselves.

A crock of shit, that. Shawn hadn't been initiated into anything except a huge joke of which he was the butt. Everything he'd been told had been a lie, and all his time and energy had gone toward nothing less than his own total exploitation. Meanwhile, he'd meant nothing to Rachel. Like everyone else at Dellwood, she'd been using and deceiving him. And when she finally decided she didn't need him anymore, or couldn't trust him, she'd tried to dispose of him. "Shoot him!" she'd called from the window. He had heard her shout those words. He could still hear them now.

It began to rain in the woods. Shawn watched as the rainwater splashed in the brook, first in little droplets and then furiously. He now knew the truth, that Ambius had tricked him into doing the exact opposite of what he meant to and that his actions had ultimately put the world in more danger than even Ambius itself could know. Yet he was being prevented from doing a single thing about it.

As he turned around and started back toward the house, the kid's proclamation from earlier reverberated in his skull: we're all on somebody else's leash until we decide to cut ourselves loose.

CHAPTER 20

Andrew Leland had told Shawn he remembered nothing about his time on the other planet beyond "bare-bones facts."

This was a lie.

Yes, he had experienced nothing through his human senses and couldn't remember things as they actually had been. But his mind had *adjusted* his memories and translated them into experiences he could understand, as the mind so often does with the incomprehensible.

Still, things were hazy even in translation, and he found his memories to be fluid and unspecific, very much like dreams. A place on that world that was neither city nor forest nor beach might be remembered as any of the three, depending on the time he was remembering. Likewise, the beings with whom he had lived were sometimes recalled as vague, faceless entities and at other times as people, though he knew that whatever they had been, they hadn't been anything like people.

He remembered her as a she and himself as a he, without knowing whether those terms had applied to either of them at the time.

"They want me to take it down," he told her one night, in what must have been the fourth year since his arrival, measuring in Earth-time. By that point, he was already revered in their world for having built the incredible shield that had protected their planet from Earth's planned attack. But if they felt gratitude to the mysterious man from outer space, they had grown increasingly nervous about his planet. Yes, with his help, they had staved off an attack, but a hostile and unpredictable world like Earth so close to their own was a continual threat, and it was unclear whether the barrier he'd engineered for them truly couldn't be breached. The threat, it was finally assessed, needed to be removed completely, and in order to accomplish that, they required him to undo what he had done, to remove the shield so they could pass through from their end and eliminate the danger permanently.

"What did you answer?" she asked.

The two of them were standing on the edge of some beautiful place, possibly a large field or a sandy beach, which was illuminated by a majestic blanket of stars.

"I told them I couldn't do that."

"Couldn't or wouldn't?"

"Is there a difference?"

"What did they say?"

"Nothing."

She looked into his eyes, and he feared for a moment that her penetrating gaze might hold a hint of judgment, that she might now see him as the others surely did, as apart, as not really one of them.

Then, without any warning besides a mischievous gleam in her eye, she snatched a medallion or pin or something else from off his chest and suddenly took off running.

He darted after her, and soon they were running side by side, playfully shoving one another as they raced beneath the night sky. To those born of her world, he knew she was considered a kind of goddess or sorceress, exalted, worshiped, revered, but to him, she was both more and less, childlike and at the same time a source of such incredible wonder that he sometimes questioned how he ever could have felt alive back on Earth. When they reached the other side of the field, they both collapsed, panting on their backs as they lay amid the stalks of the field or the sand of the beach or some other substance entirely.

He would never understand her, he knew that. Her power was said to be beyond the comprehension of all but the wisest and most intellectually evolved of their world. Just like the so-called Illumination, that strange and mysterious resource that Earth had sought to steal from them. Leland had built the cosmic shield chiefly to protect the Illumination, but he still had no real idea of what it was, why it was so powerful, or why anyone on Earth might want it.

She, on the other hand, was one of the enlightened few who did. Since he knew the Illumination was beyond his grasp, he never pressed her to try to explain it to him, though he sometimes teased her, asking who was more powerful, she or it, a question she would laugh off, probably because she understood that his teasing masked his deep sense of inferiority.

And who in his situation could help but feel insecure, unworthy, at least some of the time? In truth, he wasn't interested in understanding the Illumination. What he really wished he could understand was her.

They lay there for several moments, staring up at the stars, and then she rose to her feet and stared down at him with those intense and sincere eyes, always remembered as wide and green. Looking up at her now, silhouetted by the dazzling star field above, he was reminded of the very first time he'd seen her, bathed in ethereal light, surrounded by a vast horde gazing at her with reverential awe.

"You'll be in grave danger now," she said, her voice soft, but firm. "You have to let me save you."

He didn't respond, and she stared at him for several more

seconds, then lowered herself back down and climbed on top of him and placed her mouth upon his. She lay down on him, and the two remained that way for some time after.

The rain continued to pound the walls and roof of the old mansion. Leland stared out the bedroom window at the trees and the highway in the distance. He didn't really remember her anymore, not truly. What she looked like, what she sounded like, even much of her personality, these were lost to him. And the field had not been a field and the kiss had not been a kiss and the girl had, of course, not been a girl.

But that feeling that had passed between them, as the two of them lay there beneath the stars, that feeling had survived, was with him always, and he knew he could pass through a thousand different bodies in a thousand different worlds and he would never be able to forget it.

CHAPTER 21

When their supplies finally ran out, Shawn and Leland had been living with the kid, who called himself Miles, for two weeks. In that time, Shawn had warmed up to Miles, who certainly made better company than Andrew Leland. For the most part, he was a genial and bracingly honest conversation partner, though he could also turn cold and distant on a dime if you pressed him about his past or, for that matter, his future.

Since they'd met him, Miles had continued to show no sign that he might recognize Leland, though Leland and Shawn remained careful not to let down their guards. There had actually been one incident that had made Shawn a little uncomfortable, though he wasn't sure what it indicated, if anything, and it certainly didn't rise to the level of *evidence*, per se, of anything to be concerned about. It had occurred about a week after Shawn and Leland had arrived at the mansion. Miles had been telling Shawn a story about his grandfather, some kind of war hero, when he decided he wanted a cigarette, and Shawn had accompanied him outside to the front porch to continue the conversation while Miles smoked. As they stepped outside, they were both immediately struck by the clarity and brightness of the stars in the night sky, and for a minute, neither said anything. Then, after a long drag on his cigarette, Miles asked, "You think there's anything's out there?"

"What do you mean?" asked Shawn.

"You know. Life."

Shawn, who'd been trying to spot Andromeda in the sea of tiny white dots, looked over at Miles. He was still watching the sky, his cigarette lobbed in the knuckles of one hand while the other rested on his hip in a sort of quasi-aristocratic pose. Shawn wasn't sure how to answer him. Once upon a time, it would have been a perfectly normal and commonly asked question. But nobody asked it today! Of course there was something "out there"—the world had watched it snatch away a famous physicist on live TV! So was Miles just fucking with him now? If yes, why? Did he already suspect Leland's identity, and was he deliberately putting Shawn in the awkward position of having to either confront the subject of Bernasconi Hills head-on or blatantly and unnaturally ignore it? Or was he instead just one of those conspiracy theorists who didn't believe Bernasconi Hills ever happened?

In the end, Shawn opted for a simple and uncontroversial "Yes, I do" without elaborating and quickly changed the subject back to Miles's grandfather.

The conversation had unsettled Shawn, but not so terribly, and he didn't bother mentioning it to Leland. Ultimately, he concluded that, as with the time Miles had used the term *rocket scientist*, the incident probably said much more about Shawn's own paranoia (however justified) than it did about Miles.

It was late afternoon when Shawn and Leland got back into their Honda Civic for the first time since their arrival and set off for a shopping excursion in nearby Black Canyon City. The plan was to load up on supplies and then stay in the Atterbury House for another four or five days before moving on to the next location, leaving most of the supplies behind, in keeping with their agreed-upon arrangement with Miles. While the mansion had provided a stable and convenient cover, more than two weeks in the same spot was already pushing it. As for where they'd be heading afterward, Shawn had no idea. Leland rarely told him where they were headed next before they were about to go, and he kept him totally in the dark about the overall trajectory of their travels and where, if anywhere, their ultimate destination lay. Leland didn't need to spell out why; Shawn understood that the less he knew, the better. If he was captured by Ambius, they would surely want to know about Leland's whereabouts and any other information about him Shawn might possess. However, even if Shawn knew nothing, there was a strong possibility he might be tortured for info, which is why Leland had given him a tiny cyanide capsule that could be hidden in his tooth. Whether this was primarily to protect Shawn from the pain of torture or Leland from exposure by Shawn was left ambiguous.

In Black Canyon City, about fifteen miles from the Atterbury House, they pulled into the parking lot of a Walmart, and Shawn got out of the car. While many previous shopping outings had involved risky after-hours break-ins, this time there was no need, as Miles had surprised them with money. It turned out he had at least four hundred bucks in cash, probably stolen from his parents. He'd likely been holding out until now to see if he could trust them.

While Leland waited in the car, a nondescript baseball cap pulled down to just above his black shades, Shawn walked into the superstore and felt a surge of freedom. Hundreds of customers moved this way and that, as various staticky announcements—sales, specials, upcoming store events—rang out over the intercom. He knew which section he needed to seek out first, what needed to be obtained, but for a moment, he simply stood in place. This was the first time in a good while that he'd found himself amid a real crowd, an anonymous individual blending in with a larger whole. A *member of society.*

It felt liberating and then suddenly troubling. *Wasn't* he, after all, a member of society? And didn't that carry certain obligations? Shawn held secret knowledge that affected all these people around him and millions—no, billions—more, and the only reason he wasn't acting on it was because Andrew Leland wouldn't allow him to. *Cut the leash.* There was a bus station just beyond the parking lot; he'd caught sight of it from the car. He didn't need to remain anybody's prisoner; he could break free and finally, *finally* do the right thing. This was his big chance, right here, right now. Leland was out in the car, nowhere near him. Shawn could be on a bus headed out of Arizona before he even realized he was gone. *Cut the leash, dammit!*

But he couldn't do it. Maybe it was because he knew no one would ever believe him. It would be one thing for Andrew Leland to come out and reveal the truth, but it was quite another for Shawn, a complete nobody, to come forward with such a wild and improbable story. Or maybe, despite his disappointments and disillusionment, he still had some reverence for Leland, still trusted him, and was afraid to betray him.

Or maybe he was just afraid, period. He wasn't sure himself the exact reason, maybe didn't even want to know, but in the end, he returned to the car with a shopping cart full of food and supplies and unloaded them into the trunk and backseat of the Honda.

"We'll pack tonight," Leland said afterward as Shawn climbed into the front passenger seat. "Be discreet about it."

Shawn gave him a confused look. "Aren't we staying another few days?"

"Nope. Leaving at sunrise. No reason for him to know in advance. Safer that way."

When they returned to the mansion, they brought most of the items from Walmart down to the basement and, together with Miles, stacked them inside the closet where he'd been stashing his supplies. They didn't tell him about the things that had been left upstairs, paid for with *his* money, that would be going out with them in the morning. After Leland went back upstairs, Miles tore open one of the six-packs he'd requested, and he and Shawn shared a beer.

"You guys didn't get any of the magazines I asked for," Miles observed.

"Well, in just a few days, you'll have your SIM card back."

Miles grinned. "True that."

After they finished the beer, Shawn wished Miles good night and then started toward the staircase, but paused at the landing. He turned back to Miles, who was sitting on his mattress now, fiddling with his phone, probably gearing up for one of his marathon gaming sessions. Miles had been something like a friend to him these past few weeks, probably the closest thing he'd had to one since going into hiding. Miles had also lit something of a spark in him, even if in the end Shawn couldn't actually go through with breaking free from the ties that bound him the way Miles had done.

It didn't seem right to just disappear without a word. He knew Leland would have objected to even the slightest hint that they would be taking off tomorrow, but this wouldn't actually qualify, and anyway, Leland wasn't here now, was he?

"Miles?"

Miles look up from his screen.

"Been fun times hanging with you."

Miles looked at him a little funny, and for a second, Shawn wondered if he might suspect something. But then he smiled with something approaching genuine warmth. "Same here, pal," he said.

Shawn and Leland spent the rest of that night packing as quietly as they could. Sometime after 1:00 A.M., Shawn went to bed as Leland continued to through his maps, making preparations for wherever they'd be heading next. *It's really a shame to be leaving here*, Shawn thought as he nestled into his sleeping bag. It was by far the most hospitable spot they'd found, not to mention easily the most fascinating. He'd also miss Miles, he realized. He hoped that the kid would get out of here soon, either go back home and find the strength to face whatever he was running from or else start life anew just like he wished he himself could.

A few hours later, Shawn woke from his sleep to a noise, opened his eyes, and bolted upright.

A figure stood in the middle of the bedroom, barely visible in the darkness. With the help of the shallow moonlight streaming in from the window, Shawn's eyes quickly adjusted, and he realized it was Miles and that he was pointing a handgun directly at Leland's sleeping bag.

"Miles!" Shawn cried in a hoarse whisper, and Leland's own eyes popped open, as well.

Miles gave Shawn a quick glance without turning his head. "I ain't gonna hurt you, pal," he said. "But your friend and I, we got us some business to attend to." He smiled at Leland, who was starting to sit up. "Did y'all really think I didn't recognize the most famous man in the world? I knew you the moment you first pulled up in that beat-up Honda. Everyone on Earth knows that face, and me even more than some. I never really told y'all where I was from, did I? Little town called Annabella, Texas. Heard of it?"

"Nope," said Leland.

But Shawn had. He remembered reading articles about Annabella years ago, sometime soon after Bernasconi Hills. About how the local Presbyterian minister and the majority of his flock had jointly renounced their Christian faith and sawed the steeple off their church, declaring themselves members of a new order with a brand-new theology.

"They worship you," Shawn said quietly to Leland. "Like a messiah."

"Like a *god*," Miles corrected. "Overnight, my family, my whole town, went from normal, hardworking folk to fucking fruitcakes.

And our good, holy reverend . . . well, let's just say he was the biggest fruitcake of 'em all. Whole lotta pickles short of a barrel. I lived with it long as I could, long as I had to, and then I busted right out of there. Decided I'd rather live on my own than be part of some nutty cult. But maybe . . . well, maybe I gave up on 'em all just a little too soon. Ya know? Maybe things will change back to normal once I show 'em all that the great Andrew Leland bleeds red just like anybody else."

With slow but deliberate movements, Leland started to work his way out of his sleeping bag.

"Oh no you don't. You stay down," Miles demanded, but he looked uncertain as he spoke, and Leland ignored him, carefully keeping their eyes locked as he got to his feet. "That's my gun," he said when he was standing face-to-face with Miles.

The kid chuckled. "Don't feel so great to be on the stupid end, huh?"

Leland didn't answer.

"You got any last words, Lord and Savior?"

"Give me back my gun."

Miles laughed again. "You don't think I'm serious?"

Leland shook his head.

"Why's that?"

"You would have shot me while I was still sleeping if you were. That would have made sense."

"Maybe I just wanted to give my little speech first. Don't everybody?"

Despite his joking, Shawn noticed that Miles actually looked incredibly nervous. In fact, he looked more nervous pointing that gun at Leland now than he had when Leland had pointed the gun at him back when they first met.

"Well, you gave it," Leland said. "So what are you waiting for now?"

Shawn couldn't believe this whole exchange was actually taking place. "Miles," he pleaded, "*please* just put down the gun."

Miles ignored Shawn and regarded Leland with confusion. "I don't get it. Do you *want* me to end your life?"

"I don't have a life. But you woke me up from a pretty nice dream, and you might send me back there forever if you pull that trigger. But you won't."

"How do you know?"

" 'Cause you're a scared kid."

"You'll see just how I scared I am when I blow your fuckin' brains out."

"Go right ahead."

Miles tried to steady the gun, but his hand was shaking.

"Come on," Leland said. "Shoot me."

"No," Shawn begged. "Miles, *don't* do it."

"Don't listen to him," said Leland. "He's just like the nut jobs in your town, worships me even more than they do. Show him. Show everyone. I'm ready when you are."

"I'm not fuckin' around," Miles said, his voice strained.

"But you are," Leland said. "So get your shit together and man the fuck up. Steady your hand. Raise the gun higher."

Miles raised the gun a little, though steadying his hand was apparently beyond him right now.

"Now go ahead. If you have the balls, do it."

Leland waited. Miles's frustration appeared to be mounting as his fingers seemed unable to move, even as his index fixer hovered right over the trigger. After a few more seconds, Leland smiled.

"See? And you know *why* you can't? Because you're also just like the nut jobs in your town. You think I'm something special, and you're *afraid* of me. Pathetic. You should just pack up your shit and go right back to your cult, 'cause that's exactly where you belong. But first, you need to give me back my gun and get the fuck—"

The pistol went off with a loud blast. Shawn screamed and briefly covered his eyes with his hand. When he removed it, he gasped at the shocking, grisly scene before him. Leland stood in place, while Miles staggered backward, blood pumping out of his chest. The gun slid out of his open hand and onto the floor with a hard thud. Miles, his face full of confusion, looked at Leland and then at Shawn and remained on his feet only a few seconds longer before his legs buckled out from underneath him and he collapsed to the ground, landing on his side. His eyes went blank as a dark puddle formed beneath him.

Shawn stared at Miles's body in horror. He looked back up at Leland. The man was physically untouched. As far as Shawn could tell, the bullet had simply ricocheted off his chest, like a handball bouncing off a brick wall, right back into Miles. Leland bent down beside Shawn's body and retrieved the gun. Shawn stared at him.

"We've got to clean up this mess," Leland said.

Shawn didn't move.

"Now," Leland said, flashing him a serious look. "We can't leave any trace of this behind."

"You knew," Shawn said, his voice barely above a whisper. "You knew what would happen when he tried to shoot you. That's why you goaded him into doing it. You *knew*."

"He came in here to shoot me, and he did. Don't think he wouldn't have told the whole world we were here."

"And we would already be gone, so who gives a shit? He didn't have to *die*."

"*I* didn't pull the trigger."

Shawn clutched his hair with both hands and stared down at his feet, taking deep breaths. "Holy fuck," he whispered, almost laughing, and looked right back up. "You told him to raise the gun higher, to steady his hand. You were *measuring*. The distance between you guys, the angle, the velocity—you were making it *inevitable* that the bullet would bounce right at him."

"He was trying to kill me. Maybe you forgot that part."

"But he couldn't have hurt you at all, could he? Jesus, can *any-*

one?" Shawn looked Leland over top to bottom. "What *are* you? Did *they* do this to you?"

Leland gave no answer.

"*What the hell are you?*" Shawn demanded.

Leland just stared back at him. "The shed in back of the house," he said. "Let's see if it has any shovels."

By the pale moonlight, Shawn and Leland buried Miles behind the house, between the shed and the start of the wooded trail. Neither spoke. When they'd finished, they returned upstairs and used wipes, clothing, soap, and bottles of water to remove any visible trace of what had happened. As for Miles's belongings, they decided to leave them in the basement, untouched. Even if those items could be traced back to Miles, it wouldn't mean that much to anyone besides his family, unless it was already known that Miles was dead.

Leland decided they should stick to the plan and wait until morning to leave so they could do a final search of the house by daylight and make sure nothing incriminating had been left behind. There were only a few hours left before dawn, and Shawn decided to spend the rest of the night on the sofa in the library. He knew there was no way he'd be able to fall asleep upstairs.

As it turned out, he wasn't able to sleep in the library, either, and instead found himself just staring up through the darkness at what he could make out of the chandelier. Occasionally, he would close his eyes, but every time he did, the images he saw started them open again.

At some point, Leland entered the library, as well, and Shawn watched in silence as Leland approached a shelf, removed a book, and sat down on one of the armchairs. At first, Shawn wondered how Leland would be able to read in the dark, but this was answered by a soft sound he realized was Leland rubbing the pages with his fingers.

Perhaps, Shawn thought, Leland also hadn't been able to sleep after what he'd done to Miles, or rather, what he'd tricked Miles into doing to himself. But he quickly dismissed this idea. Leland wasn't the type to be kept awake by a guilty conscience. He watched him for a few moments in silence, then sat up on the sofa. Leland gave no reaction to Shawn's movement, though he'd surely heard him.

"You were picked up in the desert," said Shawn. "Ambius interrogated you. Why did you let them take you? You could have gotten away at any time—that's obvious now."

Leland looked at him through the darkness and shrugged. By the moonlight streaming in, each could make out the other's shape, but not much else.

"Maybe I was like you," said Leland. "Thought I could tell them the truth. And then, when I actually *met* Ambius and saw who they were, and what they wanted me to do for them, and what they wanted to do to me if I refused, I understood why the whole galaxy had cut ties with our world long ago."

"So what happened? You killed your interrogators and fled?"

"Something like that."

"Does Ambius know that you're . . . different?"

"By now, I've taken out about four of five of their hit squads, so they should have some idea."

"So then why do they keep coming after you?"

"The same reason they do everything: hubris."

"And that's why you think even if they knew what the other planet was planning, they'd still try to take down the shield."

"Yes."

Shawn was silent for a few moments, and Leland was about to go back to his book.

"Okay," Shawn suddenly said. "Well, here's what I think. Maybe you're right. Maybe if Ambius knew what you and I knew, it would make no difference at all and they'd still take down the shield and just aim to strike the aliens first. But maybe you're *wrong*. Maybe they'd take a step back and reconsider removing the *one thing* that protects our planet from being destroyed. And maybe that's what you're really afraid of. Because deep down, maybe you really *want* Ambius to take down the shield. And you *want* your old friends to come at us and do whatever it is they're gonna do. God only knows why. Maybe you're so bitter you think we deserve what's coming. Fuck if I know. But if Ambius finds out the truth and decides against taking down the shield, *nothing* will happen. In fact, even if Ambius chooses to take down the shield anyway and just try to strike first, like you say they would, they'll be prepared now and, who knows, maybe they'll actually succeed. And maybe you're scared of that, too. I don't know. This could all be bullshit, but still, when I really think about it, I can't help but wonder: Whose side are you really on?"

Leland closed his book and turned his whole body in Shawn's direction. "Whose side am I on?"

Shawn said nothing.

"Whose side am I?" Leland repeated, his voice louder and thick with scorn. "You listen to me, you fucking fanboy. My 'old friends,' as you call them, wanted me to take down that shield so they could finish off this shitty planet of ours, and I should have done it, but I refused, so I had to flee or die. I left my home, gave up everything we had there, because I couldn't bring myself to help them wipe out seven billion people. And I come back here to the world I saved, and what beautiful thanks do I get? A secret government agency tries to torture me into doing exactly the same thing I'd refused to do up there, and then I've got to run again and be chased and hunted like a fucking rabbit for all time. And you have the gall to ask me whose side I'm on? *You* gave Ambius the technology to disable my shield, the *only* thing that was keeping us safe. *You* fucked it all up, not me."

When Leland finished speaking, he was breathing heavily. Shawn wasn't sure he'd ever seen him display so much emotion. "'Everything we had there,'" he said. "What do you mean by that?"

"What?"

"You said before you gave up 'everything we had there.' Who's 'we'?"

Leland stared at Shawn through the darkness. "You and I are done talking."

In the early morning, after one final inspection of the house, Shawn and Leland packed all their belongings into the Honda and rode out. An hour later, they were already getting close to Sedona, their next destination. As Leland silently commanded the wheel, Shawn stared out at the passing scenery, the stretches of dark green forestry and the hazy, overlapping mountains in the distance. Once upon a time, as recently as Shawn's trip with Rachel to Northwestern, the American landscape had represented a special kind of freedom to Shawn. Now, it was nothing more than a symbol of his fugitive existence, his exile from civilization.

He had made up his mind. If he ever had any doubts before, Miles's death and the role Leland had played in it had proved once and for all what he'd suspected all along: that Andrew Leland was ultimately a man out for himself, indifferent to anyone and anything but his own survival. Miles's life had meant nothing to him, and Shawn's own life likely meant little more. Leland had once given up everything to do the right thing and the world had burned him, and now he was going to watch the world burn. But if the man was morally repugnant, he was right about one thing: Shawn had indeed fucked everything up. Now, he was going to make things right.

CHAPTER 22

Dr. Elliot Lepore took another sip of water and leaned back in toward the microphone, inspired by a half-forgotten anecdote, now resurfaced, that was just what he needed to lighten the mood.

"There's actually a story about Einstein that illustrates where we're at pretty perfectly," he said, an impish smile crossing his lips. "A student came to him during a final exam and said, 'Professor, the questions on this year's exam are the same questions from last year's exam!' And Einstein, he looked at the student and said, 'Yes, but this year, the answers are all different!'"

The audience laughed, and Dr. Lepore noticed that even Dr. Burke was smiling. So did he hold no grudge over Lepore's having alluded to Murata's stinging critique of him several minutes earlier? Lepore certainly hadn't meant to insult him, but hadn't Feingold, the conference chair, told him there was no need for kid gloves with anyone as established as Burke—or humble reverence, for that matter? And the audience that filled that convocation hall in the Marriott that evening surely hadn't come to see two acclaimed scientists kiss each other's asses.

Still, Lepore didn't need anyone as influential as Dr. Roland Burke for an enemy. The reference to Murata had been a fuckup.

"I think we have time for one more question," the evening's moderator, a popular science blogger, informed everyone.

A thick middle-aged woman with funky turquoise glasses was selected from the crowd and handed the cordless mic.

"Thank you so much for you time tonight, Drs. Burke and Lepore," she began. "You both mentioned earlier the *Scharnhorst effect*, which, as you know, has some implications for faster-than-light travel. I was wondering if either of you could comment on the recent rumors that scientists at NASA have begun conducting actual tests on warp drive? And if the rumors are true . . . well, do you think time travel might be just around the corner?"

The moderator turned to Dr. Lepore.

"Dr. Lepore, do you want to field this one first?"

"Would be my pleasure." Lepore looked out into the crowd and smiled widely. "Well, first of all, I want to say a few things about these supposed 'warp drive tests.' I have some friends at NASA— I'm sure Dr. Burke does, too—and these tests are extremely preliminary, to say the least. But, you know, either way, there are a great many challenges—many would say *insurmountable* challenges—to achieving warp drive. From what I understand, all these current experiments are based on an Alcubierre drive or bubble, and I think physicists like Jose Nataro have done a great job at poking some holes in the feasibility of that method. And you've also got Sean Carroll's assessment that, even if you could somehow get this going, the costs for the antimatter alone would be equivalent to something like the whole world's entire economic output for forty years. So, you know, we're talking about some expensive science.

"But I really want to focus on the second part of your question, time travel, which is kind of a separate beast, though I guess you're working off Everett's theory about using warp bubbles to go back in time. I want you to know that Stephen Hawking conducted a recent test on time travel. That's right. A test! He threw a party in his home for time travelers, and he didn't send out invitations for the party until after it had ended. Well, he sat there with wine and cheese and balloons—you can watch the videos online—and nobody showed up. So there you've got 'experimental evidence' that time travel isn't real! But, you know, seriously, the real reason—the actual reason—we know it can't happen is because it violates the causality principle. If you could go back in time, then you could theoretically kill your own grandfather before your father was born and then, well, how did you just kill your grandfather if you've suddenly never existed in the first place? Right? I'm sure you've heard that one before. It's a paradox, and the universe does *not* like paradoxes. So something will always happen to prevent them from occurring. As Hawking himself says, it might be radiation in a wormhole destroying the wormhole or virtual particles turning into real particles, but whatever happens, the universe will find some way to prevent paradoxes and the ensuing chaos they'd create. We call this the *chronology protection conjecture*, and it means that time travel, at least into the past, is really impossible. But, you know, if I'm wrong, please let me know yesterday!"

This last line drew a couple of laughs and more than a few groans. The moderator gestured to Dr. Burke, who stepped up to the microphone and adjusted his small rectangular Santa glasses.

"Is time travel possible?" he began. "Novikov, with his theory of self-consistency, thinks it is. Günter Nimtz and Alfons Stahlhofen, with their work on quantum tunneling, seem to think it is. Kip Thorne thinks it might be, and Stephen Hawking thinks no, or probably not, and Marcus Scheck thinks no, definitely not. Is time travel possible? I have no idea. I would like to think we're working our way toward it, but I can't say for sure. It's not my area, and without having poured countless hours into studying the works of these scientists or all the various attempts at unifying relativity and quantum mechanics, I won't pretend I can give you an answer. But here's what I *do* know. The universe does not 'dislike paradoxes,' nor will the universe 'find a way' to prevent them. That's plainly and simply horseshit. The universe does not have *agency*. It doesn't have likes, dislikes, and it most certainly does not have fears. It doesn't stay up at night worrying about you or your grandfather, and it's not afraid of descending into chaos. Only people like Dr. Lepore are afraid of the universe descending into chaos. They might not know what that would look like or even mean, but it obviously scares the shit out of them.

"What would happen if I tried to go back in time to kill my grandfather? That's a great question, and if and when I'm able to do that, I suppose we'll find out! But what *won't* happen is that existence itself will suddenly cave in just because the universe got so confused that its brain exploded. The universe, which has no brain, is simply *unable* to give a rat's ass what you or I do. It's there, existing, and yes, it has laws, but it doesn't *do* anything. We make the choices, we take the actions, and we are lord and master of our own futures.

"That said, I don't really consider Dr. Lepore to be exactly wrong in his views. When faced with great and historic scientific challenges, there are always those who say it cannot be done. And when they say, 'We can't do it,' they're in at least one respect correct. When it finally happens, they will surely have had nothing to do with it."

After the debate had ended and the crowd had finally filed out, Dr. Burke took a seat at the hotel bar, where he was shortly thereafter joined by an attractive young woman. Anyone who saw them there would have naturally assumed an interview was being conducted; the woman was leaning forward, holding out a small digital voice recorder, and the two were chatting amiably. That the machine wasn't actually recording or that it was Burke who was asking the questions or that Rachel wasn't actually a journalist wasn't information anyone else needed to know.

"So what's the good word? Are you through with the coherence tests?" Burke asked, changing the subject from her commute to the reason she was there as the bartender poured him a glass of Glenfiddich.

"Yep."

Discreetly, she slipped him a small USB drive, which he put in his jacket pocket.

"Was Auslander useful?"

"To an extent."

"An extent? He's supposed to be the best quantum biologist in the world!"

"He was good. We're still essentially stuck." Burke sighed with only slightly exaggerated exasperation.

Rachel glanced around and dropped her voice a few registers. "Dillon mentioned something about a house in Arizona."

Burke smiled. "A house in Arizona? He tell you any more?"

"Not really. Said I needed to hear it from you."

Burke laughed. "I can't tell if he's discreet or doesn't want to deny me the pleasure, but I like the man either way. Not just a house, an abandoned old Victorian mansion. A drifter spent a night there last week with his dog, a beagle. Dog starts barking in the middle of the night, runs out, and, whaddaya know, digs up a fucking *corpse* in the backyard."

Rachel leaned forward. "Who?"

"Some runaway kid. Anyway, he calls the authorities, and they do their usual dog and pony show and send some fingerprint samples over to Clarksburg. Guess the match."

Rachel smiled knowingly. "Starman."

Burke nodded. "But not just Starman."

Rachel's eyes widened. "So that means the story that Iranian gas station clerk told . . ."

"Exactly. Looks like they really are together. Quite the power couple, no?"

"But why would either of them kill some runaway kid in a mansion?"

"Who the fuck knows?"

"Well, are the cops launching a murder investigation?"

Burked laughed. "Course not. We took care of everything. Body doesn't exist anymore, nor does any record of the incident. But this happened near Black Canyon City, and the gas station was in New River, and I know neither of those places mean a thing to you, but what it indicates is that they're heading north and taking their sweet time about it. We should know where they are in a few days, maybe even less."

"And what then?"

"Same old shit; we'll do what we always do. Just a little different this time."

"Different how?"

"Successful, I hope. No squads this time around, not that we've even got many left. Our friend used 'em all up as target practice. We'll be using toys instead."

"Toys?"

Burke nodded. "Toys we couldn't get access to as easily in places like Trondheim or Alicante. Toys that don't go running for the hills at the sight of something a little out of the ordinary. Toys that don't die."

"Got it. And what about our other friend? You plan to take them out together?"

"One fell swoop, I should think."

Rachel nodded and looked down at her recorder as Burke observed her.

"What?" he asked after a few seconds.

She looked up, wiped her bangs from out of her eyes. "I think he might still be of value. The other one."

"Value?"

"I think he's smart enough to be worth keeping around. And

unlike his friend, he's not exactly dangerous, and I think I can maybe even turn him."

Dr. Burke laughed. "Roach, if you were in love with him, you should have told me last time!"

She stared at him in a serious way he was long familiar with. She'd been giving him that same look ever since her freshman year at Northwestern.

"All right. I'll have a chat with Upstairs, and we'll see if we can't bring your little boy in alive. For now. Just for you."

She smiled, appreciatively, sort of.

"But just answer me this one question," he continued, "if you'd be so kind."

"Go for it."

Dr. Burke raised his eyebrows and set his voice to a whisper. "*Are* you in love with him?"

Rachel rolled her eyes. "Come on, Roland. You know there's only one thing I love in this world."

"Oh? And what's that?"

Rachel leaned in close and took her time before answering. "Us."

Dr. Burke took another sip of scotch and set it back down on the bar. His breathing had become a little heavier. "Us?"

The faintest, nearly nonexistent smile formed on her lips, and she leaned in even closer so that her face was mere inches from his.

"The human race."

CHAPTER 23

The afternoon sun streamed in through the high windows of downtown Flagstaff's abandoned cigarette factory, casting twisted shadows around the room as it passed through a spiderweb of rusted pipes and scaffolding. In the corner, just below a yellow sign warning of a "275-PER-SQUARE-FOOT FLOOR LOAD," Shawn lay sideways on his sleeping bag, propped on an elbow and poring over a map of San Diego. It seemed that the best course of action would be to take a bus from Flagstaff's Greyhound bus station to San Diego, then catch a ride to La Jolla. Or maybe he could cab it; might be safer. Either way, he'd need to steal some cash from Leland before he left.

There was a chance, he realized, that Professor Glass might not remember him. But the chance was small. At Brown, and later Columbia, professors took to Shawn in varying ways, some astounded by his easy mastery of complex concepts and theories, others considering him overrated or cocky (or "snot-nosed," as one assistant professor had put it when he didn't know Shawn was within earshot). But very few would have forgotten him. Professor Glass had actually been one of Shawn's earliest champions, encouraging him to switch his major from astronomy to physics because, as he put it, "You'll never get a deep understanding of art by studying paint."

Glass had been a visiting professor from UC–San Diego, where he had since returned and had been made professor emeritus. Shawn had last seen him four years ago at a New York conference on quantum information theory, and though he had seemed frail then, he was still sharp and certainly acted as though he knew Shawn, even if it was hard to be sure he wasn't merely being polite. Either way, Shawn had remembered him as a thoughtful man with considerable personal integrity. During the years at Brown, Glass had been someone Shawn could confide in. Maybe he still was.

A door on the factory's floor level opened, and Shawn quickly returned the map to where he'd found it, scrambling on his hands and knees and tossing it back onto a pile of other maps and atlases situated near Leland's sleeping bag. He then crawled back into his own sleeping bag, closed his eyes, and pretended to nap. Below, familiar footsteps crunched broken glass and God knows what else as they ascended the steel staircase.

"Get your shit together," Leland said a few moments later. Shawn opened his eyes and lifted his head. Leland was staring down at him, wearing his standard-issue baseball-cap-and-sunglasses disguise and carrying a case of Poland Spring bottles under each arm.

"What? Why?"

"Old woman at the corner store. I paid her for this water, and she stared at me. Too long."

"So that means what?" asked Shawn. "Maybe she was just *trying* to recognize you since you're dressed like a celebrity hiding from the paparazzi."

"Time to pack up."

"Where are we going?"

"Northwest."

Just perfect, thought Shawn. San Diego was *south*west. He stage-yawned. "Could we stay another few hours? I'm totally wiped." The odds the next few hours would afford him the opportunity to steal money and slip away were practically zero. But leaving with Leland now would kill his plan completely.

"You'll sleep in the car."

Their Honda Civic zoomed down the interstate, Shawn staring out at the scenery, most of it forest, as Leland drove. If Leland's aliens truly attacked, he wondered, would there still be real forests left afterward? Or would everything be mostly scorched earth, like in some postapocalyptic movie? For a moment, he had a horrifying vision of chained human survivors doing the bidding of grotesque-looking alien overlords. He had to smile when he realized the scene had come straight from a Halloween episode of *The Simpsons*.

"So," Leland said without taking his eyes off the road. "Were you planning a trip to the zoo?"

Shawn's smile disappeared. He turned to Leland to ask what he meant, but stopped himself. He sensed this wasn't going anywhere good, and it would be wiser to stay silent.

"One of my maps was folded on San Diego," Leland said. "Not by me."

Shawn turned back to the window and just stared out. *Don't acknowledge anything*, he told himself. *Give the bastard nothing.*

"UC–San Diego, I guess," said Leland. "Tadashi Yamada is still there. So is Oren Glass, though God only knows if he's lucid. Glass might make sense. He did a lot of moving around back in the day; you might have met him anywhere." He smiled and shook his head. "You still don't get it, do you? Try this on for size. Promising young physics prodigy gets unexpectedly thrown out of his graduate program. Months later, he turns up, thin and disheveled and going on about wild conspiracy theories and doomsday predictions. Oh, and where has he been? Hiding out with Andrew Leland, of course. Do the math."

"I don't care," Shawn said quietly. "No one believed the prophets, either, but they didn't let that shut them up."

Leland laughed. "So now you're a prophet."

"I'm someone with urgent information," said Shawn, turning back to Leland. "And you're the one who doesn't get it. Back when I was obsessed with finding you, writing all those letters, do you know why I cared so much? Because despite what you were telling everyone, I believed you *knew something.* You knew something the whole world wanted to know, and you were just keeping that shit to yourself, hoarding it, when you owed it to the rest of us to share it. Well, now *I* know something, something that affects everyone. Something that is life or death, and you're demanding I just keep it to *myself.* Well, fuck that. I will not remain silent anymore. And I do not need your permission."

"You'd be making the biggest mistake of your life."

"No, I already did that, remember? I 'fucked everything up,' just like you said. So now I'm gonna try to do something about it. Maybe it will help; maybe it won't. Worst case, no one believes me and they lock me up somewhere I can't do any more damage."

"You should be so lucky to get locked up before Ambius gets to you. Not that it would really protect you from them."

"I'm not afraid of Ambius. I *am* afraid of sitting on the sidelines and watching civilization as we know it get torched when I could have done something to prevent it. So if you want to stop me, you're just going to have to kill me. You wouldn't be the first person to try to end my life just to keep my mouth—"

They both heard it at the same time. Helicopter blades, except that when they looked out the back windshield, the vehicle flying in the sky above and behind them was nothing so familiar as an ordinary helicopter. Six furiously spinning rotors extended up and out from a sleek, black circular body, underneath which protruded what looked from this distance like large skis, though they were most likely something much more sinister. Backlit by a pink-and-gray sky, the exotic hexacopter was an awesome sight to behold. Shawn had certainly never seen anything like it, though he was quite sure he knew what it was and what it was there to do.

As it began to lower itself, Leland slowed the car from seventy-five miles per hour to somewhere closer to fifty.

"Listen carefully," he said. "We've most likely been targeted by a laser designator by now. The hit will come any second, so we have to get out immediately. When you jump, aim for the shoulder and make sure to tuck and roll, then run for the forest and keep moving no matter what."

"I'll never make it to the forest."

"Probably not. Remember, tuck and roll. One, two . . ."

At *three*, the car doors flew open, and Shawn and Leland leaped out, and not a moment too soon, as seconds later, a missile struck the car, exploding it right in the middle of the highway. Shawn hit the soft shoulder of the road hard, then, without taking stock of damage to his body or the disaster on the road, rolled to his side and, in the midst of billowing smoke, scrambled to his feet, and raced downhill toward the trees. To his surprise, no missiles or gunfire followed him.

When the smoke cleared, Leland was standing in the middle of the highway, not far from the burned-out car, holding his pistol in his right hand and staring down the drone, which now hovered some thirty feet in the air in front of him, framed by the darkening sky. Unlike Shawn, Leland had been forced to hit pavement, not dirt, so his outer clothes were torn to shreds. Otherwise, save a few scratches and road burns, he was unscathed.

From up close, Leland could see that the large hexacopter was a fairly standard military model, not unlike a quadcopter he'd done some aerodynamics research for during a brief and lucrative stint in military consulting in the mid-'00s. However, this aircraft had apparently been retrofitted to include two AGM-176 Griffin missiles, one of which had obviously already been spent, as well as some additional weaponry, though it was hard to identify exactly what.

What really interested Leland right now, though, was not its capabilities but its vulnerabilities. Just as with a manned helicopter, the only conceivable way to take this baby down with just a hand-gun would be to aim for its brain. In a case like this, though, where the computer was located in an encasement, to do so efficiently, he'd first have to be closer than thirty feet away; more like just a few inches.

But there were other concerns now, as Leland suddenly sensed the slightest presence of heat on his forehead. He could practically feel the series of coded pulses he knew were now being generated on his face. These signals would soon be bounced off into the sky to be detected by the second Griffin, which would then seek out the center of the reflected signal: his face.

In a matter of milliseconds, Leland ducked and dived behind the charred remains of the Honda Civic and heard—and felt—the second missile release from the drone and slam into the bombed-out car, further decimating its remains. The drone swiftly circled around the wreckage so that it was virtually on top of him, then pulled itself back for a better angle and unleashed a torrent of machine-gun fire at him, partially solving the riddle of what else it was armed with. That was okay; bullets he could deal with, and as he handily dodged most of the firepower (an exercise in pain avoidance more than life preservation), he smiled to think of the drone pilot, hunkered down somewhere in an Ambius control center, surely cursing himself right now for having just wasted both missiles.

When the drone dropped down several feet to get closer, possibly readying itself to unleash a new, more effective weapon, Leland suddenly, in a quick blur of successive movements, leaped from the ground to the top of the charred-out Civic and then, from there, deftly avoiding the propeller blades, straight onto the body of the aircraft itself.

The hexacopter spun around furiously and even tilted, something Leland hadn't realized it could do because most multirotors can't, but he held tight. With his left hand gripping one of the rotor masts for balance and his right still clutching the gun, Leland straddled the drone's body with his legs and fired his weapon three times into the raised, glass encasement in its top center.

The drone continued to whirl and tilt, which meant Leland hadn't destroyed the operating system. Amid the shattered glass of the destroyed encasement there was, among other pieces of machinery, a small gray box with thick yellow wires protruding from it. Maybe that was it. He fired at that, but still nothing happened. Though the camera would be below the copter's body, the operating system should be right there. Not wanting to blow out everything and waste lead, he tried to search his memories from his early consulting days. He'd met with several engineers... had they ever shown him any diagrams? By now, multirotors would have gone through four or five evolutions, weaponry aside, but if he could recall the basic shape of the system, he could probably identify its technological descendant.

He didn't get the chance.

The drone pilot, wherever he or she was, had apparently made a calculated decision. A four-million-dollar hexacopter was ultimately worthless if it didn't do its job. The mission came first, the hunk of metal second. With a sudden jerk, the drone lurched back, and then, with Leland still on top of it, rammed straight into the wreckage.

Shawn watched the subsequent explosion, the biggest yet, from the edge of the woods. When Leland had told him to run into the forest and keep moving, Shawn had assumed the drone would take him out before he ever made it to the trees. When that didn't happen, he knew that he should take Leland's advice and keep on running, not least because now was probably the best chance he'd ever get to ditch him. He would run into the woods and never look back.

But not just yet.

Back at the mansion when the bullet from that pistol had ricocheted off Leland's chest and into Miles had been the moment Shawn knew he was done with Leland. But it had also been the moment when all the talk he'd heard from Rachel and Leland about intelligent alien life and cosmic shields and interplanetary intrigue had suddenly gone from science fiction to reality. Before, the whole business could have theoretically been some kind of elaborate fabrication. After all, he'd been shown no real proof for any of it. The only real evidence for aliens he had was what everyone had: the video footage from Bernasconi Hills. But in the fateful instant that Miles fired that gun, Shawn saw for himself, in person, with his own eyes, that Andrew Leland had been to space and come back something more than a man.

Now, the chance to see that new-and-improved Andrew Leland in full action mode was not one he could bring himself to miss. And watching from the edge of the woods, he hadn't been disappointed as he witnessed the awesome sight of a human being ably facing off against a military drone, a man who looked like any other, but was dodging missiles and machine-gun fire—so much gunfire that some bullets *must* have hit him though you'd never know it—a man leaping onto a drone and, Jesus, appearing to fucking wrestle with it! Keep running no matter what? Thanks, but no thanks. It had been a sight unlike any he'd ever witnessed and one he knew he would never forget.

And now that *enhanced* superman lay motionless on the side of the road, not far from where the remains of the kamikaze drone and the Honda Civic lay burning and smoking. Shawn crept out from the woods and walked up the hill to the highway. It was dark now, but the fire made everything visible enough, and the exploded drone was an incredible sight; its body and blades merged with the remains of the Honda Civic into an indistinguishable heap of twisted metal. Shawn didn't get too close in case there were residual explosions still to come. He knelt down beside the unconscious Leland, who had apparently been ejected by the force of the collision, the explosion, or both. His body, on the surface, looked remarkably intact; though his skin was covered in soot, it didn't appear to be burned, and the cuts on his face, though bleeding, looked superficial. Shawn felt for a pulse. Leland was alive.

Just then, he saw headlights coming up the road. *Shit*, he thought, *here they come.* They were actually later than he might have expected, he realized. If the drone knew where they were, then Ambius itself obviously knew, as well.

He quickly scanned the ground nearby, and sure enough, thanks to the fire, he was able to make out the shape he was looking for several feet away on the asphalt, about halfway between Leland and the wreckage: Leland's pistol. He walked over, scooped it up, and shoved it into the inner pocket of his spring jacket. Then he stood still and waited for the car to arrive.

He wasn't going to run. Not this time.

As the vehicle got closer, though, he could see that it was a large, silver SUV. Would Ambius agents be arriving in a mom car? The SUV screeched to a stop, and the shocked driver who stepped out was actually no mom at all, but a plump, middle-aged man with spiky red hair, a goatee, and a faded Styx T-shirt.

The goateed man stared at the wreckage in disbelief. "Holy fuck," he mouthed. Then he became aware of Shawn at the side of the road, and Leland, lying on the ground beside him. "Jesus!" he yelled and rushed over to them. "Dude, you call an ambulance already? What the hell happened here?"

Shawn surprised himself by reaching into his jacket pocket and retrieving the gun, which he aimed at the man's chest.

"I'm going to need your car."

Sometime later, when he had enough distance and enough time had passed for him to be reasonably confident Ambius wasn't hot on his tail, Shawn pulled over to the side of the road and activated his tablet. Though it had been rewired to be virtually untraceable, he and Leland had both deemed it good sense to keep electronic devices off as much as possible, just in case. The screen lit up now, and instead of using the GPS, which was part of what had made the tablet traceable in the first place, he checked the Internet to determine the distance between where he was now—north of Sierra Vista—and where he intended to go.

Taking Leland there would be risky. Ambius surely knew about it, even if it was unlikely that it figured too high on their radar screen. But nowhere was actually safe, and in the end, the way Shawn saw it, if there was anywhere in the country where Leland might be able to get some adequate medical assistance without creating a nationwide frenzy that would spell his imminent doom, this was going to be the place.

CHAPTER 24

The crowd in the old church house quieted, but not enough, as Hal Townsend took the stage. He waited a few moments, obviously irritated, but some geezers in the back pews still continued yammering until Carl Smith, sitting in the second-to-last row, turned around and shushed them. Several people laughed. Carl had only been voted general secretary days prior, and this just might have been his first official act in that capacity.

"All right now," Hal began. "First off, I'd like to thank all y'all so much for coming out tonight. The children have prepared long and hard for this event, so I know the last thing anyone wants is to see them all held up by introductory remarks. All the same, I wouldn't be doing my job if I had all y'all assembled before me and I didn't remind you about the annual dinner coming up next week. I know we aren't the richest town, and we aren't the richest congregation, so let me just say that every li'l penny does count. Unless, of course, you're Walt Butler, in which case we'll just throw those pennies right back at you and ask for some bills, thank you kindly."

The crowd laughed. Butler, a solid, white-bearded man sitting near the front, smiled with good cheer. He'd been enduring these awful "richest man in Annabella" jokes with that same grace for decades.

"Now, on a more serious note," Hal continued, "I want to point out that the dinner, despite our lack of advertisement, will likely draw out some, shall we say, vermin. They'll most likely be milling around out front, if we succeed in keeping 'em from sneaking in. Now I won't name names, but someone did some chatting with one of these vermin just last week, and so we had a nice little write-up in the *Central Valley Gazette* about what a lovely little bunch of loonies we all are."

Several people lacking in tact looked to Tobias Wheeler, whose face had already begun to turn red.

"Now, I ain't saying we should care what *vermin* think, but—"

"Hey now," a voice interrupted.

Hal tried to ignore it and continued, "—we do have to keep in mind that some of the people who read this—"

"Hey now!" the voice repeated. It was Tobias Wheeler, and Hal sighed and let him speak.

"That is *not* fair," Tobias said, rising from his seat. "That man didn't tell me he was from any *Central Valley Gazette*. We're in Morgan's, I'm having a cup of coffee, and some gentleman starts asking questions about our fair town. I don't know I'm on the record—should I be unfriendly? Would that have been more to your liking, a story about what unfriendly boobs we all are?"

"Tobias, I'm not blaming anyone, and I never used anyone's name."

"Oh, come on. Don't give me that horseshit."

There was audible shock from the crowd at Tobias's language in the church and when there were children present, no less.

"You're out of line, Tobias!"

Tobias glared at Hal, but sat back down.

"As I was saying before that little interruption," Hal continued, "please remember, at the dinner, not to engage with those who are only looking to mock what they don't understand." He smiled. "And now, for some short words of grace and science to introduce the youngsters, let's have a hand for Reverend Daniels."

The crowd applauded, and Reverend Will Daniels, a man of about fifty with graying curly blond hair, stepped onto the stage and smiled warmly at the assembly.

"Evenin', everyone," he said.

"Evenin', Reverend!" the crowd called back.

"First off, I'd just like to say that, Toby, I think you're quite right in what you say. You didn't know who you were talking to, and you were being friendly. I, myself, in the first years after our big switch, *voluntarily* spoke to the press a few times. I tried to explain our point of view, that we represented a serious and sincere faith and that we weren't no Waco or Jonestown or Heaven's Gate. What I learned soon enough, folks, is that the press is a lot like the house in a gambling casino. You can say what you want, present things as carefully and accurately as possible, but they will always win. So the only way to not lose is to not play.

"Now, Hal promised you words of grace and science, but far be it from me to delay the proceedings any further. I'll just note that the first song our Choir of Celestial Light will be performing tonight might sound familiar. It's a hymn we used to sing in our less enlightened, pre-Event days. The lyrics have been changed only a little, and if the words don't move you, well, the voices of the little ones most certainly will. My brothers and sisters, may I present the Choir of Celestial Light!"

The reverend left the stage, and about twenty-five middle-school-aged boys and girls appeared. As an organist began to play, they launched into a high and beautiful updated version of the seventh-century Presbyterian hymn, "Creator of the Stars of Night." They sang:

Descender from the stars of night
Thy people's everlasting light
A winter solstice gently shown
All things celestial bring you home
Our Andrew grieving ancient curse
Should doom to death a universe
Hath found the medicine, full of grace
To save and heal the human race

Reverend Daniels, gently swaying to the music beside his wife, Anne, felt a tap on his shoulder. It was Marjory, the church's long-time secretary, holding a cell phone.

"It's Dr. Rogers from the clinic," she said in a whisper louder than the average person's speaking voice.

Alarmed, Reverend Daniels took the phone and brought it to the back of the room.

"Evenin', Eddie," he said into the phone.

"Evenin', Reverend," came the reply. Eddie's voice sounded just slightly off.

"I'm at the children's performance. Everything okay?"

"Reverend, are you sitting down?"

Annabella's clinic had been operating for about thirty years. It had originally included just a doctor's office and examination room, but over the past decade or so, a pharmacy had been added and then eventually several sickrooms and even a limited ER. About fifteen minutes after his phone call with Dr. Rogers, Reverend Daniels's station wagon pulled into the parking lot. When he got out, Nurse Ellen was waiting for him by the entrance. She brought him in and whisked him down the hall to the room where the doctor was.

Reverend Daniels went inside and stopped in his tracks. An unconscious male patient lay on a gurney, hooked up to various tubing and machinery. The reverend just stared at him, scarcely able to believe his eyes, as Dr. Rogers, removing a blood pressure cuff from the man's arm, smiled.

"You believe me now?" Dr. Rogers asked.

The reverend walked all the way into the room and got closer to the patient. He leaned over him, held his hand over the man's face, but restrained from actually touching him.

"How . . . how's he doing?" he asked, a slight but audible tremor in his voice.

"Well, his heart rate is 105 beats a minute, fairly high, and he's breathing independently, but he's definitely comatose. Blood pressure's at 130 over 90, also high. Usually, we'd want to do a whole battery of blood tests, but that doesn't seem possible at the moment."

"Why not?"

Dr. Rogers put the blood pressure monitor back into a drawer and closed it, then turned back to the reverend.

"Because our needles can't puncture his skin."

Reverend Daniels opened his mouth to speak but said nothing. He looked back at the unconscious Andrew Leland, lying there on the gurney, then turned back to Dr. Rogers.

"Eddie, I don't want anyone to know about this, you hear me? This has got to be kept strictly confidential. The repercussions would extend far beyond Annabella, you can be sure of that."

Dr. Rogers nodded. "Don't worry. I've already sworn my secrecy to the young man."

"The kid you said brought him here?"

"That's right."

"Where is he now? I should speak to him right away."

"Him? Oh, he's gone."

"Gone? Well, where did he go?"

"Beats the hell out of me," the doctor said with a shrug. "He brought him in here, said something about there having been an accident, and then just took right off into the night."

CHAPTER 25

Leland had said Shawn wouldn't last more than two hours on his own. It had now been more than two days, nearly all of that time spent driving, and he hadn't so much been stopped by a state trooper, let alone mowed down by a hit squad or blown to bits by a drone. Now, though, the risk factor was about to jump exponentially. He was heading straight back into the fire.

Leland was right about what he'd said just moments before they were attacked. Shawn had no credibility, and the world at large would never take him seriously. So he had decided to come now to the one person who might.

Since Dellwood College hadn't existed in over ten years, the main entryway to the campus, a winding woodland road, had long ago been chained off. Shawn had therefore left the SUV in a small forested area just off the highway and then walked up the hill to where that blocked road began. Earlier, he had considered entering via the woods, parallel to the road, but since his intention was to make his presence known as soon as he arrived, there was no point, and he figured the sneakier he went about things, the more likely it was he'd be shot before he had a chance to talk. Dying he could deal with, but talking was the whole reason he'd come back.

Night had fallen, and as he made his way along the road, surrounded by tall oak, black ash, and maple trees and guided by the moonlight, every sound, every creak of a branch or rustling of an animal, seemed sinister. He consoled himself with the knowledge that he was basically a walking dead man, anyway, so what good was fear? Even if Ambius believed him, even if they accepted his claims about the dangers of deactivating the cosmic shield, and even if they *listened* to him and heeded his warnings, they'd surely also kill him. As long as he wasn't any use to them, he was a threat. He'd learned that the hard way, and just being back on that road, so close to the campus, brought back the sickening feeling of Rachel's betrayal.

When he reached the main campus, he saw that everything was dark. While it was normal for the lights in the main buildings to be off, at least some of the lights in the physics buildings, the student center, and the dorms should have been on at this time. Shawn walked up to the entrance of the old physics building and tried the door. It was locked. Though months of being on the lam had greatly enhanced Shawn's lock-picking skills, this particular door utilized a Medeco dead bolt, which made it impervious to any of the standard methods. Fortunately, as he circled around the building, he spotted a window that wasn't completely closed. He grabbed the bottom with his fingers and pulled up hard, managing, with all his might, to pry it open. He then hoisted himself up and climbed through. Once he was all the way inside, he got to his feet in the dark and turned on his flashlight, illuminating what turned out to be a classroom. Keeping the flashlight shining forward, he moved out of the room and into the hallway, then down the stairs to the basement level, where Laboratory B was located.

Stepping into the old lab, he first tried the lights, but they were dead. He then swept the room's perimeter with his flashlight and could see no indication that the lab had been recently used. No scattered papers, no empty Styrofoam cups. The air seemed dustier than he'd remembered, if not in the same league as the school library's. The equation on the whiteboard was actually one he recalled having worked on with Rachel shortly before his last night at the campus. That was particularly strange. It was as if the entire Dellwood operation had existed solely for him.

He left the physics building, crawling out the way he'd come in, then moved on to the old dormitory, which, unlike the physics building, wasn't locked. But if the physics lab had appeared abandoned, the dorms unquestionably *were* abandoned. Moving through the empty rooms on the second floor, flashlight in tow, Shawn couldn't find a trace of anyone's belongings or any other signs of life. The place had apparently been entirely cleared out, though there was still one room left to check.

Rachel's dorm room had always been a source of great mystery to Shawn. But his feelings for her aside, Rachel's room was unique in and of itself. Situated on a separate wing of the floor once designated for the dorm preceptor, no one was ever invited inside, and when Rachel locked herself in for long periods at a time, no one, or certainly not Shawn, had any idea what she was doing in there. Ravi once joked that the room probably contained a spa and a private Starbucks, the latter a reference to the unconventional hours she kept.

When he tried to open the door, it was locked, but he removed a small pick and torque wrench from his pocket and went to work. After about a minute or so of fiddling, the lock clicked open, and Shawn entered the room and turned on a lamp on the night table beside the door; unlike the lights in the physics buildings, the lamps in the dorm rooms still worked. The room didn't look much different from his own. A simple-looking full bed. Industrial ceiling fan overhead. Night table and dresser. The main differences seemed to be a tall mahogany bookcase, far nicer than any of the furnishings in the other rooms, and a walk-in closet. Or rather, what Shawn *presumed* to be a walk-in closet; it was covered by a wide curtain with a tacky, purple geometric pattern.

Shawn walked over and yanked the curtain to the side. Sure enough, it had been covering a walk-in closet, but not just that. At the far end of the closet were two large silver panels. Shawn walked into the closet and approached the panels, which he realized were actually double sliding doors. On the upper part of the right door, there was a tiny little hole about the size of a nickel.

There could be no doubt: he was looking at an elevator.

"Welcome back," a soft, childlike voice said somewhere behind him.

He spun around to see the bald man from earlier, his bulbous head glowing eerily in the lamplight, smiling at him and aiming a handgun. Though Shawn still had Leland's pistol in his jacket pocket, it was too late to draw it now. "I need to speak to Rachel," he said.

"No problem," the man answered. "She's expecting you."

And then the man reached out his gun and swung it straight into Shawn's right temple. Shawn dropped to the ground, clutching his head with both hands. The pain was seismic. He heard ringing and thought he felt something moist seeping from his hair through his fingers, though identifying it as blood would have required far more focus than he could muster. Already down on the floor, he felt a hard kick to the stomach that knocked the wind right out of him. As he lay there gasping, the man reached into his own pocket, removed a syringe, and inserted it into Shawn's arm, bringing on a profound sense of déjà vu.

"But first . . . ," the man said, and Shawn didn't hear the rest because he had already blacked out.

CHAPTER 26

"Where is Leland?" the voice of the bald man asked again from out of the darkness.

"I already told you," Shawn answered, blindfolded and bound to his chair. "You killed him with your drone!"

"So Andrew Leland is dead?"

"Yes! For the twenty-millionth—*aaaahhhhh*!"

There it went again. The deafening, piercing sound in his ears. When he'd first felt the earbuds go in, he'd remembered reading that detainees at Guantanamo had been forced to listen to "Born in the USA" and the theme song for *Sesame Street* for days on end, and he'd been praying for something similar. No such luck. The high-frequency noise being pumped into his eardrums had to be at least 20 kilohertz, and each burst sent him into a whirl of pain, disorientation, and acute nausea.

"If Andrew Leland is dead, where's the body?"

"Buried him," Shawn said, trying to catch his breath. "In the woods."

"So why no trail of blood on the highway?"

Shawn took another few deep breaths. "Because it's Andrew Fucking Leland."

He immediately regretted swearing.

"*Aaaaaaaaaaaaah! Shiiiiiiiiit!*"

As pain and nausea engulfed him again, he could hear the maniacal shrill laughter of the bald man, like a baby squealing with delight.

"Ultrasonic, you know, has become popular now in pest repellents," the man declared. "Sends mice and rats fleeing as it scrambles their brains."

With that, he sent yet another burst through Shawn's headphones.

Shawn reeled. "I need," he said, between breaths, "to speak to Rachel."

"What you *need* is to tell me the truth. So no blood because he was Andrew 'Fucking' Leland, but still dead. Dubious, dubious, dubious."

"He is dead," Shawn said, fighting the urge to vomit. "I swear to you."

In a nearby room, Rachel, watching on a monitor, shook her head.

"Where is all this going?" she asked the stiff Ambius intelligence analyst sitting beside her. "I don't give a shit about Leland right now; I want this kid on our side."

"A little discomfort is usually the fastest way to make that happen."

"Yeah. Worked like a charm with Leland."

In the interrogation room, Shawn was wondering how much more of this he could take. In his tooth, he could feel Leland's cyanide capsule, but this was nowhere near the level where he'd have to think about that. Still, this was pretty damn unpleasant, and he wasn't sure if he might be on the verge of some permanent damage. He could, of course, just tell this psychopathic freak all about the cosmic shield and the dangers of disabling it, but that was probably useless, and if he was going to die tonight, he wanted to die with the knowledge that Rachel, a real scientist who understood all the implications, had heard the full story straight from his own lips.

"So if you and I were to go for a ride," the man asked, "you could bring me to the location of the body?"

"I mean, it was in the middle of the woods, but yeah, I could do my best."

He could worry about that later.

"Please," he said, "let me speak to Rachel."

"Hmmm. Ask me again to speak to Rachel."

Shawn said nothing.

But that didn't matter.

"*Aaaaaaaaaaaahhhhhhhhhhhhhh!*"

Shawn lurched forward and puked all over himself, which sent the man into yet higher shrieks of delight.

Then there was a shuffle of movement, possibly a door opening and closing. The blindfold was suddenly removed from Shawn's face, and Rachel was staring down at him, the bald man gone, the two of them alone in a darkened room. If he hadn't known her better, he might have thought she'd looked just a little concerned.

"You have something you want to tell me," she said.

Shawn took a few deep breaths. "If this is good cop–bad cop and you're the good cop, I am truly fucked."

"Believe it or not, I actually want to help you."

"I'm gonna go with 'not.'"

Rachel walked around him and untied his wrists from behind his chair. "Come on. Let's get you cleaned up."

A short while later, Shawn, now in a clean white T-shirt, sat with Rachel in a weird ovular room carved from rock with no windows and no furniture besides the retro, bright red egg chairs on which they sat. On their short walk from the interrogation room to here, they had crossed a high, grated metal bridge, from which

Shawn could get a quick glimpse of the vast, subterraneous space where they were, apparently a series of large caverns housing a network of interlacing bridges and stairways and offices built into the bedrock. In all, it had reminded him of his favorite building from Columbia, the futuristic Alfred Lerner Hall, but crossed with the Batcave. Below the bridge on which they walked, he had glimpsed various people—scientists, security personnel, worker drones whose precise jobs Shawn couldn't guess—moving in and out of offices, going about their routines, some chatting, some wheeling lab equipment or other machinery, some just staring up curiously at Rachel and Shawn.

"This is more than some abandoned college," he said now.

"True."

"Was this always underneath the campus?"

"Not until the school moved out."

"And this is the 'Docks'?"

She shook her head.

Figures, Shawn thought. The awesome facility where they built spaceships and experimented with advanced alien technology was obviously not anyplace they'd bring him.

"It was all bullshit," he said. "Every single thing."

She didn't respond.

"But lying to me, that was the least of it, wasn't it? That was the *minor* betrayal."

"Shawn, you risked your life to come here. Was it just to tell me how pissed off you are?"

He glared at her. But he got her point and took a deep breath. "I know the truth about the shield," he said.

"Which is what?"

"That you weren't using me to help you build it. Leland had already built it—you were using me to help you *destroy* it."

"Okay."

"You can't do that."

"Why not?"

"After Leland built it for them, for that . . . civilization . . . they decided that it wasn't good enough. Maybe we would find some way to breach it or take it down. You know, who knew what we were capable of? So they asked Leland to deactivate it, to remove it so they could go after us. Take us out for good, make sure we could never try to harm them again. But he refused. He *refused*, Rachel. And he knew they would kill him for not cooperating, so he escaped and came back here, came back to Earth. Came back home, where you guys captured and tried to torture him. *You guys*, not the government, not the fucking CIA or whatever bullshit you fed me before. Rachel, the cosmic shield protects both worlds from each other. If you take it down, mark my words, they'll strike us so fast, you won't have a chance to do anything about it."

Rachel leaned back in her chair and stared at Shawn for a few moments. She seemed to be considering something. Finally, she spoke. "Shawn, do you have any idea what it is that we want to do?"

"To steal something. Some kind of . . . *resource*."

"And you don't know what? Leland didn't tell you?"

He shook his head.

"What did he tell you about their planet?"

"Nothing, really. Said he couldn't really remember it anymore because he experienced the whole thing as something else."

"What do you mean *something else*?"

Shawn didn't answer. He wasn't sure himself what that meant, and he was also getting the feeling he may have said too much.

"What? He somehow *became one of them*? Is that what you're saying?"

He just looked at her. She waited another few seconds, then smiled. "Either way, you're telling me he didn't even remember the planet, yet he was still *convinced* that they were so much more powerful than we are, that if we removed the shield, they would obviously be the ones to strike first."

"They're an advanced alien civilization."

"And what are we?" She stood up. "Come on."

"Where are we going?"

"You've always felt out of the loop, haven't you, Shawn? I'm going to bring you in. All the way in."

Rachel led Shawn out of the room, then across another metal bridge, which led to a large double door in the rock. The double door slid open on their approach, and they walked through it into a dark and rather dank tunnel. At the end of the tunnel, they reached a wide and intimidating iron door. On its left was a combination thumbprint-iris scanner. Rachel put her left eye and her right thumb to the appropriate screens, and the door slid open. The two of them entered a large white room, clearly a science lab, and then Shawn saw it right away, right there in the middle of that room, and right away he understood.

After several moments of just staring, he finally managed to speak.

"How?" he asked.

Rachel smiled. "Stealth operation carried out by one of our best. By the time they realized it was gone, the shield was already back up. Seems like Andrew Leland underestimated us. You, too."

"What is it? Some kind of . . . *flower*?"

Indeed, the object sitting on a table in the center of the room, measuring about three feet in both length and height and encased in a glass dome, had many of the characteristics of a flower, specifically a lotus. Emerging out of a square box of soil, it consisted of large petals in a particularly brilliant shade of violet, which encircled not a normal stigma or ovary, but instead some kind of large, green, and vaguely gelatinous orb, which reflected and distorted the surrounding room like a mirror ball.

The overall picture was undoubtedly strange, but stranger still was an intangible aura of foreignness the whole object seemed to give off, as though its uniqueness was itself a physical quality, as though the object somehow occupied a slightly different level of reality from everything else in the room. In that sense, it was truly unlike anything Shawn had ever seen before.

"It's not a flower," Rachel said. "It's a machine. It obviously has plantlike characteristics, and it contains organic material. But this was built."

"By them."

"Yes."

"Why?"

"We're not exactly sure. What we do know is that about a thousand years ago, their sun was said to be on the verge of burning out. Then, around that time, they built this. Well, they're still around."

"So you're saying you think this flower . . . *machine* somehow restored their sun?"

"Maybe. Or maybe it helped them replace it."

"Uh-huh. And, uh, how, might I ask, could it do that?"

"We don't know yet."

"Really? That's a shock."

"We have a theory. Some preliminary testing seems to possibly even support it. But it sounds crazy."

"I'm all ears."

"We think—and this is still just a theory—that it might utilize a kind of *reverse* photosynthesis. Instead of converting light energy into chemical energy, it somehow converts chemical energy into light energy."

"It would need to do more than just convert energy; it would need to produce nuclear fusion."

She nodded.

"Okay, then. A cyborg flower that creates nuclear fusion. That might have once created a whole *sun*. And do you have a theory on how this thing could produce *any* fusion, let alone the kind of fusion ignition you'd need to create actual stars?"

"None whatsoever. We've been trying our best to study it, but the problem as we see it is that this thing is in an 'off' position right now, and we've got no idea how to turn it on. It might not even function at all on Earth for all we know. We've been working with Roy Auslander and a few other quantum biologists, plus some botanists from the Kunming Institute, but we haven't gotten far with any of them." She paused. "Or, to put it another way, why do you think you're still alive?"

He looked at her in shock. "You have *got* to be kidding. What is this, round two? Are you completely nuts? The last time I helped you guys, you tried to *murder* me, remember that?"

"I remember you and I were chatting in your room, and then you decided to jump out the window."

Shawn was almost too stunned to respond. "I jumped out the window because your buddy was standing out in the hallway with a fucking gun! You were about to have me killed!"

"I was trying to *save* you, Shawn. You fucked up that meeting with Burke at Northwestern. He wanted you disposed of."

"Why? Because I told him we needed to try to act responsibly and not screw over other planets? What, so that meant I wasn't dedicated enough to the mission and I needed to die?"

Rachel didn't answer, and Shawn shook his head. "Jesus."

"You act like everything is so simple, so black and white. It isn't. Point is, I was trying to give you a second chance."

Shawn nodded. "You were trying to get me to say that I would actually do anything, no matter how fucked, for the sake of our precious Earth. And if I didn't say that, or if you didn't believe me, you were gonna have Baldy come in and blow my brains out right there in that room. Sorry, I wasn't going to play your game."

And now he turned away from her. He could feel emotions rising in him that she had no right to see. "I heard what you called out," he said, his voice suddenly soft. "What you yelled out while I was running for the woods. 'Shoot him.' You said those words, Rachel; you told him to kill me. Am I wrong?"

She started to speak, stopped herself, took a deep breath. "No, you're not wrong," she said. "I won't deny it, and if you hate me now, I can understand that. You have every right. I lied to you, Shawn, and I betrayed you, and I don't expect you to forgive me. But you have to understand that we're not individuals here. We are part of a larger race whose survival is in some serious fucking jeopardy. On this planet, we might be on the top of the food chain, sure. In the galaxy, not even close. We need to progress, and we need to progress *fast*, much faster than we have been if we're going to have any future at all. Ambius might seem dirty to you, unethical, duplicitous, but you have to appreciate that it is on the front lines in the war against our extinction and that everything it does needs to be seen in that light."

"Right. Like stealing valuable resources from other planets."

She shrugged. "Sometimes to not wind up on the bottom, you do whatever you can to get to the top."

"Wow, eloquent. So I guess I really shouldn't take any of this personally. I mean, guys like me and Andrew Leland, we're just some of the eggs you've got to break to make your omelet. Sorry, not break. Pulverize with a drone."

"Let's talk about that drone, Shawn. Don't you find it just a little odd that you survived that strike?"

He gave a skeptical look. "What do you mean?"

"The drone that killed Leland. Or that you *say* killed Leland—I don't believe he's actually dead, but that doesn't matter right now. *You* were supposed to be a target, too. I talked Burke out of it."

"Sure. That thing sent a missile at our car while we were *both* in it."

"And what do you think, that you both jumped out just in the nick of time?"

"I don't give a shit. You're a confirmed liar; you admit that. But if you're telling the truth, then I can only guess you spared me 'cause you thought I could help you figure out how your little plant here works. Well, you should have let me die. That's never going to happen."

"Is that so?"

"You've got an object here you think can produce real nuclear fusion. And from that spiel you just gave about the food chain and our place in the universe, I'm assuming you've got some pretty ambitious plans for it. Something that could possibly alter our position radically, put us far ahead of everyone else, right where you and Roland Burke think we belong. Well, good luck and Godspeed. You'd have to be insane to think I'd want anything to do with you or your psychotic cohorts ever again. Not a fucking chance."

She didn't respond, just stared at him for a few moments, as though weighing his words. Finally, she nodded. "Okay, I get it." She pressed a button on the wall, and the iron door slid open. Two armed guards appeared.

"But before you give a final answer," she added, "how about you take some time to think it over?"

Shawn stared at the guards. "How much time?" he asked, his expression blank.

Rachel smiled. "All the time you need."

CHAPTER 27

The dining room of Reverend Daniels's house was rich with the fresh aromas of home cooking as the family sat around the table eating a delicious dinner of roast beef and sweet potatoes, prepared with typical love and expertise by the reverend's wife, Anne. As the reverend and Anne dug in, Kayla, their six-year-old daughter, was building a short and compact tower of sweet potatoes on her plate.

Reverend Daniels watched with a smile and leaned in. "Try to make it lean a little like the one in Italy," he said softly.

Anne shook her head. "Come on, Will. Don't encourage her." She turned to her daughter. "Potatoes are for eating, sweetie. Now, drink some juice."

The reverend laughed and helped himself to some more roast beef.

"How was the fund-raising meeting?" Anne asked.

"Oh, fine."

"They resolve that silly fuss over the library wing?"

"Uh, yes. Yes, they did."

He turned his attention back to his food, while Anne watched him a moment longer.

Kayla's eyes suddenly lit up. "Hey, Papa. Wanna see the painting I made in Mrs. Harrison's class today? Mama saw it before."

"Sure, honey!"

Anne interrupted. "But first, baby, finish your yams."

But Kayla had bounded off from the table before Anne had finished her sentence. Reverend Daniels continued to eat his beef while his wife watched him for another few seconds.

"Honey, is everything . . . *all right*?"

He paused and looked up at her. "Sure, just fine. Why?"

"It's just . . . I don't know, you seem a bit distracted lately."

"Well, honestly, sweetheart, I don't see how a man can have his full bearings when you've prepared as delectable a feast as this."

"Oh, Will, give me a break," she said with a laugh.

"Everything is fine, sweetie," he said. "And I promise, if it wasn't, you'd be the first to know about it."

She nodded. For a few seconds, they ate in silence.

"He'll come back," Anne suddenly said, softly. "He's full of confusion, that's all. He still loves us, and he still *respects* you. And I know he misses his baby sister. He'll come round. Believe you me, he'll be comin' home any day now."

Reverend Daniels nodded. "Amen," he said.

Kayla returned carrying a small drawing depicting a cartoon figure wearing some kind of headgear, which she displayed theatrically for her father.

"Like it?"

"I *love* it!" the reverend replied. "What is it?"

Kayla looked shocked. "It's Andrew Leland!"

"Oh!" Reverend Daniels replied, nodding in fake recognition. He squinted. "What's that he's got on his head?"

And now Kayla turned mad. "It's a fisherman's hat!" she declared, the annoyance in her voice palpable.

"But why's he wearing a fisherman's hat?"

"Because he's in disguise as a fisherman!" Kayla exclaimed, at this point totally exasperated. She put the drawing back on the table and went back to eating her sweet potatoes.

"Oh, well, now that you say so, yes, yes, that makes sense. That's a terrific drawing, honey!"

The girl smiled forgivingly and scooped a heap of potatoes into her mouth. "Papa," she asked, speaking with her mouth full, "why's Andrew Leland hidin'?"

"That's a really good question, honey," Reverend Daniels responded, and he put down his fork and knife for a moment and looked at his daughter thoughtfully. "I wish I could give you an answer that's just as good as your question, but the truth is, we don't really know for sure. We can only guess that it's because he's not ready to give us his message. And that when he is, he'll come."

"But why not?"

"Well, again, we just don't know. The only person who could answer that is Andrew himself. All we can do is hope that when he's good and ready to give it to us, we'll be good and ready to receive it. In the meantime, we've just gotta sit tight and wait."

Kayla shook her head and pouted. "Micah says waitin' is for horsecockies!"

Anne's eyes widened in shock. "Kayla! We do not use that kind of language, not here at the table, not anywhere!"

Reverend Daniels laughed, but stopped quickly after a sharp glance from his wife. He wondered, though, if she was also secretly amused by this inventive swearword that indicated Micah's father might be spending too much time at the racetracks.

"Your mama's right, pumpkin," he said. "But there might be some point in what Micah says; a lot of people don't like waiting. I don't like it much myself, but then I wonder if maybe that's what faith is all about. Maybe faith is always just waiting. And hoping and praying and believing that whatever you're waiting for, sooner or later, is really gonna come about."

The reverend could see Anne smiling at him out the corner of his eye, no doubt at the absurdity of this impromptu sermon delivered to a six-year-old who obviously wouldn't appreciate it. And he knew his wife was probably right, but then again, what difference did it make whether or not the girl understood? Because the whole point was surely about to become irrelevant, anyway.

The long wait was finally going to be over.

At around ten o'clock, Reverend Daniels told Anne that he was going out to visit a patient at the clinic who hadn't been doing well and who wished to keep things private. As he drove over, he felt a little guilty that he'd allowed Anne to think his recent distractedness was as a result of their son. Of course he missed their boy and thought and wondered about him all the time, but he was also firmly convinced that once the truth became known to the world, once the message had been revealed, the kid would come right back home, ready to repent for all his waywardness. Now, the stunning revelation would be happening even sooner than he'd expected.

When he arrived at the clinic, Dr. Rogers was inserting the largest needle he'd ever seen into an unconscious Andrew Leland's arm.

"It's a jab stick," Rogers explained as Reverend Daniels entered the room. "They use it for elephants. We had it ordered special yesterday."

Reverend Daniels closed the door behind himself. "How's he doing tonight?"

"Better. Heart rate has steadied and blood pressure's now at a healthy 116 over 75. Breathing is good, too, if a little irregular. And his reflexes . . . well, to say they've improved would be an understatement."

"What do you mean?"

"Here, let me show you something."

Dr. Rogers opened a drawer and removed a small rubber hammer. He then lifted up Leland's left leg and repositioned it so that it was dangling slightly off the edge of the gurney.

"Watch closely," he said and, very gently, tapped the spot right below Leland's knee with the hammer.

After a second, Reverend Daniels shook his head.

"Was something supposed to happen? I didn't see anything."

Dr. Rogers smiled. "That's exactly the point, Reverend. His leg moved so fast you can't hardly see it. All his reflexes are the same way, like lightning. And I don't think that's all, either. You're still dead set against an MRI or CT scan?"

"Absolutely, Eddie. We can't take him off these premises; the exposure is way too dangerous."

"Well, I've just got a funny feeling that if we did do any of those tests, we'd find that the bones underneath his skin aren't like any bones we've ever seen. If they're bones at all."

The reverend smiled and shook his head in wonder. "You see what's happening, Eddie?"

"What's happening, Reverend?"

"Everything! It's all happening, and it's beyond our wildest dreams. When he comes out of this thing, he's gonna have a hell of a thing to tell us, just you wait. To tell the *world*. The time has come, Eddie." He paused, stared at the doctor. "You don't seem convinced."

Dr. Rogers shrugged. "With all due respect, Reverend, without us here circulating his blood and giving him the proper fluids, this man would be dead."

"Okay, but don't you see? We're all part of the plan. And it's all coming together now, like pieces in a puzzle."

"I can appreciate that, Reverend, and when I look at that gurney, I see a very special man. But a man nonetheless, and a man who, while no doubt remarkably different from other men and in astounding shape given his present predicament, is still in a pretty bad way."

Reverend Daniels chuckled. "Oh, Eddie, you would have said the same thing if you'd seen Jesus bleeding on the cross."

"I probably would have, Reverend."

Reverend Daniels walked over to Leland's bedside and leaned in close. "Andrew," he whispered into his ear. "Don't worry. We're here, we're waiting for you, and we're not giving up, so keep pushing, keep on moving. We're ready to receive you. And we're ready to receive your word." He turned to Dr. Rogers. "You think he can hear us when we talk?"

Dr. Rogers shook his head. "While nothing's for sure, at this stage, he'd still be in what's called the 'true coma' phase. He wouldn't be having any sensory perceptions whatsoever."

Reverend Daniels stared at Leland, lying flat on the gurney with his eyes closed, looking so peaceful.

"What about dreaming? Could he be having dreams?"

Dr. Rogers shook his head again. "At this stage right here, we can safely assume that his mind is basically shut off," he said. "He is nowhere, and he isn't dreaming, he isn't thinking, he isn't anything. If he's experiencing anything at all, it's nothing but blackness."

CHAPTER 28

The colors swirl before his eyes. Crimson, violet, neon yellow, some colors that Leland feels he can't recognize, let alone name. Swirling before him like smoke, hazy and translucent one moment, stark and clear and so damn bright the next, constantly moving, forming spontaneous works of art, cloudy abstract images, until suddenly they are no longer clouds, no longer abstract, no, they are taking shape. They are becoming more and more defined, crystallized, until they form a room or some version of a room, a bedroom or some *bedroom-like place* from back there, and he knows this room he is in, though this surely isn't what it had looked like then. Now, he can hear her calling his name from somewhere else, somewhere beyond the room . . .

"Andrew!" she cries out again in her soft honeycomb voice, and he runs to the window and looks up and out into the night, and there is a spiraling rope bridge ascending straight from his bedroom window up into a haze of lavender mist.

"Andrew!" she calls once more from above, from somewhere beyond that mist.

He knows tonight is the night, and he crawls out the window and proceeds to climb the bridge, moving higher and higher, not daring to look down at the steep nothingness below, only up at the misty unknown above, and soon he's moving through that mist, more colors, not just lavender but cherry red, midnight blue, hot pink, swirling around him as he does, and all of a sudden, he has found himself *passed through*, in the clear, standing on some extremely high plateau with that entire world spread out below him like a blueprint for itself.

And here she is, smiling, those wide and brilliant green eyes sparkling, and she approaches and kisses him on the lips.

The night he is reliving in this dream is the night they have both been planning for. He is a wanted man, a traitor marked for death, but she will lead him to safety and restore him to his original human body. Then he will fly away on a spaceship specially designed for him, and, following an advanced and secret formula of his own devising, he will attempt to pass through the cosmic shield at such a speed and angle that he will wind up on the other side in the *present* instead of the past. He will probably fail at that, but if he somehow succeeds, he will return home to Earth, and his entire time on this world will fade into obscure memories and hazy dreams like the one he is experiencing right now.

"Are you ready?" she asks as their lips part.

"I'll never be ready," he answers. The same thing he said the first time he lived this moment.

"If you stay here, they'll finish you."

"Or I could just do as they ask and take down the shield."

"And watch your whole world be destroyed?"

"The most destructive world in the galaxy. Maybe we deserve it."

"Some of your kind do. Many more don't." She extends her hand. "Come. We don't have much time."

He reaches out, takes her hand, and the two of them leap from their spectacular height into a massive cloud below, and soon the cloud gives way to that blueprint, that map, their entire world below getting closer and closer, wider and wider. He can see a suspension bridge far below, tall and stately and orange, he *knows* this bridge, and it's getting bigger and bigger until suddenly they are right on it, and now they are running across it, hand in hand, moving at the speed of a car or a train, but they are running or some *version* of running, something *like* running, some way in which they are moving very fast. He turns to his left and there's a magnificent city passing by, glowing majestically in the night, dense and tall with an enormous skyscraper with burning antennas, and he recognizes that, of course, it's the Chicago skyline—he spent time there as a child, and it looks just like it looked then, no Franklin Center yet, no Trump Tower—and he turns to his right and there is another city, this one even larger and grander and also lighting up the night with dazzling skyscrapers and towers, and who in this galaxy or any other wouldn't recognize the Big Apple? And up ahead, the two giant orange towers from which the bridge's suspension cables descend—yes, of course, the Golden Gate Bridge—and the sky above is filled with shining stars, and the sea below is dark and full of mystery as they race across the bridge.

Just then, they hear a sound they feared but knew they'd hear eventually: helicopter blades. They glance over their shoulders, and in the distance behind them, up in the night sky, are hundreds of strange flying black vehicles with six rotors apiece, moving together in a menacing flock formation.

They are after him.

"Come," she says, and suddenly she leaps over the side of the Golden Gate Bridge, dragging him with her, and there goes Chicago in one insane blur, and now they're falling so fast, and beneath them, where is the water? No water, as he would expect, but instead yet another city, this one flat and neon and thick with blue smoke, but though they're falling toward it, it's not getting any closer. They are *falling*, he wants to cry out, and it is *not getting any closer*. But no sooner has he made this realization when suddenly it rushes up at them, and they pass right through it as though it was all an illusion or yet another cloud of mist of neon yellow, midnight blue, fuchsia. They continue to fall, hand in hand, and now he can see below them a dark and vast sea rising up, and just as they're about to hit the water, she says, "Don't be afraid," and an ancient-looking rowboat glides in beneath them, and they land gently and gradually into its hull.

The boat drifts and sways in the darkness, sandwiched between the twinkling sea of stars above and the sea reflecting those stars below, and they are surrounded by enormous cliffs on all sides, and in the distance he can see a great Gothic structure with bat-like gargoyles and spires and a bell tower and, somehow above all of that, a giant silver dome.

"What's that?" he asks.

"That's the observatory," she answers. "That's where your body is." She pauses. "Your *real* body."

She picks up one of the oars and hands him the other, and they begin to row, softly and gently in the direction of the observatory. He looks at her face, wondering if he can still discern the sweet, inno-cent, and mischievous child inside of her. But that child is nowhere to be seen, not tonight. Tonight she is all steely resolve, all mission. She is his savior and also everything he will lose by being saved, and he knows that the price is too fucking high.

But then, as he watches her, she suddenly starts to fade, every-thing starts to fade, the boat and the water and the Gothic observa-tory in the distance, and he can feel the surface on which he lies and foreign protrusions in his body, and he can hear the distant murmur of voices, medical terms being bandied about somewhere close by.

The real world is trying to break through, but he's just going to hold on to this dream that much harder, for as long as he can.

He's lived this night before, he knows that, but everything must have been different. It *had* to have been. For one thing, he hadn't had a name to be called, and for another, she and he are far too much like people right now, and they were nothing like people back then. And, of course, there was no New York City on that world or Chicago or Golden Gate Bridge, and those are just some of many reasons why he knows that everything must have been different when it had actually happened in real life. But if different, then different only in the details, in the specifics. The heart will remember what the mind no longer can. He's lived this night before, and it was nothing like this and it was everything like this.

CHAPTER 29

Shawn Ferris lay on his stiff cot, staring up at the ceiling, whispering to no one: "Dynamene, Dysona, Dyukov, Dwingeloo . . ."

He'd been in the cell over two days, and in the first day, he'd gone through all the major physics theories of the twentieth century and their corresponding years, and in the second, all the theoretical physics laws named after people who were still alive, and now he had taken to naming all the minor planets, in alphabetical order to the best of his abilities. All of this had been in an effort to stave off insanity, though to anyone watching, that surely would have seemed ironic.

"Dzhalil, Dzhangar, Dzhanibekov," he continued, then paused. Was that it for the Ds? He was pretty sure it was. *What is the first planet to start with E? Eamonlittle? No. Eades?*

He took a deep breath.

I'm going to die in here, he thought, not for the first time. His cell was six by nine feet with gray concrete walls and consisted of the cot, an industrial silver toilet bowl, and a security camera pointing downward from the corner of the ceiling.

Rachel's words from before now echoed in his ears: "We're not individuals here . . . we need to progress, and we need to progress *fast*, much faster than we have been if we're going to have any future . . ."

Facing the prospect of a lifetime in this cell, he had to admit her arguments suddenly seemed far more persuasive.

"Ambius might seem dirty to you . . . it is on the front lines in the war against our extinction . . . everything it does needs to be seen in that light . . ."

Shawn stared at the security camera above him. A thought that had occurred to him earlier now came back to him once more. The idea had originally come to him sometime after he'd made his *quantum tunneling* breakthrough, which had occurred sometime before he began naming physics theories.

He toyed with this thought again. He didn't like it, but what choice did he have?

Fuck it, he decided finally. He was done with this cage.

Shawn got to his feet and stood up on the cot and stared right into the security camera above him. Besides the cyanide capsule in his tooth, Shawn had managed to smuggle one other object into the cell, a sealed two-inch ampoule of a chemical compound known as amyl nitrite, which he'd hidden in a sock and which he now held between the middle and ring fingers of his right hand, jutting out from behind so that as long as his palm stayed facing the camera, the ampoule wasn't visible to it.

"Hey!" he shouted at the camera. "I'm ready, okay?" He paused, put both hands around the camera, and stared into its lens. "I'll do it!" he shouted, then added, "I know what the machine needs!"

He released the camera from his grip and stood there for several minutes, up on that cot, waiting. He was hoping to immediately hear footsteps, for the big steel door to suddenly open, for fresh air to come rushing in—he could almost taste it—but nothing happened, and he reminded himself that it was probably very late at night, possibly early morning.

"Hey!" he shouted again at the camera, a note of desperation creeping into his voice. "I said I'll do it!"

He got back down and spread out once again on the cot. He stared up at the ceiling, going over some of the vague science in his head, his tunneling breakthrough, though to call it a breakthrough might have been a stretch.

Suddenly, he heard a noise. A *click*. He sat straight up and watched as the big steel door slowly opened to reveal Rachel, looking alert and standing with a large security guard, thankfully not the bald man. If *he'd* been there, Shawn would have probably gotten queasy from the sight of him and lost all resolve.

Rachel eyed Shawn skeptically. "You're not fucking with us?"

"I need to see the plant. Right now."

Accompanied by the guard, Shawn and Rachel made their way from the cell to the dank tunnel that led to the lab. At the lab's entrance, Rachel told the guard to wait outside, she was good from here, and then she once more applied her eye and thumb to the appropriate screens of the security scanner, and the large iron door slid open, and she and Shawn entered.

The lotus flower remained on the table in the center of the lab, and like a fun house mirror, its orb rendered wildly distorted reflections of Shawn and Rachel as they came in.

Rachel turned to Shawn expectantly. "All right. What have you got for me?"

"Well, first of all, I'll come clean. I exaggerated. I have no idea what this thing needs, but I really needed to get the fuck out of that cell."

Her eyes widened. "Are you—"

"Hey, that's nothing compared to what you did to me, right? And, come on, was it even plausible I could have come up with anything real while lying on my back staring at the ceiling? But I did have a *thought*. A starting point, maybe. An avenue of exploration."

She gave him a hard look. "Okay. What?"

"Few years back, I read an article in some journal about scientists in California looking for evidence of quantum mechanics in plant life. Well, one of the big things they discovered was that in photosynthesis, there was some evidence to suggest electrons actually move through plants using quantum entanglement."

"Okay."

"But there was also strong evidence of energy moving through plants using not quantum entanglement, but quantum *tunneling*."

Rachel waited a beat. "Okay."

"So. Where else do we see quantum tunneling? Where is quantum tunneling *absolutely essential*?"

Rachel thought for a second, and it hit her. "Nuclear fusion."

"Bingo. If you want to understand how this thing really works, I would bet a shitload of money there's a connection between the quantum tunneling in photosynthesis and the quantum tunneling in nuclear fusion. That's what you should be looking at."

Rachel stared at him for a moment, then turned to the plant and said nothing for a little while. She seemed to be contemplating what he had said, although with her, you could never really tell. After a few moments, she turned back to him.

"Shawn, I really want to work together with you on this. But we *need* to be able to trust one another. I need to know that all the bad shit is behind us."

He looked at her, took a deep breath. "You gave me a lot of time for reflection in that cell. I know what happened, that it wasn't your call and that you didn't really want to hurt me and tried to avoid it. That doesn't mean I'm cool with it or that I'll ever be cool with it, but I can just barely understand it. It's the breaks. Like you once said, what's at stake here is a lot bigger than you or me. You're going to be experimenting on this thing, on this plant that may or may not be able to do the incredible things you say it can do. There's no way I don't want to be a part of it."

Rachel smiled. "I'm very glad to hear that, Shawn." She turned back to the plant and shook her head. "Jesus, I can't wait to see the look on Burke's face. He delivered a paper on quantum tunneling just a few months ago at Cal Tech. You really are a genius, you know."

She then noticed that Shawn was breathing a little heavier and looking at her funny, with just the slightest, slyest smile. "You okay?" she asked.

"Fine," he answered. "It's just the last time we were in a lab together and you called me a genius, I'm pretty sure you followed it up with a kiss."

She laughed, a little embarrassed. "Oh, did I now?"

He nodded.

"Hmmm." She gave him a sideways glance. Then she turned in to him, slowly leaned in, and kissed him full on the mouth.

The kiss lasted a long time.

And then it lasted too long.

She tried to pull away, but he held her head from behind, keeping it in place while refusing to pull his mouth away from hers.

Finally, she broke free, gasping and coughing.

"What the fuck?" she exclaimed, out of breath.

He stared at her. He wasn't smiling anymore.

"What the *fuck*, Shawn?" she repeated. "What was that?"

"Cyanide capsule. It was in my mouth. Now, it's in your stomach."

Her eyes went wide. She immediately leaned forward and shoved two fingers down her throat. She began to dry heave, but nothing beyond spittle was coming out.

"I never bit down, so the toxin wasn't released," Shawn said. "You won't start to feel anything for at least another fifteen minutes when the capsule starts to dissolve inside you. Then you'll experience weakness. Shortness of breath. Vertigo."

She swung around at him, bloodshot and teary eyes full of rage. "I'm gonna fucking kill you!"

"You could, but then you'd be joining me right after. You probably want to know where the antidote is first."

"Where is it? Tell me—we can *make* you tell me."

"Like your friend made me tell him where Andrew Leland was? How much time do you think you have to fuck around with here?"

"Dammit, Shawn, where is it? Tell me *now*!"

"I'll tell you, but definitely not now. You're gonna help me get out of here first. All the way out and without any issues. Oh, and I'll be taking this with me."

He wrapped his arms around the soil box at the bottom of the flower and hoisted the whole thing off the table, glass dome and all. The lotus's intangible weirdness seemed to almost course through his own body as he held it against his chest, but he would have to ignore the sensation for now.

"Sorry," he said to Rachel, "but this is stolen property."

When the guard saw Shawn carrying the large, strange-looking flower out of the lab and into the tunnel several minutes later, he did a double take, but Rachel nodded that it was okay and informed him they wouldn't need his escort from here on out. As Rachel led Shawn across a long bridge overlooking some sort of garage, neither of them spoke. As it was the middle of the night, very few people were out and about, but now two figures were moving toward them from the far end of the bridge. When they got closer, Shawn recognized them as Ravi and Megan, the married couple with whom he'd worked at the campus many months before. Megan was dressed in her traditional outfit of turtleneck and pleated skirt. Both registered surprise at seeing Shawn.

"Shawn!" Ravi exclaimed. "Hey, you're here!"

"Hey, Ravi," said Shawn.

"Shawn's working with us again," Rachel cut in, her voice low. "We'll be conducting some light experiments with the flower aboveground."

Ravi and Megan both looked taken aback to hear that, though it was unclear what they were reacting to: that Shawn had rejoined the team or that the lotus flower was being taken aboveground.

"Well," Ravi said to Shawn, with a weak smile, "welcome back into the fold, man!"

"Thanks, buddy," Shawn answered, his tone unmistakably icy.

By the time Rachel and Shawn reached the elevator at the end of the bridge, Shawn could already hear a change in her breathing. On the ride up, he stared straight ahead at the elevator doors, but he could feel her eyes glued to him as her breathing grew louder, raspier.

He wouldn't look at her. As resolved as he was in the righteousness of what he was doing, he knew that seeing her right now in the state she was in could still weaken him.

When the elevator doors slid open, Shawn was surprised to find they revealed not the inside of Rachel's dorm room but instead the lobby of the sports and rec center, a building he'd previously assumed to be totally defunct. The visages of sports heroes from decades past gazed down at them from posters on the high walls as they crossed the lobby and exited out into the night.

Outside, Shawn still tried to avoid looking at Rachel as they made their way across the path toward the road that led out of the campus, but he could tell that her walking was less steady now and that her breathing had worsened further. Even so, for someone who'd swallowed cyanide, she was still in reasonably decent shape. When they reached the beginning of the road, he stopped and turned to her.

"Okay. Here's fine," he said.

He knew he should have enough time now to get back to his car and make a clean break, and he worried that if he pushed her further, she might not make it back down to save herself.

"On top of the security camera in the cell," he continued,

"there's a small ampoule of liquid. You'll want to inhale what's in it for at least thirty seconds. Also, before tomorrow tonight, you should get yourself an injection of sodium thiosulfate to be safe."

Rachel said nothing. Her chest was heaving, and her eyes no longer showed any trace of anger or even fear. Just a quiet sadness that seemed almost alien to her face. She looked at the flower in Shawn's arms. "What are you going to do with it?" she asked. Her voice was strained and barely above a whisper.

"Take it far away from here. From any of you 'scientists' who don't know the first thing about the meaning of that word. You know what the funniest part is? When it came to *my* life, it was all about the bigger picture. The ends justified the means. When it came to *your* life, you let me walk right out of here with everything. Good-bye, Rachel."

Shawn turned around and disappeared up the wooded road and into the darkness. Rachel turned toward the recreation center and began to make her way back. Walking was much more difficult now. Her lungs seemed to be fighting harder and harder for air, as though her chest were closing in on itself, and there was a pounding in her head accompanied by severe dizziness. The trees and buildings around her seemed to be wiggling, dancing. The rec center looked to be about thirty yards away. As she pressed on, she passed a large, thick oak tree and paused for a moment, holding onto one of its branches to regain her balance. She decided to take just a few moments to rest and leaned herself against its wide trunk and let herself slide down to the ground.

She sat there beneath the tree, taking in big gulps of air, and closed her eyes tight, trying to fight off the vertigo. She should get back up, she realized. The rec center was probably only twenty yards away now. She had enough time to get back down to the base and take the antidote. If she moved fast enough, she could tell them all what had happened, and they might still be able to catch Shawn before he reached the interstate. They could bring him back, together with the plant.

But she made no move to get up. Instead, she remained seated where she was, at the base of the tree, transfixed by the old television program playing in her mind. An aging game show host with dyed red hair and wearing a plaid suit and bowtie was smiling before a small, dimly lit studio audience, reading a question off a teleprompter.

"For twenty-five points, which of the following was the name of the theory that explained superconductivity and nabbed the scientists Bardeen, Cooper, and Schrieffer the Nobel Prize in 1972? Was it—"

Before he could read off the choices, the bubbly twelve-year-old contestant from Australia had already slammed down her buzzer.

"The BCS theory!" she called out with a wide grin and in her thick Aussie accent.

"Well, I hadn't finished the question, but that's still correct!" the host declared.

The crowd cheered.

"Next question! For fifteen points, in the publication *Optica Promota*, which of the following scientists—"

The girl's buzzer sounded again.

The host laughed. "I haven't even finished the *first* part of the question, Roach! I'll let it go this time, but please, for the future, let me finish the questions. What's the answer?"

"James Gregory!"

"That is correct again!"

More cheering from the crowd as the child beamed. Such a precocious little girl, people murmured. A child prodigy. A real genius!

Rachel opened her eyes and took in another deep breath. Her heart felt like it was beating a mile a minute. She could see the rec center, only some sixty feet away. She should really get up now, she thought. She could make it. She could save her life.

But she didn't move. She could still hear the murmurs of that studio audience as she closed her eyes for the last time. Such a precocious little girl, they were saying, a child prodigy, a real genius! She could become anything she wanted in this world.

She would go on to do great things.

CHAPTER 30

Dawn hadn't yet broken when Shawn pulled the car over to the side of a dark wooded road somewhere, he estimated, between Owatonna and the Minnesota-Iowa state line. He removed the flower from the passenger seat and carried it some distance through the trees and then placed it down amid a pile of broken branches and twigs surrounded by sycamore trees. A yellow moon shone through the spaces between their trunks, and, by its light, Shawn could make the lotus out pretty well, its pale green outer leaves, its large and brilliant violet petals, its shiny bulbous orb. A flower, a plant, a machine, whatever it was, it was at once strange-looking and glorious.

From his pocket, he removed the small metal cigarette lighter he'd taken from the glove compartment of the SUV. There was an etching on its side of a pirate ship.

Could he really go through with this? He knew that by most estimates, the sun would begin its long, slow death in about four or five billion years. It would swell to 150 times its current size and brighten to 5,000 times its current luminosity, and then it would reverse course and shrink and cool into a small white dwarf that would eventually fade away. Humanity may or may not still exist by that point. More likely, some highly evolved descendant would be lording over the world. Either way, this flower, this *thing*, could be the key to the Earth's continued survival in a sunless future.

For a moment, Shawn allowed his imagination to run away with itself. He could see the flower being hidden away somewhere, maybe in Fiji or the Marquesas Islands or somewhere else at the far side of the world, someplace where it would be exposed to light and rain and somehow preserved for billions of years, a secret handed down from modern man to generation after generation until perhaps, eventually, the secret would somehow get lost. A lapse in tradition, a break in the chain. Then, one day, four billion years from now, with the sun already entering into its long-predicted demise, some future advanced humanoid would accidentally stumble upon the beautiful lotus, stored away, possibly with an ancient inscription nearby, explaining what it was, where it originally came from, and how it would now save the world from the oncoming darkness.

Shawn smiled at this futuristic fairy-tale vision and then let it float away. Deep down, he knew that the Earth itself would not exist in four billion years if this thing were allowed to exist now. Nuclear power at its current limited stage of development and usage was already fraught with danger. The catastrophic destruction that could be wreaked by a device such as this one once again falling into the wrong hands was beyond what he could even imagine.

He ignited the lighter, bent down, and lit one of the plant's outer leaves. For a few seconds, the fire seemed to remain burning in just that one spot, localized, but then it began to spread and expand. He stepped back and watched as larger flames began to dance their way across the lotus's leafy outer layers, gradually engulfing its beautiful violet petals.

Soon, the entire flower was burning.

Shawn stared, transfixed. He was aware that the strange, high-pitched sound he was beginning to hear coming from the flower was likely the result of the plant emitting ethylene in reaction to the intense heat. Still, listening to that eerie whine and watching the lotus's leaves and petals writhing and wavering and ultimately withering in the flames, he couldn't help but imagine that it was in fact screaming, that it understood what was happening, knew that it was dying.

One part of the lotus remained untouched by the flames. In the midst of all the smoke, that large and gelatinous green orb in the center of the flower seemed almost to be watching him, like a gigantic eye. And then, as Shawn stared back at it, he realized that it was slowly expanding. He could see his own distorted reflection in it getting bigger as the orb widened, first to the size of a beach ball and then bigger still, so grotesque and yet totally magnificent, a pale green color brought out by the flames in a shade not quite like any Shawn had seen before, and he wondered whether this thing was about to burst.

It was then that it occurred to him that he had no real idea what this flower was actually made of, nor what sort of chemical reactions might be induced from heating it up. When he had decided to destroy the lotus by fire, he had been conceiving of it as a flower, somehow giving no thought to the very obvious fact that it was so much more than that. Now, he was seized by a sudden panic. Would that gelatinous orb explode? If so, of what magnitude would the blast be? Could heating up the flower and whatever was inside of it actually trigger the ignition of nuclear fusion?

The absurdity of destroying what was essentially a small nuclear reactor by *fire* now seemed to him so glaringly obvious that he wondered how he ever could have missed it. What had he been thinking?

In the end, the orb didn't explode. Instead, it eventually began to soften and liquefy until it collapsed into a bubbling soup-like substance in the center of the flower's burning petals, where it remained for several minutes before it eventually boiled out. What was left of the husk of the flower didn't explode, either, and continued to burn and burn until there was nothing left.

The color of the sky had begun to change from black to a deep, tangelo orange. The night was coming to an end, and as Shawn snuffed out the last embers from the fire with a canteen, he wondered for just a moment whether it could all have been some kind of sham. The body of the flower had given way to no metal exoskeleton underneath, no fancy network of wiring, no final fireworks of wild chemical reactions, nothing besides the orb that was at all indicative of anything other than standard organic plant matter. In truth, had he ever had any proof that this thing had otherworldly origins besides the word of a known liar? None at all.

But the thing itself had been proof enough. Its bizarre appearance was one thing, but that was nothing compared to the strange sense of otherness the flower exuded, that unclassifiable unreality that had struck Shawn the first time he'd seen it and had never dissipated. He couldn't explain it, but it was something like the difference between an object in real life and an object in a dream. It felt like it belonged to another plane of reality, and yet here it was in our world. Or rather, here it had been.

No more.

As dawn broke and the color of the woods took on a deep burgundy hue, Shawn stood and stared at that small mound of ash that was now all that remained of the plant. Soon, the wind would scatter it, and then it would be as though the flower had never been there, not at this spot, not in these woods, not anywhere in this world. He should go now, he realized. It wasn't safe to stay in one spot for so long, especially with sunrise not far off. But he stayed standing there for just a few more minutes. He had done the right thing, he was certain of that; he had no regrets. All the same, he couldn't escape the feeling that he had just destroyed the most strange and wondrous thing he would ever encounter.

CHAPTER 31

The window in Leland's room at the clinic looked out upon what must have once been a courthouse or municipal building, an isolated redbrick structure whose ivory pillars still looked regal and impressive, while the rest of it appeared dilapidated, with boarded windows, missing roof shingles, and the white paint on the windows and door frame chipped and yellowing. Out in front of it, in the center of a circular driveway, was a small tiered fountain long out of use, and at this moment, two young teenagers, a boy and a girl, were circling it on bicycles. The boy, Leland could see, was faster than the girl, and though she tried to keep up with him, it seemed that for every cycle she made, he made two. She kept trying.

"I'm sorry, I'm afraid I just don't understand," said Reverend Daniels, seated in a chair beside Leland's gurney. "I mean you were *there*. You *had* experiences."

"I wasn't me. Not in any normal sense."

"So you don't remember *anything*?"

"Nothing."

Daniels shook his head wistfully. Then his eyes suddenly

alighted, and he smiled knowingly. "Wait a minute," he said. "Is this some kind of test?"

Leland sighed and shook his head. When he had first regained consciousness, he had intended to leave immediately, especially when he'd realized where he'd ended up. However, the doctor had explained to him that having just awoken, he would be placing himself in grave danger if he didn't wait at least a few days before leaving, and yes, he was well aware that Leland was no typical patient, and no, that would not protect him in the slightest from severe post-coma neurological complications. He needed a limited time for rest and monitoring. As Leland didn't feel 100 percent, anyway, he had reluctantly agreed. He'd been enduring these insufferable conversations with the reverend since.

"You have to understand," the reverend was saying, "we gave up everything we had ever believed in, everything we were, just for you."

Leland could see the desperation in the man's eyes. And there was something else in his expression, too, something vaguely familiar, though Leland couldn't place it. "I didn't ask you to," he replied.

"No, you certainly didn't. But that was the most beautiful part about the whole thing. You never asked anything of us, but we gave it freely. Our love, our devotion. Our faith in your message."

This was too fucking crazy. What to do with this poor, sad idiot? And how much more of this could he take? He took a deep breath and turned to the reverend.

"Okay," he said. "There is *something*. A vague, distant memory. From up there. I'll try to remember if I can."

He shut his eyes for several moments, and when he opened them, the reverend was gazing at him reverentially and expectantly.

"There was some sort of . . . *shaman*," Leland said. "I can't remember what he looked like, but all the others said he was very wise. I was seeking answers, just like you. I sat down in his tent or whatever it was, and he told me things."

"What things?"

Leland shut his eyes again and furrowed his brow in concentration.

"He said . . . he said science could take our physical selves to all kinds of spectacular places, geographically. The farthest reaches of the heavens. But our *real selves*, he said, our souls, are stuck on the ground until we realize that the big stuff happens only in the infinite space inside of us. The 'Great Infinity Within' is what he called it. It's in there, he said, that you'll find true salvation, true discovery, and adventure."

Leland opened his eyes. On the reverend's face was an expression of sheer wonder. He looked like he might just burst into tears.

"I think I understand," he whispered.

"Good," said Leland, pretty certain he didn't.

There was a knock at the door.

"Pardon my interruption," said Dr. Rogers, peeking his head in, "but, well, we have a visitor."

The reverend looked shocked. "For who?"

The doctor gestured toward Leland.

"That's impossible!" the reverend exclaimed. "No one knows he's here!"

With the two of them seated in wicker chairs on a back porch overlooking the forest behind the clinic, Shawn recounted for Leland everything that had occurred between the drone attack on the highway and the death of the mysterious lotus flower. He tried to leave nothing out, from the unique, rock-embedded architecture of Ambius's underground lair to how the flower had looked as it was perishing in the flames. When he was finished speaking, Leland didn't respond. He just sat there in silence for several moments, seemingly lost in thought.

"The Illumination," he finally muttered, more to himself than to Shawn.

"The what?"

"That's what it was called, that flower you burned. Or, you know, what it was called in my memory, at least. But they never told me what its actual power was. They said what it did was beyond my comprehension."

Shawn gave a confused look. "Maybe how it *worked* might have been beyond your comprehension. But what it *did*, at least on a functional level, was fairly simple! It produced nuclear fusion, created new stars. Why would that be beyond your comprehension?"

Leland had no answer, so he just continued to stare out at the Texan hickory trees. Shawn did the same, and, after a while, Leland got a funny feeling that maybe Shawn was waiting for some sort of formal recognition, some pat on the back. Maybe he wanted to hear that he had done a good job. That he had saved the future of the human race by destroying the potentially dangerous Illumination. Or maybe that he had ultimately been right to return to Ambius and confront them, that contrary to all Leland's warnings, it had all worked out for the good.

"Glad you're alive," was all Leland said.

"Thanks," Shawn replied with a hint of a smile. In truth, he couldn't have cared less about validation from Leland.

Shawn spent that night at a nearby Motel 6. Though Reverend Daniels had offered to put him up in his own home, Shawn was concerned his presence might place the reverend and his family in too much danger. Leland, meanwhile, remained at the clinic, and at around 8:00 P.M., the reverend arrived at his room with a glass of tea and a worn Braille copy of *Don Quixote* from the local library (though curious, the reverend thought it wiser not to ask Leland why he had requested a book in Braille). After Leland thanked him, the reverend lingered uncertainly in the doorway a few moments. Leland looked at him expectantly.

"May I ask you a question, if you don't mind?" Reverend Daniels asked. "Just to clarify something?"

"Sure," Leland answered. In seeing the reverend's nervous, unsure expression, he had suddenly realized with a jolt of recognition why he looked so familiar. How had he ever missed it?

"What you said earlier today," the reverend began. "Do you mean that your message to the world is that there's a piece of outer space inside all of us and we can find the answers there?"

By now, Leland had lost all patience with this whole business. "My message," he said, "is that there is no message."

"What? I don't understand."

"I have nothing to tell you people. I'm sorry that you wasted so much of your time. And your community's."

"No, that can't be. You're testing me!"

"This is not a test."

"Everything's a test. Every minute of every hour of every day is a test. And I won't fail you, you hear me? I believe in you! With all my heart and soul, every fiber of my being. I will *not* fail you."

"I'm sorry about your boy." The words surprised even Leland. He hadn't meant to say them; they had just come out.

A shocked Reverend Daniels was about to ask Leland how he knew about his missing son, but he stopped himself. Of course Andrew Leland knew about him! He knew all, the seen and the unseen. He surely knew where the boy had run off to, as well, but now was not the time to ask about such things. The message itself had yet to be declared. For some mysterious reason, Leland was holding out now, playing coy, testing him. But soon, all would be revealed. He was certain of that.

"Thank you," the reverend said with a smile. Leland, however, didn't smile back.

When Daniels finally left him, Leland continued to read, though he found himself continuously distracted. Not by his conversation with the reverend but by his earlier conversation with Shawn, which he continued to go over in his head. Shawn's question bothered him greatly. Shawn was right; the Illumination's power had ultimately turned out to be quite straightforward: it could produce nuclear fusion and create new stars, create suns. So why had the leaders on the other world always claimed that the nature of its power was completely beyond Leland's mental reach, something he could never truly understand? Had they all just underestimated his mental capacities? That answer seemed unlikely, especially given that they knew he had already built for them a powerful cosmic shield whose precise workings they themselves didn't fully comprehend.

A more plausible and disturbing explanation was that, as a *nonnative*, he had been deemed simply not trustworthy enough to know the truth, to hold information that had such enormous implications for the survival of their world. As the Ambius scientist had explained to Shawn, when their planet's sun had died out, they had somehow used the Illumination to create a new one. It was obviously the most important resource they had, and truthfully, given that their own general populace didn't know much about it, he, an émigré from the most hostile planet in the galaxy, shouldn't have expected to be any exception. He had helped them, yes, but he still wasn't genuinely one of them, and he never would be. (He supposed he eventually proved this once and for all when he refused to take down the shield so they could destroy Earth.)

Most troubling of all was that *she*, too, had always told him that the powers of the Illumination were beyond his abilities to comprehend. But she, too, must have known this wasn't exactly accurate. So did that mean she hadn't trusted him, either?

Leland read for a while longer, trying his best to ignore these unanswerable questions. Eventually, after an hour or so, he put down his book and went to sleep.

In his dreams, he and she were standing on some elevated platform, staring out on a vast expanse of outer space. He couldn't see her face, but he knew it was her, could sense her presence. And then, suddenly, the imagery changed, and he wasn't sure where he was anymore or whether she was still with him or what exactly he was looking at. Whatever it was, though, it was absolutely stunning, an enormous whirlpool of light or energy or gas, colors swirling at its center.

And that center was heating up, he could see that, and the colors were changing accordingly, brightening and intensifying. Something was about to happen . . .

He awoke in a cold sweat and sat straight up.

It created stars, he reflected. *The Illumination created stars.* That's what it was, that's what it did! The terrible truth was starting to dawn on him, and now he struggled to remember exactly how Shawn had described the Illumination's appearance.

A flower! A flower with beautiful violet petals encircling a shiny green core.

Violet, green.

Leland could feel his heartbeat quickening. Those two colors had passed through one ear and out the other the first time he'd heard them. Now, they pounded in his skull, and he clutched his head with both hands, trying to control the panic and horror that were steadily rising to the surface.

And what had Shawn done with the Illumination? He had taken it into the forest and set it on fire, burned it down to ash, utterly destroyed it.

"No," Leland whispered repeatedly, shaking his head. "What did you do, kid? What did you fucking do?"

As usual, Shawn had simply been doing what he thought was right. Leland knew that. Nevertheless, at this moment, he hated him more than anything on Earth.

In the morning, Andrew Leland's room was empty and his few belongings gone. The doctor informed the reverend, who immediately summoned Shawn, but Shawn insisted he knew nothing, that Leland hadn't indicated to him any plans to leave.

Days went by, and when it became obvious Leland wasn't coming back, Shawn left town, as well. Meanwhile, not the reverend, the doctor, nor the nurses could figure out why Leland had taken off so abruptly, though all hoped that whatever the reason had been, he had left in good condition and of his own accord. Under orders from Reverend Daniels, it was resolved that no one else in the town should ever know who had been their guest for several unforgettable days.

Afterward, the reverend tried to move on, to lose himself in church affairs, distract himself by spending more time with Anne and Kayla, but he struggled. After years of hoping and praying, the Bearer of the Great Message had finally arrived and cryptically declared that *the message was that there was no message* and then disappeared without a trace. *What did it all mean?*

All he could do was reflect on an old quote from John Adams: "Admire and adore the Author of the telescopic universe, love and esteem the work, do all in your power to lessen ill, and increase good, but never assume to comprehend."

His runaway son, meanwhile, never returned home.

CHAPTER 32

Summer had finally arrived for the students and faculty at Pennsboro College, but there was still the usual vexatious business of tidying up loose ends. Professor Armond Jordan's eyes drifted to the Saturn-shaped wall clock in back of his office, lingered there for several seconds, then glided back down to the young, broad-shouldered Thor look-alike who was seated across from him, watching the professor with nervous anticipation.

Professor Jordan forced a smile through his exasperation. "I appreciate your predicament, I really do," he said. "I wouldn't want to see the Meerkats playing without you, either. Problem is, you're telling me that if you were to take the final again, right now, you wouldn't do any better! So how can I possibly raise you to a B?"

"I know, Professor J. I don't wanna lie to you is all. I just don't think I have the right head for all this."

"Okay, but if you don't have the head for this, can I ask why you signed up for the course in the first place?"

The student shrugged. "We had to take a science. Everyone else was taking geology, but I love *Star Wars*, and I thought this would deal with more of that kind of stuff."

The professor smiled sadly. "Yes, well, I suppose we could have spent a little less time on Newton and Einstein and a little more on Jabba the Hutt. I'll make a note for next year." He sighed, stared at the desperate student before him. "All right. Look, son. There's a planetarium over on White Street. If you can give me a full ten pages on the history of the planetarium and at least *some* account of how the damn thing works, I'll give you that B. But don't go advertising it, okay?"

The student's eyes lit up. "Thank you so much, Professor J! I really owe you one."

"Well, if you do wind up scoring the winning touchdown in a bowl game, I'm going to expect a full analysis of why your acceleration, velocity, and speed made the victory inevitable."

"Sorry?"

"Never mind. Just a joke."

When the student had walked out the door, Professor Jordan opened his drawer and removed a small flask of Tennessee whiskey and took a quick swig.

Star Wars. Wow.

Once upon a time, having recently received his Ph.D. from MIT, he'd had his sights set on several Ivy League programs in the Northeast. A series of family illnesses, some run-ins with nasty academic politics, and at least one case of bona fide racial discrimination had derailed these ambitions, and Pennsboro, which he'd once considered nothing more than a way station, had eventually become home. Still, you made the best of it, and there were surely worse physics programs one could wind up at. Almost definitely.

Grace, his soon-to-be-retired secretary, buzzed him.

"Dr. J, there's a young man here to see you."

He leaned into the speakerphone. "If it's another student

asking about a grade change, tell him I've blown my brains out; he should take it up with my next of kin."

"He's here about the ad."

"Send him on in."

Seconds later, a young man appeared in the office, medium height, thin, scruffy facial hair that wasn't quite a beard. He introduced himself as Mike Williams, and Professor Jordan instructed him to take a seat across from him.

"So, Mike, you have a résumé?"

"Not with me," the young man replied. "I was passing through and saw the sign and thought I'd stop in just to hear about the position. I can get it for you later, though."

"Sure, sure, that's no problem. Have you ever been a departmental secretary before?"

"Nope. This would be the first time."

"Ah, okay. And what makes you interested in the job?"

"Well, I've always really loved physics and figured that working all day inside a physics department would be a pretty great environment."

"Mm-hmm. You have any kind of formal background in physics?"

"Well, I almost majored in it in college. Took lots of courses, but didn't end up going for the degree."

"What areas of physics did you study?"

"Special relativity. Quantum field theory, string theory. Bunch of other stuff."

Professor Jordan looked at the young man as though suddenly seeing him for the first time.

"Where did you study?"

"Roxbury Community College."

"Must confess I haven't heard of it. What areas of quantum field theory did you study?"

"Gauge theory and supersymmetry, mostly. Also some of the stuff Hugh Watkins has been saying about superstring theory."

"Huh! Tell you the truth, I wouldn't have thought undergrads would be getting exposure to those sorts of things. What do you think of Watkins's superstring theory work?"

"I think the whole thing is nonsense, to be honest."

Jordan laughed. "It's complete bullshit, isn't it? Five, ten years from now, everyone else will realize it, too. Meantime, the fad will just have to run its course. Why didn't you finish the degree, if you don't mind my asking?"

"Uh, you know. Fate, circumstances."

"Mm-hmm. Well, I'll be honest with you, Mike. We're not exactly a hub of scientific innovation here. The environment at this department will be not unlike the environment of any other department at this school, which is to say, not unlike the environment of an old-age home. That said, you get in your paperwork and everything checks out with administrative services, you've definitely got the gig."

"Thank you so much, sir!" the young man replied. "Is it okay if I take a few days to think about it?"

"By all means!"

Outside, the maple and holly trees were in full bloom, and the summer sky was a beautiful creamy blue. As he got ready to leave the campus, "Mike Williams" turned around and took one last look at the physics building. He had asked for a few days to think about it, but in truth, there was no decision to be made. Shawn couldn't take the job, not this one or any other. Employment, friendship, romance, all things indicative of a consistent, stable existence were simply not in the cards for him anymore.

But he could still dream.

As he got into his Toyota Corolla, which he'd stolen after discarding the old SUV in New Mexico as a precautionary measure, he took off his T-shirt and exchanged it for another. He changed his clothes at least three times a day and never drove wearing the same outfit he'd worn while walking around. Sometimes he wasn't sure whether he was being rational or whether life on the run had simply made him completely obsessive-compulsive. Either way, he now judged himself to be more paranoid than even Leland had been, and that scared the shit out of him.

He still wondered about Leland sometimes. It was over two months since the last time he'd seen him, when he'd vanished so mysteriously from that clinic in Annabella. That sudden flight had been strange, but in the thousands of hours he'd spent with Leland on the road, he'd never been able to get any real handle on the man, so why waste time trying to understand him now? In physics, you might spend decades researching and experimenting in the hopes of finally solving some great mystery. With other people, you weren't so naïve.

He hoped Leland was still alive, though, and figured that if he, himself, hadn't yet been caught, even though he'd stolen the lotus flower *and* didn't have any special abilities to protect himself with, then Leland was no doubt doing just fine, outrunning Ambius and probably more than a little happy to be on his own again.

Shawn didn't think about Leland too much, though, and he thought about Rachel even less, a fact that surprised him. He wasn't sure if it was because he'd hardened himself against her or, as he suspected might be more likely, he'd built a wall around the whole subject, another "impenetrable shield," this one to protect him from himself.

One image that occasionally came back to him, though, was that strange, sad look that had crossed her face in the last moments before he left her. Of all the expressions he would have expected to see on her—rage, fear, desperation—sadness seemed strange, out of place, especially for someone as cold and calculating as she was. Yes, after all the hope she'd pinned on that flower, she surely must have been horrified to watch him steal it from her. But sad?

He wondered, could it be that what he had seen had been a hint of regret? Remorse, even, for everything she'd done to him, everything she'd done in general? A small trace of humanity?

It was possible, he supposed, but not likely. Either way, he certainly wasn't going to dwell on the matter.

Most of the time, he just thought about his next meal or his next bed or where he could stock up on canned vegetables or soap—the usual mundane concerns of a wanted fugitive. He didn't know why he was still alive, why he had made it as far as he had, but he was under no illusion that he was likely to survive much longer. If they had caught up with Leland in Alicante, Spain, they would catch up with Shawn in the United States.

And when they did, he had decided, he would die grateful. All his life, he had dreamed about whatever mysteries might lie beyond the horizon of our everyday existence, about the adventure he knew awaited in the larger universe of which our own planet was only a small speck of dust. These preoccupations had gotten him into science in the first place and had taken on obsessive dimensions once he'd come face-to-face with the footage of Leland being abducted in Bernasconi Hills.

In the end, he had actually gotten a few small and magical glimpses of that world beyond the world. Just enough to know it was really there. He had seen strange and mysterious sights, things he now felt as though he'd only imagined but knew he hadn't. A human being facing off against a military drone on an Arizona highway at sunset. A miracle flower from light-years away dying in a Minnesota forest. These were no doubt mere windows to things far more incredible, things unimaginable, but windows were much more than most people would ever get to see.

Except sometimes a small taste makes the hunger burn that much deeper. At night, when he closed his eyes to fall asleep, he sometimes still saw that flower, the "Illuminator" or whatever Leland had called it, burning away in the darkness of the woods. In his mind, he could still see that weird green orb, staring out at him from amid the flames, shining and expanding, abask in its unfathomable otherness. The wider existence he had longed for since childhood, that higher realm of magic and mystery where the familiar laws of physics and chemistry no longer apply, where truly anything can happen, that world of *science fiction but real*, he had finally gotten to experience a small piece of it. But it was a world in which he, Shawn Ferris, was not destined to live.

CHAPTER 33

And one by one the nights between our separated cities are joined to the night that unites us.

—PABLO NERUDA

The Sonoran Desert, which covers large swaths of the southwestern United States and northwestern Mexico, first came into being over eight million years ago during the Miocene Epoch, the same period of time in which the ancestors of humans are believed to have split from those of apes. The desert extends over an area of more than one hundred thousand square miles and is considered one of the most biologically diverse in the world, home to some sixty species of mammals and hundreds of species of birds, reptiles, and amphibians, not to mention thousands of varieties of plants. When the sun goes down, these various forms of life join forces to create a mesmerizing song, whose star performers include the screech owl, with its incessant repetition of four notes, the hooded skunk, with its rhythmic scratching and digging, and the Mearns coyote, with its mournful and melodious howl.

Tonight, this symphony was rudely interrupted by a far less native sound, the thunderous roar of a 1980s-era Harley Davidson XLR, as the pitch blackness was likewise pierced through by the bike's beaming headlight, streaking its way across the desert floor.

Andrew Leland had been in Mexico for over a month now but hadn't yet been ready to return to the desert. Instead, he'd been holed up in a tiny inn in Juárez that doubled as a whorehouse, covering the walls and floor of his room with marker ink as he attempted to work through his labyrinthine equations. Now, here he was at last, and he still wasn't ready for what he was about to do, but he was as ready as he was going to get, which would have to suffice.

Though it had been over three years, it didn't take him long to find the cave he was seeking, actually an abandoned gold mine that stood adjacent to a large saguaro cactus. He parked the motorcycle outside the entrance and, with a backpack and flashlight in tow, went inside.

Guided by the flashlight, he followed the path of the old cart tracks down through a limestone tunnel. The air was shallow and stale, and he could hear bat wings fluttering about somewhere in the deeper recesses of the mine. After about twenty minutes of walking, the tunnel he was in suddenly opened up into a wide and magnificent chamber full of shimmering stalactites and stalagmites.

And at the far end of this chamber, blending in with the cragged rock, there it stood, untouched and exactly as he'd remembered it, tan and pentagon shaped and about the size of a large sedan. Its sloping roof was covered by a series of hard interlocking plates that were reminiscent of certain herbivorous dinosaurs and which made the whole thing look far less aerodynamic than it actually was.

Leland almost felt wrong to be seeing it now, if only because he had never intended to see it again. He approached with slow, deliberate steps and, when he reached it, slipped his fingers onto the color-coded keyboard-like panel below its circular door and inputted a four-digit combination that, simple as it was, he was surprised he could still recall. The circular door opened, extending outward with a soft *whoosh*, and Leland hoisted himself inside the ship.

Once he'd settled into the cockpit, he strapped himself into his seat and stared at the instrument panel. A maze of oddly shaped monitors, switches, and indicators, the panel, which would have been utterly foreign looking to an airline pilot or astronaut, had been designed by her specifically for him, just like the rest of the ship, and he was again surprised at how quickly it all came back. He hit the switch to activate the panel, and everything lit up like Christmas. He then removed a crumpled sheet of paper covered in scribbles from his backpack and, with his eyes flashing between the paper and a keypad on the panel, punched in the appropriate coordinates.

The plan was anything but simple. He would first need to fly this thing on his own to the mesosphere, about three hundred thousand feet from the Earth's surface, at which point the ship's autopilot, as determined by his coordinates, would take over. Then, at the very end of his journey, eleven and a half light-years away, he would retake manual control of the ship and bring it in for the close.

Assuming the ship still flew, the initial ascent would likely go fairly smoothly. The next step, however, the autopilot phase, would be fraught with danger, as it depended entirely on the accuracy of his calculations, in which he had only moderate faith. The final stage of the trip, where he would resume control of the ship and fly it straight into the cosmic shield, if he'd made it that far, would be the real moment of truth.

Shawn had claimed that to calculate everything just right so that a spacecraft could pass through the shield and wind up on the other side still in the present day, and then to successfully *execute* these calculations, was virtually impossible. This was correct, yet Leland had managed to pull it off when he'd escaped back to Earth the first time. Now, though, what he needed to do was an even less optimistic proposition, involving murkier math and science and requiring significantly greater aerial finesses. He would need to hit the cosmic shield at such a speed and angle so as to wind up on the other side, at their world, *not* in the present, *nor* thousands of years into the past, but just far back enough to reset the course of events and make everything right.

Just far back enough to undo all of Shawn's damage.

Even if he succeeded at the time travel part, there were perilous side effects to consider, with the implications of time travel itself being chief among them. At least as far as he was aware, no living creature from Earth or anywhere else had ever actually traveled backward in time. While theoretical physicists had all kinds of strong opinions on the subject, it was impossible to truly know what sort of chain reaction doing so might unleash, what great paradoxes might result or what cosmic catastrophes they could trigger. Would the space-time continuum self-destruct, as many believed? Would the fabric of existence itself tear apart at the seams?

Did he really care?

This was his only chance to save her. If his actions somehow managed to destroy the entire universe instead, it was a risk worth taking.

With all his preparations now in place, he grabbed the joystick and put his foot to the pedal. The engine revved up, five hundred thousand horsepower at six thousand revolutions per minute. At least as far as driving went, the ship seemed to be working fine, and he deftly steered it out of the chamber and into the tunnel, then along the old cart track and up and out through the large hole from which he'd entered, back into the desert.

The bike was right where he'd left it, and he took a last look at that splendid machine, which he'd stolen from some gangster in Torreón, then hit the pedal hard and gunned the ship across the desert floor at a speed about which a Harley Davidson XLR could only dream.

As he zoomed through the darkness, the g-forces inside the cockpit building up and pushing him farther and farther down into his seat and the dark silhouettes of dunes and rock formations zooming by through the cockpit window, he imagined that he wasn't riding through the desert but across the Golden Gate Bridge, with the electrifying New York City and Chicago skylines on each side lighting up the night like in his dream. He could see, in his mind's eye, her bright green eyes, her mischievous, childlike smile, all of her immense wonder and beauty.

But of course he had always known, from the time he had first come back to Earth, that he couldn't remember what she had *really* looked like, what she had really been. And that although he always remembered her as a beautiful woman, she could have just as easily been a horrifying ogre in reality or a bizarre insect or even some kind of plant.

Some kind of *flower*.

She always used to laugh when he would ask her who was more powerful, she or the Illumination. Why she had kept the truth from him, he couldn't know now, but he did know that if he had known it back then, that she *was* the Illumination, that it was *she* Earth had been after, *she* whom he had built the cosmic shield to protect, he never would have left that place. Instead, he would have immediately agreed to deactivate the shield when he was asked, even though it would have meant facilitating the destruction of his own people.

As the ship lifted off and he felt the g-forces intensify, he thought back to the last moments from his last night with her, the night he had dreamed about earlier, the night she helped him escape. In his memories, at least, they were standing in the observatory beneath its wide silver dome. In the corner of the room was a large table covered in a tarp, beneath which, he understood, lay his original human body. She was holding in her hands a small, thumbtack-like object, which he remembered from his encounter with the avatar who had first transformed him into one of them. Though he had been told that his body had long ago been disposed of, this was obviously a lie, and now that incredible initial transformation process would be reversed, and he would return to his old self.

"You should know," she said, gesturing toward the tarp, "I had one of our technicians make some adjustments to it. For an experiment, I told him."

"What kind of adjustments?"

"Just a few minor things. You'll see when you return to Earth."

He smiled. He could only imagine what sort of "adjustments" she might be referring to.

"All right," she said, stepping forward with the small pin. "We'd better do this before it's too late."

"Wait," he said.

"What?"

"I want . . . I want something to remember you by."

She thought for a moment, then reached into an inner pocket of her silky violet robe and removed a dazzling crimson jewel and held it out to him. "A rose rock from a volcano that destroyed one of our largest cities over a million years ago. I've kept it with me for many years as a reminder of the impermanence of great things. It will be in your ship when you board as a man."

"I'll keep it with me forever," he said. "But I want more than that."

"What do you want?"

He smiled and looked her in the eyes. "I want to see for myself why they call you 'goddess.' I want a miracle."

She stared back at him for a moment without saying anything, and he feared she was going to say what she'd always said, that her power was beyond his abilities to comprehend.

But she didn't this time.

Instead, she smiled.

There was a small, round elevated platform in the center of the room, and she stepped onto it and motioned for him to join her. He walked over and got on, as well, and then it suddenly began to rise, extending upward from the floor. He looked up at the dome ceiling above them, and the retractable shutter began to open up, revealing the stars. The two of them continued their ascent until they had passed through the opening and were outside, at which point the platform stopped ascending and kept them in place, level with the top of the dome.

They stood there, wordlessly, surrounded by the night sky, and the night sky was like nothing Leland had ever seen. In every direction, there were glittering masses of colorful interstellar dust and gas, nebulae, magical and kaleidoscopic, and there were star clusters everywhere, like pink and blue and yellow and green snowflakes, and spiral galaxies all around that looked like giant neon Frisbees.

In the far distance was a dark gray cloud of what he assumed to be gas, and she was staring at it with the most intense expression he'd ever seen on her or anyone. Suddenly, as if by magic, the cloud began to move, to swirl, collapsing in on itself and taking on an increasingly circular form as its gravity pooled more and more gas into the great whirlpool of its center.

And, as he watched, that swirling center began to visibly heat up, the colors of the gas moving about inside of it shifting from black and gray to orange and yellow.

Andrew Leland, world-famous physicist, knew very well what he was seeing even if he couldn't quite believe it. The heat was now going to reach eighteen million degrees, and the hydrogen atoms would combine and form helium.

Nuclear fusion.

He turned to look at her, standing so still in her brilliant violet robe. Her green eyes, trancelike, remained fixed on the events taking place within the center of the collapsing cloud. He knew that she was controlling everything. Whether by sheer will or some other way far beyond his innately human ability to grasp, she was making all of this happen. He turned back to the cloud just in time to witness the inevitable cosmic explosion of nuclear energy and the birth of a brand-new shining star.

He didn't try to fight the tears. It was the most beautiful thing he had ever seen in his life. Soon, he knew, the gas and dust from the former cloud would begin to spread out and away from the star, giving it space, clearing the way for it to shine brightly and freely for the next several billion years.

He turned back to her, and now she was looking right at him. That trancelike expression was gone, her eyes were suddenly soft, and her only focus was him. He opened his arms and let them enfold her, and she put her arms around him, as well.

They knew that he should be going, that every second counted now. But they continued to hold each other. They could both already feel the distance of the light-years that would soon separate them and the even greater distance that would exist between who they each were. And so they didn't want to let go.

In a universe of infinite time and space, they never should have come together to begin with, this strange and unlikely pair. But they had, a goddess and a man, though in this moment, really no more than two lonely souls, clinging to each other amid a great and mighty storm of moons and stars and worlds, untold secrets and mysteries, desperately trying, for just a little while longer, to keep it from pulling them apart.

ACKNOWLEDGMENTS

Although it would be impossible to individually thank everyone who helped with this book, this comes close. First, thanks to my editor, the insanely talented Brendan Deneen, who believed in this story when it was a three-line idea and expertly guided it into becoming an actual book. Thanks, as well, to my associate editor, Nicole Sohl, and the entire team at St. Martin's Press, including Thomas Dunne, Kenneth J. Silver, and Cameron Jones. Kudos, also, to my eagle-eyed copy editors, Sara and Chris Ensey, and to David Curtis on his spectacular cover design.

I'm incredibly fortunate to be represented by the amazing and dedicated MacKenzie Fraser-Bub of Fraser-Bub Literary. Many thanks to her, and thanks also to the folks at Trident Media, especially Scott Miller and Chelsea Grogan.

In developing this story, I harassed countless people for feedback, but benefited especially from conversations with Murray Young, Jeffrey Helmreich, Joshua Halpern, Ronen Verbit, Ronn Blitzer, Joseph Fruchter, Mordechai Juni, Elliot Schimel, Brandon Gold, Esther Friedman, Leo Helmreich, Charlotte Wendel, Alessandro DiGiovanna,

Kalman Honig, Jessica Schechter, David Steiner, Rivka Schwarcz, Joshua Werber, Leora Botnick, Daniel Friedman, Joshua Saidlower, Paul Marcus, Nathaniel Fintz, Elana Lehrer, Ari Gilder, and Vinnie Rothberg. I'm particularly indebted to the following early readers: Robert Knepper, Diane Kolatch, Greg Starr, Ryan Pliner, Alexandra Elbaum, and especially Deborah Halpern. I'm also grateful to Yonah Lemonik, Adam Solomon, Lt. Col. Yaakov Bindell, and Rebecca Weiser for their technical expertise, and to Bernard Velinsky and Jill Silverman, early literary mentors. A special thanks goes to Terry Steiner, Nadja Rutkowski, Yvette Mang, Myrna Gabriel, David Tse, and everyone else in the wonderful TSI family. And I could never have made it to the finish line without the uninterrupted peace provided by The Writers Room.

Last but not least, thanks to two more early readers of the manuscript: William and Helaine Helmreich, great writers and even better parents, whose love, support, and endless encouragement were indispensable in the writing of this book. Love you guys!